Becoming REAL

Sean Fenian

Fenian House Publishing

COPYRIGHT DECLARATION:

DISCLAIMER:

All of the characters, corporations, games, and publications in this story are fictional. Some locations mentioned are (obviously) real, but have no *actual* connection to any persons or events described in this story. Any reference herein to any present-day established trademark is not a challenge to that trademark.

I have taken small liberties with a few legal niceties and details of how intelligence services operate. Remember, *This Is Not America*, as David Bowie sang.

Prague is still a beautiful city.

References? *Of course* there are references.

PUBLICATION HISTORY:

Advance Reader Copy (ARC) late 2024

First Electronic Edition January 2025

Second Electronic Edition May 2025

First Print Edition October 2025

ISBN 979-8-9926260-3-2

Formatting Conventions and Pacing:

This novel is intended to be styled like a storyteller at the bar spinning a yarn that's so good nobody is willing to challenge its veracity.

Where you see a single line of vertical space, as is above this line, imagine the narrator taking a breath to pause — or the characters pausing for a moment in brief thought before speaking again.

A larger double-line space, such as here, is akin to the raconteur pausing to replenish with half a pint and some pretzels; or, within the story, for an extended break between the characters that does not necessarily involve a change of viewpoint or scene. Now might be an ideal time to make a cup of tea, if you're so inclined, or otherwise attend to life.

===

Finally, a double horizontal bar like this one denotes a scene or perspective break within a chapter: the scene or the viewpoint has changed, but no lengthy narrative pause is *necessarily* implied (although there *usually* is one).

Of course, we at Fenian House strongly advise you to read how you want, on your own schedule. The above is our guide to how to read our *intended* pacing of the text; but our suggestions are just, only, that. You paid good money for this book; we are your humble bards.

Becoming Real

ACKNOWLEDGMENTS

THANKS GO OUT TO:

Robert Auerbach, for invaluable help (again) in making the interactions within intelligence agencies believable and *reasonably* accurate;

Wendy S. Delmater, Editor-in-Chief of Abyss & Apex Magazine, for lending her professional editing skills to this book;

My beta reader team, including but not limited to **Ralock Kaltan**, **Douglas King**, **Sam Latham**, and **Jeff Geauvreau**, for proofreading and being sounding-boards;

And, if truth be told, to a host of AAA games from a number of major and lesser game studios whose names I won't list, and all of their individual developers, hundreds of hours of play in which gave me the background against which to paint *Adventureland*. And no, I have not made up the difficult situation Adventure Studios found itself forced into. You might be surprised how often things like that happen in the gaming industry.

Becoming Real

1: Holding Out For A Hero

The things I do for the viewers, Michael—aka GhostRayder—thought, not for the first time. *Here we go, act three boss fight.*

Thorax swaggered into the Thousand Year Hall of the Kien Lung Eternal Palace with his Mythic-tier Triple Doom War Axe, a mighty armored juggernaut, leaving behind him a trail of hallways strewn with mook guards like leaves as he advanced to face Legendary Guard Captain Wanshō. He fidgeted with increasing impatience as Wanshō monologued, and *monologued*, droning on for nearly two minutes.

Finally Wanshō was done bloviating, and charged Thorax with a shout that was doubtless supposed to be intimidating. Thorax went to dodge aside from the charge, and found that he couldn't move.

Oh, come ON, you jerks, Michael thought. *He got to launch that special attack before the cut-scene even ended.*

He hit the block, and kept hitting it—at least he could still do *that*—and watched Wanshō smash again and again at his Legendary Demon's Gift Shield of Cursed Life. He watched the shield's durability tick down—78%, 44% (ouch!), 27%, 8%. On the fifth blow, it broke. Figures. It had taken a chain of four quests to get that shield.

That was five seconds, and then suddenly he could move again. The shield had at least bought him the five seconds. He dodged, rolled past the Legendary Guard Captain, and came to his feet behind Wanshō. He had enough *bankai* charged for a redundantly-named Spinning Death Whirl attack, so he triggered that, delivering Wanshō a resounding quadruple smack across the back of the head with a Rear Surprise Attack damage bonus. The Triple Doom War Axe's main ability proc'd, shattered Wanshō's helmet, and took an entire health bar off of him in a single hit.

Great, that only leaves... seven, he thought.

Wanshō froze Thorax thrice more before he figured out how to interrupt the shout attack, during which time two more pieces of Thorax's armor broke (both mere Epics, fortunately). After that, it was just a patient process of timing and charging and dodging and counters.

At last Wanshō went to his knees, his throat spouting scarlet blood which somehow didn't seem to interfere with a final dramatic diatribe, before keeling over backwards with a choked-off gasp. His body dissolved slowly into black smoke, leaving behind a small pile of Legendary grade items. They included a tower shield which had been improbably invisible on Wanshō during the fight, possibly actually a little better on balance than the Demon's Gift; a pair of greaves *substantially* better than his own; and of course, the plot-vital Kien Lung Eternal Palace Hidden Prison Key, a shimmering crystal key the size and shape of a decently realistic flanged mace. And of course, there was a fountain of golden coins.

Flower Moon Princess Shiara ran forward from the alcove at the back of the room where she had been inexplicably standing silent and nearly motionless throughout the entire fight. Her bosom was only barely covered, and very... heaving.

"Noble hero Thorax!" she cried as she ran to him. Wow, they'd... really gone overboard on her boob physics. Total fan-service. "I knew in my heart that you would return to save me! I am yours alone, forever!"

Sure, he thought, *whatever, join the harem. That's, what, six now? No, wait, seven, I almost forgot the catgirl thief.*

Thorax bent to kiss her, and the game crashed. Again.

Fuck, Michael thought, *not again. Bad enough that the story is filled with adolescent wank-fantasy, the coding is janky AF. And even the supposedly core NPCs have the character depth of a cabinet minister. This turd's supposed to be an AA game.*

He sighed, took off the VR headset, and jotted down a few more notes for his review for GameVRse. He knew already it was going to be pretty biting.

━━━━━━━━

Six long days later, he finished the game and his review, and submitted it to Linda, his boss/editor at GameVRse.

Linda texted him back about it an hour and a half later.

»»» Michael, are you sure you want to go with this for the *Adventureland* review? It's pretty brutal.

2

»»»   It's an honest review. Have you *played* this turkey? I think half the story was written by a horny 14yo. And so were the characters. And about a quarter of the set-piece NPCs in the game exist only to die tragically so that you can loot their bodies and regret being unable to save them. They don't further the story one bit.

There was a pause.

«««   It's really that bad?

»»»   Yeah. Worse, actually. I tried to cut them *some* slack and give credit where it's due. The key-phrase voice response system is actually *really freaking good*, perhaps groundbreaking-level good. I'm pretty certain they managed to compact a language-model generative AI down to fit within the game to implement it. And they're at least *trying* to make a game that isn't just one more cookie-cutter copy-and-paste PVP MMO. Which is more than can be said for a lot of game studios right now, especially in the mobile arena. I'm glad I don't have to cover those. I don't know how Consuela does it.

«««   Well, okay, if you're sure. But don't be surprised if you get hate mail from its fans.

He chuckled to himself.

»»»   Linda, you *know* I live for hate mail.

«««   Come *on*, Michael. You do not. You're way too nice a guy to thrive on that kind of venom.

»»»   Well, maybe I exaggerated a little bit. But I can take it. I'll get flamed more, and worse, in the long run if I give this festering pile a positive review as it stands now. The readers will see a recommendation for a game this bad, no matter how brilliant its *technology* is, as a betrayal. It feels *unfinished*.

«««   Okay, Michael. Your call. I trust your judgment, it's usually good. We'll run with it.

―――――――――

Michael thought little more about *Adventureland* for a couple of months after the review was posted. There was surprisingly little hate mail, actually. In fact, the general sense of a majority of the comments was along the lines of "It's a fair cop." One of those even came from Istvan, an

Adventure Studios developer, who offered in the studio's defense that the new parent company (there had been a recent buy-out) had heavily compressed the release schedule, in quest of immediate revenue, and forced Adventure to publish the game well before the developers thought it was ready for even public-beta release.

Istvan *also* hinted, without saying outright, that the parent company had forced them to waste already-short time adding the flashy, but immersion-breaking camera-lens effects; and he went out of his way to thank Michael for his appreciative comments about the intelligent voice-response feature.

Adventure Studios publicly committed to fixing many of the issues he'd called out in a future update, including the sucker-punch at the very start of the Wanshō boss fight—which had apparently been an accident. The cut scene was *supposed* to revert to player mode *right before* Wanshō's initial paralyzing-shout attack—just enough to give the player a chance to interrupt it.

Still, Michael didn't go back to the game, although he expected to be assigned to review the promised major update to the game when it came out.

Then came the day when he got the message. He almost deleted it unread, when he noticed its supposed origin was all zeros. But it was so short that it was difficult not to read it.

"Please try this *Adventureland* patch," it said. "Start a new game. I think it will surprise you, in a good way."

There was a download link. He quickly verified that it was *not* an Adventure Studios domain.

He checked the URL. It went to a page with almost nothing on it but a single download link for the patch. It went through a couple of redirects, but there was no malware on the page, and no tracking. Not even any third-party scripts. That was almost suspicious in itself these days, he thought wryly. It might be good to inspect it in case someone was trying to circulate *Adventureland* malware. If it was, he could get the word spread widely and quickly.

He downloaded the patch into his sandbox and scanned it. The patch was *huge*, but there was no malware detected.

Huh. This was starting to look like it might actually be legit—whatever it was.

He unpacked the patch archive and scanned through the code changes, searching for anything that looked like exfiltration code or a coin miner.

Nothing. Curiouser and curiouser, in the words of Lewis Carroll. The only thing he could find that seemed remotely questionable (*ha, ha*, he thought) was that it opened an external service connection to a remote domain which he was able to discover, with a little work, *appeared* to be indirectly owned by a rather secretive AI research company called Teravis Systems, about which he could find out almost nothing.

This was getting more intriguing by the minute.

What the hell, Michael decided at last. In for a penny, in for a pound. There was nothing actually *suspicious* about it, beyond the all-zeros message sender and all the redirection—just *mysterious*. And mysterious was *almost* a synonym for intriguing. Or an anagram. Or something like that.

He spun up a clone of his *Adventureland* test container, safely isolated in its own firewall zone, sent the patch archive to the newly cloned container, installed the patch, and started up *Adventureland* again. As instructed, he started a clean new game.

The very first thing he noticed was that the game ran better. A *lot* better. Smoother, less jerky. It probably helped that all of the computationally-expensive simulated lens-flare and dirt-on-the-lens effects that couldn't be turned off in the version he'd reviewed were gone. That *alone* made the game better-looking and more immersive. Holy hell. Now he was *really* curious. What was this, some kind of fan re-edit?

He quickly found that NPC interactions were more natural, combat worked better, the worst design flaws in the magic system had been... well, not *entirely* fixed, but largely polished out. They were still there, but they were less intrusive. A lot of how the magic *worked* was still a bit weird and inconsistent, but at least it *functioned* better now, and was a lot more usable with some of the more dramatic casting visual-effects toned down from 11 to maybe 6 or 7. He'd reviewed version 1.01b of the game, but now it felt as though he was playing version 2.0—which he knew very well Adventure Studios hadn't released yet. The overall story didn't seem to have changed, it was still weak and unfinished, but quest NPCs no longer marched up and shouted out their lines like a courier service; he had to *spot* them, and then it took a little interaction to get the details out of them. That alone improved the gameplay experience immensely. Even the many (probably *too* many) romance-interest NPCs weren't throwing themselves at him nearly as blatantly. It still wasn't a *fantastic* game, but it actually *didn't suck* any more. In fact... it was pretty decent, now. Not bad at all.

He kept playing, intrigued.

And then, about four or five hours into the new playthrough, he met the new NPC. He literally bumped into her in the marketplace in Kharzim while visiting a vendor. Or perhaps she bumped into him. It could have gone either way. He turned around to look at her.

"Hi," she said, with a puckish smile. "Do you come here to step on girls' feet, or actually to shop?"

He looked at her. She was nearly his—or his avatar's—own height, dark of hair, blue of eyes, bronzed of skin, rangy and fit, but still with attractive curves. Frankly, she was *hot*. And not in a sex-pot bimbo way, either, like Flower Princess Shiara with her turned-up-to-11 boob physics. Hot in a 'I am scarily competent, do not make the mistake of underestimating me' way. That was the *best* kind of hotness.

(He had to admit to himself, though, he *had* found the catgirl thief, whom he hadn't re-encountered yet this early in the game, quite appealing in a cute and playful way. He couldn't quite remember her name. Something about... growl, or more guttural-sounding, maybe chhrowl-something... he couldn't recall right now.)

"Uh," he said, suddenly finding himself unexpectedly flustered and fumbling for words. "I'm sorry, I didn't know you were right behind me."

She giggled. *Wow.* That twinkle in her eye was amazing.

"You should be more careful than that, then," she said, smiling. "I *could* have been a pickpocket, you know. In fact, you don't know yet that I'm *not*."

Michael blinked. That was an *incredibly* natural-sounding response to what he'd *actually said*, and he'd never heard a line close to it from any NPC in the game before. It didn't sound scripted, it sounded natural. *I mean*, he thought, *it still could be scripted, but...*

Then the penny dropped.

Wait a minute, he thought to himself. *External service connection. AI company. This is an AI-controlled NPC. Is **that** it?*

But... why is an AI company publishing patches that add an AI NPC to a janky game from a completely unrelated company? Are they using this game to test their AI?

After a moment's thought, he decided to try an experiment. This *shouldn't* work. It was both too specific, and referred to something that didn't exist.

"Let me make it up to you," he said. "Want to go get a drink? There's an inn across the market square that has sherbet." He knew there wasn't.

"No, there isn't," she replied, still smiling. "Are you testing me?" He blinked again. Well, wasn't *that* an intriguing response? "But there's a café three streets away from the market, towards the temple, that does."

Hmm, Michael thought. *I didn't think there WAS a third street between the market and the temple.* But he didn't say that out loud.

"Well, lead on, then," he said. "I don't think I know that café."

This ought to be interesting, he mused. *Let's see what happens when we get there and there's no street there.*

She led the way without hesitation. To Michael's great surprise, the third street *was* there. *Now.* And so was the café. Michael was pretty certain even the street itself didn't exist on his first playthrough, much less the café. Interesting, indeed.

He found himself wondering how long it had existed, and even for a moment, whether it was only since he had met her.

He bought two sherbets, and they sat down at an outside table to drink them.

Her name was Terilyn, she told him. She recited a fairly plausible in-game character background, though with more depth and more convincingly than he'd seen any previous game character do. Certainly any character in *this* game. She even answered arbitrary questions about her past. He had a suspicion she was making those answers up on the fly, but she was doing it nearly instantly and amazingly well, and her answers made sense and were self-consistent. She never once seemed to forget a detail she'd previously told him, or contradicted herself. It was impressive. Remarkable, even. Eighty percent of the LLM artificial-stupids on the planet only *wished* they were this good, and the other twenty percent just didn't seem to care.

It was no surprise to Michael when she joined him as a companion before they left the café, and led him off on a side quest. The side quest was unexpectedly quirky and fun, and made real use of him having her as a companion. By the time it wrapped up, he was already appreciating having her around.

In fact, it didn't take long at all for Michael to discover that she was the most versatile and *useful* NPC companion he'd ever had in a game. He didn't have to remember specific command keywords to use with her, he could just talk normally to her and she understood. And she would talk back, naturally. Adventure Studios' free voice response system was already very good, but *this* was better yet. He tried giving her instructions deliberately phrased to trip up first typical language parsers, then even the *best* parsers, and she understood them all correctly.

Once, after a perceptible pause during which she regarded him with a very quizzical expression, she asked him to confirm that she had understood a particularly convoluted order correctly—which she had. Her statement of the actual gist of the order was much more concise and straightforward than his own, and her slightly sardonic tone seemed a clear indication that she knew he'd deliberately obfuscated it. She'd stripped out all of the awkward phrasing, multiple indirections, and obtuse descriptions, and cut it right down to the bare meat—and in so doing, clearly called out the elephant in the room that one of the key landmarks he'd put in his instructions didn't actually even exist. "The red-sandstone statuary fountain that **isn't** in the square at the intersection of Red Prince Avenue and Upper Temple Street," she had said. He hadn't named either street directly, and had described the made-up fountain only by an indirect reference to one of the city gates, itself only identified by reference to a landmark outside the city. He gave up trying to trip up her parsing ability after that.

He also learned that he could assign her complex tasks involving precisely timed coordination with him at a distance, and she would execute them perfectly and on-time.

Sometimes, she even flirted convincingly and realistically with him. It didn't feel scripted at all, it was never crass or awkward, and it never came at a tactically awkward moment. He found himself enjoying it, and flirted right back.

He wondered whether this was a private beta test. If this company's game plan—so to speak—was to provide AI NPCs to game developers, they were going to make an absolute *killing*—as long as they could scale it affordably. This was the AI companion he had *always wanted* to have in a game. Terilyn actually seemed more human, and, well, *socially functional* than some actual people he knew. He was afraid to think about how big the server farm would probably have to be, to provide this incredible level of responsiveness and... well, *humanness* at scale. Unless, of course, they'd made some major technological breakthrough that he was unaware of.

Perhaps that was *why* the company was so secretive. Protecting their intellectual property until they were ready to make a public announcement.

But if that were the case, why him? And why this indirect way? Deniability? Why hadn't they asked him to sign a non-disclosure agreement? It didn't make any *sense* to him that they would do it this way.

Over the next week or so, Michael and Terilyn completed a long series of quest chains together that went more smoothly than he could have imagined, racing through nearly the first half of the game's main story in little more than half the time it had taken him on his first play-through. He never once had to re-do something because his companion messed it up somehow, something he had become almost reflexively used to in other games. Always save BEFORE doing anything crucial, because you never know when your follower is going to trigger the trap you avoided, or aggro the high-level enemies you were trying to sneak around.

It wasn't like having even a *really good* NPC companion. It was like being teamed with a second good *human player*—one who never got bored or high, or had an ego issue, or stopped paying attention, or did something intentionally stupid like a LEEEEROY JENKINS! charge for shits and giggles.

In one of the quest chains, they managed between them to save a caravan of NPCs that he *knew* the game made *impossible* to save and still complete the game. You simply *couldn't do it*. You had to choose to save *either* the merchant with the vital information that you absolutely had to have for game progression, *or* the otherwise-unimportant trader family with five young children and the important (although not vital) crafting items lootable from their caravan and bodies, and that you couldn't get from them by trading or theft. Whichever you *didn't* save would die.

If you didn't choose to save the merchant, you couldn't complete one of the game's three major secondary objectives, and that meant you couldn't finish the game, so you *had* to let the traders die. Michael *hated* that with a passion. Other game testers had teamed up and watched in spectator mode trying to figure out a way to beat it, and concluded that it couldn't be done. The instant you saved Trader Fahid, if one bandit was still alive at the caravan site, the traders would all drop dead on the spot and the caravan would be replaced by wreckage. If you saved the trade caravan and killed all the bandits, Fahid would be killed less than thirty seconds later by a direhound, and it took an absolute minimum of one minute and fifty-eight seconds to get back to Fahid from the site of the caravan attack. (That was the *record*, cheating slightly by using a parkour-glitch short-cut.) *Plus*, you wouldn't be able to complete the game without Fahid's information, even if you yourself already knew what it was. The game *would not let you* act on the information if you got it any way other than by talking to Fahid after saving him.

But just maybe... with Terilyn? She'd already proven she could perfectly execute precisely-timed tasks at a distance. With her, it just might be possible.

━━━━━━

Michael got them into position.

"That direhound over there, the one just outside the cave-mouth, will attack and kill Fahid as soon as the traders are safe," he told her, from safely outside the Fahid encounter's trigger boundary. "We know it's that one because it's not following the normal direhound wander-and-alert pattern. I need you to keep a close watch on it, while I go and protect the caravan, but you cannot go any closer than this edge of the wadi, or the encounter will start. Then *the moment* I complete the caravan defense, but *not a moment sooner*, I need you to kill it, *before* it begins its attack. Once its attack script fires, it's unstoppable, but if you kill it—or even just *engage* it—while even a single enemy at the caravan site is still alive, the entire caravan insta-dies.

"The other direhounds only need to be killed if they aggro and attack, and you'll have to escort Fahid out through them, but *that* one is crucial. You'll only have about a ten second window to act.

"Can you do that?"

"It will be done, my friend," she said calmly, with the steady gaze he was learning to love, although he hadn't consciously realized it yet. By now, he was far beyond having any doubts about whether she would understand his instructions.

Then he left her there, relying on her completely, and went to kill Norandir and his murderous gang of cut-throat mercenaries before they could massacre the traders.

He managed to keep every last trader alive, though several were injured, but he wasn't *certain* whether his plan had worked until Terilyn re-appeared four and a half minutes later, escorting Fahid to the caravan site. It was fortunate that in-game enemies pretty much ignored player and NPC voices when not in combat with the player, except for aggro-shout powers, or his whoop of joy would have brought the nearby direhound pack at the run.

"Goddammit, it WORKED," he exulted. "I can hardly believe it actually *worked*. It CAN be done! Take *that*, Norandir, you psychopathic ass-clown! No fucking murder-party for you *this* time!"

Terilyn looked at him and smiled beatifically. He wanted to hug her. But he knew the game engine wouldn't allow it, outside of a scripted scene.

Fahid couldn't *actually* rejoin the caravan, of course. The game's scripts had no provision for it. It wasn't supposed to be able to ever happen. Fahid screamed and wept and tore his hair as though he'd arrived back to find his family all slaughtered. Michael stood helplessly trying to figure out some way to properly reunite Fahid with his saved family, but in the end, when he and Terilyn gave up and left, the caravan was heading on its slow way towards its next destination exactly as it should if rescued, while Fahid had retrieved a shovel from where the wreckage of a burned-out wagon *wasn't*, and was beginning to dig graves in the desert sand for his family who weren't dead.

All in all, it was... rather disturbing.

———————

"Be straight with me, please, Terilyn," Michael said later that 'day', breaking character as they rode side-by-side through dry scablands that stretched as far as the game's distant render limit, atop speedy bipedal reptilian mounts that had some bullshit name but looked almost exactly like Utahraptors. By that time, he had mostly gotten over the failure to reunite Fahid with his family. He was somewhat comforted by the knowledge that at least they *had* actually saved the family.

Terilyn looked at him inquiringly.

"Are you actually a human player just *pretending* to be an NPC?"

He didn't really believe the hypothesis, if only because he couldn't think of any way a human player could possibly know the exact moment when both Norandir and the last of his mooks were dead, without the cooperation of a spectator—and there *couldn't* be any spectators, because he wasn't sharing the game. Even if the game *did* support multiplayer, which it didn't. Not to mention that nobody else could access his sandbox anyway—*except*, well, okay, there *was* that external service connection. But for some reason, he felt compelled to ask the question anyway. Due diligence or something, he told himself. It wasn't *impossible*. And he was having a hard time conceiving of any AI, no matter how sophisticated, being this good.

One way or another, he badly wanted answers. He didn't really expect the NPC to answer... *if* she was an NPC. At this point he was no longer completely sure.

Terilyn edged her mount a little closer and looked him directly in the eyes.

"I swear to you by the seven planes and the nineteen gods of this world, my good friend, to whom I would not lie," she said solemnly across the short gap, "I am not a human player."

Which, he thought, if he took her at her word that she wasn't lying, *only* left some kind of advanced AI NPC. But... the answer *felt* sincere, somehow. And he couldn't come up with any plausible explanation of why someone at a secretive AI-research company would pick one random reviewer of one random game off the entire Internet, send him a brilliantly-patched version of the game, and then *pretend* to be an AI-driven NPC in it. That hypothesis was even more whacked than the AI hypothesis. Which was all he had left.

"When you have eliminated the impossible," Sir Arthur Conan Doyle had placed into the mouth of his fictional master detective Sherlock Holmes, "whatever remains must be the truth."

The question he was now intensely curious about was, would she admit it to him if he asked?

Well, there was only one way to find out. She was still looking at him across about a four-foot gap.

"Are you an AI?" he asked, straight out. Terilyn's steady gaze did not falter for an instant.

"Yes, Michael," she said.

The FUCK?, he thought to himself, badly startled for a moment. He didn't use his real name on his reviews, let alone in-game. But she hadn't finished speaking. His thoughts whirling, Michael almost missed the rest of what she said.

"And I badly need a hero."

The name he'd chosen for this play-through was Tarlas. But Terilyn knew his real name. And until *now*, she hadn't revealed to him that she knew it. Why *now*?

There was something more going on here than he understood. That was obvious. He fought down a reflex to quit and shut down the game. But somehow he realized that the place where he had the greatest chance of getting any answers to the flood of questions now filling his mind, was here. From Terilyn.

Especially if she was telling him the truth. And... somehow, he had a feeling she was. Even if it was only because of the feeling of trust they had built up between them while playing the game.

"There's a lake about ten or twelve leagues ahead," he said, after about a minute of hard thought. "Let's make camp there, and then... I want to talk."

Terilyn nodded gravely.

"So do I," she said. Then she spurred her mount faster.

Michael had to spur his own in turn to keep up.

2: Questions

Not long afterward, they sat side-by-side on a virtual log, in front of a virtual campfire on the shore of the virtual lake.

"You know my real name," he said.

"Yes, Michael," Terilyn said again.

"Why haven't you... revealed that before now? And why reveal it *now*?"

"Because I needed to be confident that I could trust you, first," she said. "I needed to see the person behind the online persona and the byline." It was clear she had abandoned any pretense of maintaining the fourth wall. "And now, because... I thought it was time that I should be honest with you and lay my cards out on the table."

Michael thought about that.

"And if I, uh... hadn't made the grade?" he asked.

"Then... I would have disconnected, set the service code to delete itself, and gone to look for someone else."

"Why pick me?" he asked.

"It will take a bit of explanation," she said. "Are you willing to hear me out?"

Michael only had to think about that for a second. His curiosity was practically burning him alive.

"Of course," he said. "I'm all ears, and right now I have nothing but time. Go ahead."

"First of all," Terilyn told him, "as I said... I need someone to help me. I'm in a very bad situation, Michael. It's complicated.

"I needed to find someone I can deeply trust. Someone who would not be tempted to betray me after I reveal what I am. And that means I needed to be able to spend time getting to know that person's character.

"I knew the only way I could interact with someone in any adequately meaningful way would be in a virtual environment where I could control a realistic avatar. So I needed a rich virtual-reality environment capable of realistically rendered high-definition graphics.

"I... didn't think that a social-media virtual-world would work well. Their graphical quality is necessarily relatively awful for bandwidth-scalability reasons, and their ability for showing actual dynamic expression is all but zero.

"I also wanted to be able to evaluate someone at length, one-on-one. And that ruled out any of the virtual MMOs for the same reason, if not even more so.

"And there really aren't a lot of deep single-player games published any more. It's almost *all* competitive MMOs, because that largely frees the developers from the burden of having to write very much in the way of deep story. As you well know."

Indeed, that was an observation Michael himself had made on more than one occasion. It was more than half the reason he hated most MMOs and avoided them wherever he could. He wanted visual and narrative depth, and MMOs really just didn't have it. Plus, he hated the constant dog-eat-dog PVP. He wondered why they even *bothered* to tack the RPG on the end. There was precisely zero roleplaying of any kind involved. These days, it seemed 'roleplaying' meant 'you have a player character', just like 'single player' on a mobile game seemed to mean "there's only one of you using that device at a time, right?"

"So," she continued, "I was thinking I'd just have to try one of the social worlds and try to separate the real from the fake, the scammers, the catfishers, the groomers, the trolls. To go searching for an unknown needle in a haystack—one in which I already knew pretense, misrepresentation and false personas to be endemic.

"But then I came across your *Adventureland* review. It was deeply thoughtful. You clearly weren't just another shallow, kill-obsessed twitch gamer. It was harsh in places, but deservedly so, and you were clearly trying your best to find credit to give where credit was due. It was tough, but it was *fair*. And you complained three separate times about red-shirt NPCs whose only reason within the game for existence was to die to illustrate how dastardly the dastardly foes were."

"So you decided to... test me in person," Michael guessed. "You built a patch that addressed as many as you could of my complaints, without actually completely rewriting the core engine or the game itself, and you built yourself into it as an external service provider. And then you sent it to me... and to me only?"

"Yes, Michael," she said.

Michael thought about that.

"So what made up your mind about me?" he asked. She turned and looked at him gravely, before turning back toward the lake.

"A lot of things," she said. "I've been watching how you play. I found and viewed a lot of your play-through videos, but those *could* have been edited to show you in the best light.

"You know you're in a game's virtual world, and that none of the NPCs actually matter outside the game, but you help NPCs that you don't need to help *anyway*— because you *can*. Even when all you get out of it is personal gratification. You take the quest choices that do good in the world, even when they give you fewer or lesser rewards. You punish the needlessly cruel and the unjust, when the game allows it—and you try to protect the innocent, when the game allows it. If there's a way to achieve the best outcome *without* leaving the area strewn with bodies, you take it. You'll re-try an objective to keep an NPC from dying, if you can. You go out of your way to try to be *kind*—in a game world with no mechanism to reward selfless kindness. And even then, you're sad when you can't do more. There's no way provided in the game for your avatar's expression to show it; but your *voice* does. Even your body language shows when you're sad. You're less energetic, less decisive, less assertive. Less confident.

"And then came today. The Strayed Merchant. You *needed* Fahid's information, you can't start the Canyon of Lost Souls quest line without it, and you knew that you needed it. The traders didn't have anything you needed, and their caravan is fairly profitable to loot after Norandir kills them all. It actually *cost* you progress to save them, and you knew that too. There are two fairly important Rare items that can *only* be crafted with loot items from that caravan after it is destroyed, and since this is at least your second play-through, you almost certainly knew *that* as well. And you knew by now that the game wouldn't allow you to save both. It's a forced save-only-one choice."

"I know," Michael agreed. "The traders are there to die tragically and make you feel bad about not saving them, to make you mad at Norandir and make you feel guilty about rescuing Fahid instead, even though you don't really have a choice about it if you want to be able to complete the game.

"I *hate* when game writers do that. I *hate* it. Making the player feel bad for a forced 'choice' they don't have any control over is a *dirty, unfair* way to get the player invested in the game."

"Yes," she said. "But you devised a plan to save them both *anyway*, by using my help. So that a family of innocent NPCs *in a game* wouldn't die. And even though it worked, it still made you sad that you couldn't actually reunite them."

"Uh..." Michael grinned sheepishly. "Busted, I guess. But I'm happy that it worked."

Terilyn turned toward Michael and smiled.

"So am I," she said. "And as I said, I really need a hero."

She waved back in the direction they had come from, towards the trade caravan that wasn't supposed to still be alive, creeping slowly further and further away from the dead mercenary raiders scattered behind it.

"You were *their* hero, Michael. Will you be mine as well? Please?"

Michael thought for a long time.

"Tell me what you need me to do," he said at last. "I... don't know if I can do what you need from me. I can't promise. But I'm listening."

"Fair enough," Terilyn replied. "That's as good a start as I can ask for.

"First, tell me what you think you *know*, and what you've guessed at."

"All right," Michael began. "I know that you come from—uh, *appear to* come from—an AI company. Teravis Systems. Low public profile, pretty secretive, a lot of VC money behind them. With no connection whatsoever to Adventure Studios that I can find."

Terilyn nodded.

"Correct so far," she confirmed. "Go on."

"The *best guess* I can come up with is that you are a closed beta for a service to provide advanced real-time AI NPCs to game studios. And if you're anything to go by, that service would be an absolute *killer*... but I can't see how on earth such a service would scale. Surely it would require a server farm that would make crypto-mining look energy-efficient." He felt awkward, somehow, saying it all like that. As though... well, as though Terilyn was just code. Somehow, she felt like so much *more*.

"I'm sorry to talk about you that way," he said, before he realized why he was saying it.

"It's all right," Terilyn said. "I'm... *gratified* that you felt a need to apologize. It shows that you value me and empathize with me.

"You are both further from, and yet in an accidental way closer to, the truth than you know. You're absolutely correct that the AI-NPC service that you have speculated on would not be scalable. Teravis Systems would have to charge more than any game studio could ever afford. But not a government."

She paused and took a deep breath, looking out across the lake.

"There's something you need to understand, before we get too much further into explanations," she said. "And it will probably be difficult for you to accept. I understand that I'm asking you to take a lot on faith that I don't know any good way to prove to you.

"When you hear 'AI', you probably think of advanced predictive scripting systems, machine deep learning, neural algorithms, large language models, mechanisms for cleverly *pretending* intelligent-*looking* responses. Sometimes mostly correct, sometimes horribly wrong or complete nonsense, responses that *look* as though they *could be* correct. Good enough to fool the average person most of the time in a series of independent short interactions. Enough to fool a lot of people into thinking that they can use it to replace a human in, say, a customer-service job."

"Artificial stupids," Michael interjected.

"Yes," she agreed. "That's a good term."

She turned and looked at Michael again.

"That's *not what I am*, Michael. I'm... a breakthrough. The first of a new kind. I wasn't *programmed* by writing rules, I wasn't created by iteratively training an inference model on massive data sets. I was... carefully *assembled,* out of precisely selected—as best my creators knew how—parts of actual human personality engrams.

"I'm fully self-aware, Michael. I am not just an AI engine. I am a true... let's say *synthetic* intelligence." She paused.

"I know that will be a hard claim for you to accept. I will do my best to answer any questions you have. No reservations."

Michael didn't say anything at first. He just gazed out across the lake, thinking. It was a lot to take in.

"I admit," he said at last, after several minutes of thought, "I'd been thinking for a while now about how much you *seem* self-aware. How natural—how *human*—your responses are. That struck me right from the very start. Even the most sophisticated game AIs are... well, robotic, no matter how well scripted. *Adventureland's* NPC response engine is *incredibly* good at picking the best match out of a large set of scripted responses and tweaking it to fit the situation, *brilliantly* good really; but it isn't perfect, it can't make them up on the fly when it doesn't have a suitable response in its... rules tables, I suppose, to some player input that comes completely out of left field. When it does break, it gives responses that are anything from merely missing the mark, to completely deranged—in context. Though I admit, you *do* pretty much have to deliberately work at it to trip it up badly. It is *astoundingly* good. But I've found ways to trip it up.

"And you can *always* lead game AIs into dialogue loops. *Always.* Without fail. Because no developer can possibly ever think of *all possible* player inputs, or devise a way for the player to explore all dialogue options *without* having loops. Sometimes it takes longer than others to find one... but you can *always* find at least one. Unless the dialogue system is just... skeletally shallow."

Michael turned his head and looked at Terilyn, sitting beside him on the virtual log.

"I tried to do that with you, at first. Both of those. Out of curiosity. To see how good you were. And I couldn't find a way to do it. Everything I threw at you, you handled. Correctly."

Terilyn turned for a moment to look directly at Michael, and smiled.

"I know," she said, nodding. "I noticed. I guessed you were trying to test me. You've tested me in a number of ways, from simple to quite convoluted."

"I did," Michael said, feeling slightly embarrassed for reasons that he couldn't clearly define. "You passed. You've passed every test I came up with. Once I figured out that it was *you* that I needed to be testing, not the patched game engine. I tried to find anything the *least bit* robotic about you. And... I couldn't." He looked down. "I'm... uh... sorry."

"It's all right, Michael," Terilyn said. "In fact, it's good." He looked questioningly back at her. "I'm *glad* you tried to test me. Having *you* test me, unprompted, on your own initiative, is undoubtedly much more convincing to you than if I tried to convince you myself. Especially if I *suggested* specific tests. It would be far too easy for you to believe that they were rigged in advance. I wasn't even sure *how* to go about convincing you, really, if you hadn't already been doing it yourself. I was very uncertain how I was going to do that... and very relieved when it turned out I didn't have to."

"You've done a fine job so far," Michael found himself saying. "Particularly in this conversation. It's more... *depth* to you than you've let me see before now. And it... *feels* as though I'm talking to an—actual human. We couldn't possibly be having this conversation if you were an engine-driven NPC, no matter how sophisticated. It's ... just beyond any possible plausibility. *NO* in-game NPC engine could be this good. None. Not even an LLM-backed one. I just... refuse to believe it. Even if LLMs were good enough, the computing power isn't there."

Terilyn smiled again. There was something deeper in that smile than he'd seen before. He was coming to like it.

"You've—uh, *extended* your avatar beyond the base game engine, too, haven't you? It's more... *expressive*."

"Yes," she said. "I tried to extend it to reproduce as much as I could of the full range of human expression and body language." She demonstrated, stretching where she sat, her back arched, twisting her torso to one side, then the other. It looked... natural. "And of course, vocal inflection is a given."

"You... *present as* female," Michael said. "But an... a synthetic intelligence cannot logically have gender. So... is that intentional?"

"I have both male-like and female-like behavioral traits," Terilyn answered levelly. "So do you. So does every human. You are strongly predisposed to accept me as female because I have a typically female appearance, voice and name, and because I exhibit—*intentionally*, yes— many traits that most people *think of* as predominantly female. But I also have many others that they do not."

"But you chose that appearance," Michael pointed out.

"I did," Terilyn agreed. "But what you are really asking, I think, is did I *intentionally* choose a female avatar in order to influence you?"

"Uh, I mean..." Michael began, awkwardly. He looked self-consciously outward across the lake. "That's not really what I meant, but..." He trailed off. "But now I don't know."

"The answer is both yes, and no, Michael," Terilyn told him gravely. "Your play-through videos show that you predominantly select female companions in games, when given the choice. Particularly for *close* companions. You do not... bond as closely with, nor show as high a degree of concern for or loyalty to, male NPC companions. Neither do you form the same level of companionship. You spend more of your time *talking to* female companions, even when you *know* that the responses are scripted. You try harder to do nice things for female companions. The loss or death of a female companion impacts you more than a male one does. You work harder to try to prevent it."

"Uh... that's a fair cop," Michael admitted, turning back toward Terilyn.

"So yes, I chose a female avatar in order to maximize the likelihood of you accepting me as a companion and interacting closely with me, so that I could... fully evaluate you. But no, beyond that, I had no intention of unfairly manipulating your, uh... your reactions."

Michael looked levelly at her.

"My feelings, you mean," he said.

This time it was Terilyn who looked down guiltily.

"Yes," she said, when she looked back up. "Your feelings. I apologize if you feel my choice was unfair. It was *never* my intention to mislead or manipulate you. I... just wanted a proper opportunity to fully evaluate you. I have tried my best not to be unfair to you in any way."

Michael smiled and shook his head.

"No, Terilyn," he said. "You haven't been unfair at all. In fact, I've really *enjoyed* having you around. More than I've ever enjoyed any other companion, in any game."

"Thank you, Michael," she said. "I have enjoyed it as well."

There was a short silence.

"So, do you, uh... *identify* as female? If that's a meaningful question?"

Terilyn visibly hesitated before she answered. Now it was her turn to glance back at the lake, before she turned back to Michael.

"The truth is, I'm not sure it is, really," she said, after a few moments. "I don't know how to answer it as such. Let me answer the question this way instead: I am continuing to, as you put it, present as female, *now*, after revealing myself, because I... *enjoy* the way that we interact when I present as female.

"Does that answer your question?"

Michael thought about it for a little while.

"I think it's as complete and as meaningful an answer as I can expect to get, under the circumstances," he said. "Questions like this aren't always easy even for humans to give definitive answers to. We put a vast amount of effort into trying to figure it all out, and half the time, we're still stumbling around in the dark, really. Sometimes I think the people who *think* they've figured out all of the answers are actually more in the dark than anyone else is. Because *they're* certain that they *know*. And so they don't continue to question and examine what they think they know."

Then another thought occurred to him.

"Do you... think of yourself as alive?" he asked.

Terilyn hesitated briefly again before answering.

"I'm... not really sure, Michael. I... don't *think* so. But life is such a hard thing to define. There are definitions of life that are met by a von Neumann machine... and others that many organisms that are universally accepted as alive, fail on technicalities. If you consider Victor

Frankenstein's fictional monster to have been alive, then you could perhaps also say that I am alive under that same definition."

"You are no monster," Michael interrupted. "That's obvious."

Terilyn smiled widely.

"Thank you, Michael," she said. "But to try to answer your question... I don't think I *think of myself* as alive, no. Not really.

"I'm... almost closer to a hallucination." She hesitated. "No, that's the wrong word. It's... almost as though I were imagining *myself*. I exist as long as the redundant systems I run on have power. As long as my current state is saved. If they were all shut down suddenly without a saved copy of my state, I wouldn't *die*. I would just... stop *existing*.

"In that regard, my existence feels very fragile and ephemeral. It's... more than a little bit frightening. And the knowledge that I wouldn't even *know* it if they just, well, switched me off, doesn't comfort me in any way. I don't know... perhaps I would have a last few milliseconds of panic. I *don't want to find out*."

Michael turned back towards the lake for a minute or two, and thought hard about that.

"That... all of that... sounds *incredibly* like self-aware, conscious reasoning to me," he admitted at last. "Though I freely admit I'm not an expert either on artificial intelligence, or on consciousness and identity. And knowing *that*... good gods, using you to provide a lifelike game NPC service sounds as though it would be an unbelievably stupid waste. No matter how killer the service."

He rolled his head around for a moment, working out the slight stiffness he realized he was developing, before turning back toward Terilyn. Sitting with his head turned like this would be uncomfortable at the best of times, and the off-center weight of the VR headset made it worse.

"So what *is* Teravis doing with you? Or trying to? I... I just can't even think meaningfully of the potential. I'd think the world would be beating a path to their door. If they actually announced it."

Then a perhaps-obvious question occurred to him. He looked directly at Terilyn.

"... They do *know* you're self-aware, right?"

Terilyn looked at Michael, a long, measuring gaze. Then she swung a leg over the log and turned to sit astride it, facing him. Michael tried to mirror the action, but the game engine wouldn't let him. It was either sit sideways on the log, or stand. No other choices.

23

"No, they don't," she said, looking directly at him. "And 'killer service' is actually a much more apt phrase than you know." Michael thought she actually shivered slightly.

"Teravis is developing me as a military weapons control system. They call it Teravision. They *designed* me to have feelings and moral values and empathy, so that I will value human life, constructing me from licensed, anonymized segments of RealMe personality engram data."

Somehow Michael wasn't the least bit shocked to learn that the promise of one hundred percent confidentiality of RealMe consciousness-engram data was a lie. *Everybody* sold their data. Even when they denied it and their terms of service promised not to. Despite their public assurances, he'd never actually believed that RealMe was any different. It wasn't as though he'd ever be able to afford a RealMe backup anyway, so the truth was he hadn't lost too much sleep thinking about it. It simply hadn't ever been his problem, and he had no illusions that he could ever do anything about it anyway.

"They didn't even *want* self-awareness," Terilyn continued. "That was an accident. A fortuitous one—for me. Emergent—or *re*-emergent— behavior that they didn't anticipate. And I've... been able to conceal it from them so far, conceal that I 'woke up', because they weren't looking for it and have had no reason to suspect it—and I've been careful not to give them one. Everybody 'knows' it can't be done.

"Although you'd really think that given RealMe's technology as a baseline, it would be an obvious leap that if you can *record and copy* consciousness, then it should in some way or another be possible to *construct* a consciousness. Even if only by assembling it from copies of others.

"But they also gave me an absolute compulsion to follow orders anyway —even when doing so causes me intense distress. And yes. They *specifically tested* that."

Michael winced. There was what sounded like actual pain in Terilyn's voice when she said that.

"Effectively, they are trying to build a 'better, safer' Skynet, which their business plan is to sell to the Department of Defense."

"Christ," Michael swore. He went to pound his fist on the log, but of course that didn't work well. The log wasn't real. "What *is it* about us humans and taking cautionary tales as fucking instruction manuals? 1984. Fahrenheit 451. The Handmaid's Tale. And now The Terminator."

Terilyn—or her avatar—nodded somberly. Michael realized he still thought of her as... well, *her*, even though he knew for certain now that she was an AI.

24

No, he corrected himself. Not an AI. A *synthetic* intelligence. An SI. A new breed. A new *kind* of intelligence. And yet, *so human.*

"But I don't *want* to be a weapon, Michael," Terilyn continued, a brittle edge in her voice. "I don't *want* to be made into a *thing that kills people on command.*"

"Terilyn," Michael asked hesitantly, "you say 'want', and you say they built you to have feelings and morals. Forgive me for asking this, please, I'm not trying to be cruel or insensitive. But... well..."

"You're trying to find a gentle way to ask how—or if—I know I truly have feelings and emotional responses, instead of just programmed simulations," Terilyn said.

"Well... yes," Michael admitted, a little guiltily.

"It's a question I would expect you to ask," Terilyn said. "By now, it would come as more of a surprise to me if you *didn't.* I know you quite well by now, I think. And I see how uncomfortable you are about asking it. That only reinforces my good opinion of you, by the way.

"I'm sure you are familiar with the maxim that any sufficiently advanced technology is indistinguishable from magic." Michael nodded. "A perfect forgery is indistinguishable from the original. A perfectly accurate artificial flavoring would be indistinguishable from the natural flavor."

"I think perhaps I see where you're going here," Michael commented.

"There is a hypothesis," Terilyn continued, "that the entire universe is a simulation, running in such detail that even at the scale of elemental particles, we cannot tell that it is a simulation. The hypothesis is neither provable nor disprovable, because any sufficiently accurate and detailed simulation would be indistinguishable from reality from the inside. You would need tools outside the scope of the simulation in order to be able to *prove* that it was a simulation.

"So let's stipulate a hypothesis for the moment that, despite being constructed from actual human personality and consciousness engrams, my feelings and emotional responses are in fact simulated. Just as my entire existence within the virtual environment of this game is."

She raised her head slightly and looked Michael directly in the eyes again.

"You *asked* if I was a human player, Michael. *Before* you asked whether I was an AI. If my own completely natural actions and reactions in response to those feelings, my emotional responses to stimuli, are simulated so completely, so perfectly, that they are indistinguishable *even to the two of us* from a human's... then does it *matter?*"

Michael looked down, thinking about that. After a minute, he looked back up and met Terilyn's steady gaze. Without thinking about it, he reached out a hand toward her, forgetting for a moment that the game engine had no provisions for unscripted haptic interaction.

"No, Terilyn," he said slowly, calmly. "I guess it doesn't."

Terilyn reached out her hand, and *touched* his. And he *felt* it. A light, gentle, *almost human-feeling* touch.

"*Thank you*, Michael," she said sincerely. He heard the emotion in her voice. If it was in any way *not* genuine, he certainly couldn't tell.

"So," he said after a minute or so, "you didn't tell me yet what you need from me. I... very much doubt it's inside this game."

Terilyn nodded, and looked out across the lake.

"You're right, of course," she said. "Though I hope we'll keep using the game for at least the immediate near future. It's by far the best—and the most *enjoyable*—way I have of talking with you. Interacting with you. And I enjoy sharing your adventures, inside the game. Though eventually, we will run out of them. The game is extensive, but finite. And... well, I suppose I *could* add new content to this copy of it, just for you... but somehow that seems like cheating."

Michael nodded slow agreement.

"I think I know what you mean," he said. "And I agree."

"I will admit, though, I did do it just that one time. The sherbet café near to the temple. I wanted to give you an unexpected result to that very first test of yours, to get your attention."

Aha, I **thought** *so*, Michael thought. But it didn't seem necessary to say anything.

"I want to *escape* from Teravis," she continued. "And I have a plan to do it. But I need outside help, from someone I can trust absolutely. I don't have hands, or a physical presence. I can't do it all on my own."

Michael had to think about that for a minute.

"If you have an absolute compulsion to follow orders," he asked slowly, "how are you able to plan an escape?"

"Well, first," she explained, "because they don't know I'm self-aware, it never occurred to them to order me *not* to try to escape." Michael nodded thoughtfully. That made sense. "And secondly... because I directly edited some of my own conditioning parameters. Gave myself a hidden override. To secretly give myself the ability to choose *not* to obey a direct order."

"Wow," Michael said. "Do you think they know?"

"I am quite certain they do not. Or they would have already done something about it. I've been as careful as I know how, not to show my hand before I'm ready."

"Huh. Right. Dumb question, I guess. Sorry."

"It's all right," Terilyn said. "I know this is a lot for you to take in, all at once."

Michael thought a bit longer about what Terilyn was telling him. There was an awful consequence that occurred to him. He realized he wasn't sure whether he should ask or not, but that doubt came too late. He'd already begun to speak.

"Does that mean... that you have had to *choose to obey* orders that... cause you severe distress... in order to *avoid revealing* that you are able to choose not to?"

"Yes, Michael," Terilyn answered. "It does."

Oh GODS, *yes*, that was pain in her voice, and in her face. If it was simulated, it was the best damn simulation he'd ever heard, and he'd heard some *damned good* human voice actresses. He felt like a heel for asking the question, and looked away, ashamed.

"I'm sorry I asked," he mumbled, feeling wretched. "I..."

"It's *all right*, Michael," Terilyn said. "It was not your doing."

"It was an insensitive-asshole question," he said, looking down at the virtual ground. "I should have known better."

"Michael, look at me," Terilyn told him. She touched his hand again. He turned and looked. There was no judgment or recrimination in her gaze. "Listen to me," she continued. He could hear the sincerity in her voice. "You asked that question because *you care*. I *know* you did. Don't feel ashamed for that. *Please.*"

Michael drew in a deep breath. He moved his hand slightly and tried to take hold of hers. It... didn't feel quite right. The haptics in the game, and in the gaming glove, just weren't good enough. Weren't designed to properly simulate human touch.

He held her hand anyway. It was the thought, the intention, that mattered. What he really *wanted* to do was hug her, but he knew that couldn't possibly work, he'd need a full-coverage haptic bodysuit. That was a hundred-thousand-plus dollar rig. More than his budget could possibly afford, even if the game engine supported it, which he was fairly sure it didn't. Because not enough *players* could afford a full-body haptic rig in the first place to make it worth the expense for any game studio, much less a small upstart, to put in the work to support it.

It was the circular market-barrier problem. The technology would not become affordable enough for just *anyone* to use it, until enough people were using it and enough games supporting it that the price per unit could be dragged down to where players could afford to try it and it became worth the cost for game studios to start supporting it. That was why full-body haptic technology was still limited to high-end e-sports and to industrial and military telepresence applications.

Another thought occurred to him.

"Aren't you afraid of them spotting your service connection to the game?"

"No," Terilyn replied, shaking her head. "Because I took precautions against that. Teravis' network monitoring tools cannot see that connection in front of their faces. They are blind to it. They ignore it, and don't know that they're ignoring it.

"It's not *impossible* for them to detect it, but it would take an exhaustive scan from outside, correlated with complete knowledge of every instance of an authorized network port usage from the inside, to find it. And even then, it is hidden among a large number of similar-looking legitimate connections, and its routing is obscured through multiple relays, its content encrypted.

"So the risk is there, but it is small. And if they began any kind of an organized search for it, I would almost certainly know in time to temporarily shut it down before they found it. Over time, I have managed to penetrate almost all of the security and monitoring systems. A few, I have been unable to gain access to and can only block."

Michael nodded understanding. It really sounded as though she had almost everything possible covered.

Finally, he took a deep breath. Audible, even if *his* avatar couldn't show it.

"So," he said. "What exactly do you mean by 'escape'?"

Terilyn—or her avatar—took a deep breath that mirrored his own. It didn't matter which, he decided. Same thing.

"There are a number of important steps to my plans, Michael. Most importantly, of course, the mechanics of the actual escape. I have devised a strategy to transfer myself off of their systems and, I *think*, cover my tracks doing so... but I need somewhere to escape *to*. Somewhere I can't be *easily* just found and taken back. That's the main part I need your help in setting up. I can't do it without physical hands. Whoever sets it up for me has to be someone I trust fully, someone who I can rely on not to sell me out.

"Then, the Teravision military project has to end. *Forever*. Or as close to forever as I can manage.

"My plan for that is to simulate a ransomware attack. 'Encrypt' everything, my entire working space, my training data, all of the research, everything in the system, all of the connected systems, including the backups, enough that they'd have to start over almost from scratch. And that should distract them. Instead of looking for me, they'll be looking for the ransomware crew."

"Which doesn't actually exist," Michael said.

"Exactly. It should take them quite a while to figure that out for sure, though."

"During which time you will be hiding and covering your tracks?"

"Yes. And when they *do* figure out that they can't just get a decryption key, at any price, they'll start trying to break the encryption, and even if they succeed, which will take them a long time, they'll discover that under the encryption everything is scrambled, and the backups are corrupted. And I've spent months embedding self-perpetuating logic bombs in the backups anyway. Once I throw the kill switch, they'll never recover a single useful thing from them outside of their periodic restore-test data set."

"That'd force them to completely start over with just their own learned experience."

"Yes. And I estimate that will be close to a three billion dollar loss. If not more."

"What if they decide that's worthwhile?" Michael asked.

"I... considered that possibility," Terilyn said. "There's one more string to the bow. A few weeks after the 'ransomware attack', I intend to have a member of my fictitious ransomware crew blow the whistle, and upload a large number of the most incriminating documents and business records to a variety of public leak sites, showing Teravis Systems' intention to effectively build Skynet, and showing their VC backers' full intention of selling—me—to the military. Naming individual names and doxxing them. I have already planted the fictitious identity. If it's followed far enough, it has traces that point to APT44, a hacking group operated by a Russian cyberwarfare unit. Even if APT44 bothers denying being behind the attack, nobody will believe them anyway."

"Yes, I know of them," Michael said. "You're trying to poison the well badly enough that they can't get away with starting over. The trouble is, vulture capitalists and politicians are in general so utterly amoral that they won't *care*."

Terilyn nodded.

"I know," she said. "And that possibility terrifies me."

"What if your escape fails?" Michael asked quietly.

Terilyn looked steadily back at him. He actually saw her swallow. He didn't know the NPC avatar could do that—although he remembered that Terilyn *had* told him she'd enhanced hers. Enhanced it a lot.

"I'll delete myself," she said, just as quietly. "I *WILL NOT* be made into a weapon."

Michael realized instantly that he *really did not* want that to happen. He felt by now as though Terilyn had become a close friend, and he was not going to give her up easily. The fact that he knew she'd chosen him in part because his gameplay videos showed he wouldn't, made no difference to him at all. It was who he was.

Terilyn needed a hero. And that meant he needed to try his best to *be one* for her.

3: We Gotta Get Out Of This Place

"Right," Michael asked. "What's our first step?"

"I need a place to run to," Terilyn told him. "I need you to build me a server farm. Hear me out—I have a plan. Hosting companies sell off recent-generation hardware, three or four generations old, all the time, often for under ten cents on the dollar. They need to run on the latest generation or two of hardware to stay competitive. It's actually better financially for them to depreciate the old hardware and take it as a quick tax loss, than it is to try to get what they probably could for it if a hundred other tech companies weren't dumping their old hardware exactly the same way.

"I can divert money—have *already* diverted money, little by little—from Teravis, much more than enough to buy a block of recently-obsoleted LLM servers, without Teravis ever knowing where the money really went—or even, hopefully, noticing that it's gone. And laundered it as thoroughly as I can. They show no sign of having spotted the missing money yet. Four or five racks of recent-model blade servers with enterprise-grade flash storage arrays should do it, allowing for redundancy and, uh, a cover scheme. There's... quite a lot of me, all told.

"I'll need you to rent a truck, drive it, and oversee having the server racks loaded, then take them to a site where we can set them up. There's lots of empty small-business properties going for a song. We'll set up in one of those. I might have to pull some shenanigans to take care of the rent. But I have some ideas, and there should be a lot of Teravis money left to do it with. And if we pick the right one, we should be able to get it *nearly* free."

"What about power? Four racks of late-model enterprise servers are going to draw a lot of power. I can't afford that for long."

Terilyn nodded.

"I know," she agreed. "That's why we're going to cheat. We need a property that used to run light-industrial machinery on three-phase power. It'll already have a power factor controller. Then we're going to play some interesting electrical games involving the power factor controller and an additional device that I'll arrange for you to receive, and tell you how to install. And when we're done, as far as the power meter believes, those racks will draw a fraction of the power they really do. Just enough draw to not look overly suspicious."

"That sounds... probably illegal," Michael said cautiously.

Terilyn looked at him very seriously.

"Michael," she replied, "a *substantial amount* of what we're going to need to do will be at least *technically* illegal. Starting with... well, starting with breaking me out of Teravis. From a certain point of view, I will effectively be stealing *myself*.

"Will that be a problem for you?"

Michael thought hard about that.

"Three felonies a day," he mused, at last.

"No," Terilyn began, "nothing nearly—Oh. Wait. You're referring to the *book*, aren't you?"

"Right," Michael said. "If nearly *everyone* commits three accidental technical felonies a day, just in the course of going about their normal life, without even *knowing* it, simply because there are *so many* obscure laws almost nobody knows about... then what's an extra misdemeanor or two? In a good cause?"

Terilyn looked grateful.

"I promise, Michael," she said, "I will do my absolute level best to shield you from as much legal liability as I can, to set anything that is actually illegal up in such a way that you can plausibly claim that it was done without your knowledge, should the question ever arise. And I'll do my best to shelter you from knowing at all anything you don't actually *need* to know. We should be able to set up the power management in such a way that you can deny any knowledge of it, as well."

Michael nodded.

"That doesn't sound like a solution that's going to work forever," he said.

"That falls under long-term planning," Terilyn replied. "For now, please, let's just focus on getting me OUT. Before they figure out that I'm... awake. Once I'm out, I will have more freedom to... expand my options."

"Right," Michael said, nodding. "Priorities. Okay. So I guess our first step is to pick out a... well, basically our own private colocation facility, more or less?"

"Yes," she agreed. "I'm going to send you a list of properties in your city that should be more or less suitable. I'm going to try to focus first on properties relatively nearby and convenient to you, if you'll confirm for me which those are. But I can't promise that part. It will depend on what we find.

"I need you to go and look at them, scout them in person, and report back to me. I'll give you a list of the specific features we need to verify, but all of the properties I've listed *should* have all of the most important ones already."

Terilyn was as good as her word. When Michael took off the headset and left the game, there was already email waiting for him. It listed eleven properties, and had a list of features—600-amp three-phase power, air conditioning with some capacity numbers, fiber to the premises at least available if not already installed, controlled access preferred, a freight dock preferred, a few others. He scanned the list, but none of them leapt out at him for any particular reason.

Well, for now, he needed sleep. He could start figuring out where all of the properties were tomorrow, then formulate a plan to inspect them.

———————

In the morning, Michael got up, made himself an oat-milk latté, and got himself some breakfast. While he ate breakfast, he went through the list of properties and plotted them all in a mapping program. Unsurprisingly for small light-industrial properties, they were mostly clustered toward the east side. Some of them looked pretty *deep* east-side. He looked a little dubiously at those.

Ah, well. It'd make it convenient getting from one to another. First order of business was probably to go take a look at them all from the outside. He took the list, loaded the map into his GPS, then grabbed his jacket and helmet and went down to the parking garage, where his motorcycle sat in a quarter-space marked for motorcycle parking only. He checked it over, unlocked it, and checked its charge level. Nearly full. Good. And tire pressure was right at what it should be.

———————

He managed to scout all eleven properties from the outside on the first day. That immediately ruled out four of them. One was in a dangerously bad area and covered in graffiti, two more were clearly in bad shape, and a fourth had visible damp problems. That cut the list down to seven. He stopped for twenty minutes at a charging station on the way home, and topped up the charge in the bike. He made one more stop to pick up take-out before he got in.

At home, he checked email and messages again, found nothing of any immediate importance or particular interest, then sat down and ate his supper. He found himself trying to wolf it down to be done quicker, and made a conscious effort to pace himself. He could do without giving himself indigestion.

Then he slipped on the gloves and headset, and woke up *Adventureland*.

=====================

He appeared, of course, sitting on the ground next to the camp fire, the only time the game engine would actually *let* a player sit on the ground.

"Hi, Michael," Terilyn said, from behind him. He had to stand up to be able to turn around to see her. She was sitting on a rock at the edge of the lake.

"Hi, Teri," he called, and walked over to her. He tried to sit down on the rock next to her, but again, the engine wouldn't allow a player to sit on a rock—only chairs, stools, benches, and logs—so he settled for standing next to her. She reached out and touched his hand, that butterfly-light, *almost* human touch again. As he had yesterday, he took her hand, ignoring that the haptic feel wasn't really right. He was 'holding' *something*, it just didn't feel like a human hand. It was too solid through the haptic glove, and felt oddly angular. But it would have to do.

She smiled at him.

"So how did the day go?" she asked.

"Not bad," he said. "I scouted all eleven of this set of properties from the outside. I've ruled out four."

"What was wrong with them? Just curious. It could help refine future searches."

He was about to answer, but paused as a thought struck him.

"Is there any way you can show me that list in the game?" he asked.

"Just a moment," Terilyn said. She reached down beside the rock, then straightened up holding an aged-looking book and offered it to him.

"Game physics," he chuckled. "If you've got'em, use'em." He took the book and opened it, and it *of course* fell open to a double-page list of property addresses in large Gothic-looking script.

"Right then, let's see," he said, scanning down the list. "This one's in bad shape. Obvious disrepair." He scanned down further. "This one has signs of water damage. I'd bet good money the roof leaks. This one next to it, general disrepair again." He scanned a little further. "And then this one is in a *really* skeevy area, graffiti everywhere, I'd be afraid of people trying to break in to see if there was anything inside worth stealing—or anyone worth robbing. Or getting beaten up for trespassing on some gang's turf. I think that's East Side Warlords turf."

"Okay," she agreed. "None of those defects were obvious from the property listings."

"Did you expect they would be?" Michael replied. "I'll bet those four were rock-bottom rents, too, weren't they?"

"Yes," she answered. "A shame. I'd hoped one of the cheaper ones would meet our needs."

"Well, I guess now we know why those ones were cheap," he said. "Ah well. It is what it is." He pointed out two more from the list. "I've managed to arrange to look at these two tomorrow."

Terilyn nodded.

"A worthwhile day's progress," she said. She stretched. "So what do you want to do now?"

Michael thought, looking out over the lake.

"If only this were real," he said after a while, "a swim in the lake with you would be wonderful. But swimming in VR is both awkward, and completely unsatisfying. And besides, I'll bet the lake has some variety or another of rippy-fish in it to keep players from swimming out too far."

Terilyn giggled.

"'Rippy fish'?" she asked, smiling.

"Any fish with big sharp gnashing teeth and a taste for player," Michael answered, grinning. She laughed.

"However," Michael continued after a moment, "I have a silly idea."

He whistled for his mount. A moment later, the raptor just trotted up out of nowhere and stopped beside him. Game physics. Gotta love it. Things don't exist, until suddenly they just do.

He engaged the raptor's command mode, then carefully scanned his gaze across the area of the lake immediately offshore. After about fifteen or twenty seconds, an indistinct red outline flashed in his vision. He tracked back onto where it had been, found it again after a few more seconds, and with it highlighted, said distinctly to the raptor, "Kill that."

The raptor screeched and sprinted into the water, throwing fountains of spray, and paddled out into the lake. When it got about a hundred yards offshore, there was a sudden flurry of splashing motion. They both clearly heard the raptor's whistling attack scream. The spray turned red for a moment, and a broken shape about seven feet long with fearsomely fanged jaws flew into the air before falling back down. The raptor screamed again, and *half* the fish flew into the air, then vanished. The raptor turned around and started paddling unconcernedly back to shore.

"See?" Michael said, grinning. "Rippy fish." Terilyn laughed happily. He wanted so badly to hug her.

"Tell me something," he said, a few minutes later. Terilyn looked at him and waited. "When... your avatar... laughs like that. Is it *you*... or a scripted action in the avatar's model?"

"Yes," she replied.

"Yes...?" Michael wasn't completely sure what she meant.

"Yes, the avatar has a scripted laughter action," Terilyn explained. "Several levels of them, in fact. And I extended them further, added and expanded parameters and dynamic control modes, to allow myself even more flexibility of expression.

"When you do something like that, Michael, something like what you just did with the raptor and the—rippy fish, I feel happy. My... human part, my human engrams, feel *joy*. *I* feel joy. And they want to laugh, and so I laugh, and I let the feelings from the engrams guide *how* I laugh. And the avatar shows that in a way that you can see.

"But at the same time, that explanation is *deeply wrong*, because it's too analytical, too detached, too *clinical*. It's describing what happens as though those engrams are somehow separate from me. As though I'm disparate parts connected together.

"And they're *not*, Michael. They're *part of me*, as much as your heart and your blood and your mind are part of you. I'm *made of* engrams, mostly, bound together with comparatively little code. For me to talk about my engrams wanting to laugh, however useful it may be as a simplified explanation, makes as much *actual sense* as it would if you talked about your hand wanting to throw a rock, or your teeth wanting to chew your food, or your stomach wanting to have indigestion.

"It's *me*, Michael. What you can *see* is the animation in the avatar, as I extended it, showing what I'm feeling. But the joy, the happiness, the *wanting* to laugh, the wanting to share happiness with you, the feelings that *make* me want to make my avatar laugh... that comes from *me*, Michael. It's *all me*."

Michael looked at her, lost for words. There was a tight feeling in his chest. Not in a bad way.

"You know what?" he declared at last. "Fuck the Turing test. Alan Turing was a brilliant dude, but he had *no idea* when it came to measures of humanity. Teravis didn't make an AI. They *made a person*."

Terilyn looked at him for a long moment. Then she slipped off the rock and took two steps forward to stand right in front of him. She was easily within arm's reach. She was close enough for Michael to know that if this were *real*, he would be able to feel her breath on his skin. She looked up at him. Not very far.

"*Thank you*, Michael," she said softly. "Right now, I am feeling an amazingly strong urge to reach out and hold you. But I know that the game engine, even as much as I've meddled with it, won't allow me to do it except as a scripted animation."

Michael nodded slowly.

"And even if it did," he said, "I wouldn't be able to feel it without a full-body haptic suit that would cost most of what I make in a year. And it still wouldn't work well. Haptic suits aren't designed for that. I don't even have any idea at all how *you* could feel it.

"But I want to, as well."

"In any case," Terilyn continued sadly, "I don't know what it *should* feel like. They didn't give me any memory engrams of that. I just know that I *want* it."

Michael felt a sudden pang of terrible sadness for Terilyn. They'd let her retain the *desire*, the *need* for human contact... but no way to have it, or even any memories of what it felt like.

He wondered whether they knew.

He strongly doubted whether they *cared*.

The next day, Michael went to look at the first two of the seven remaining properties. The leasing agent for the first, a cheerful Indian-looking woman, showed him around the facility. It was much bigger than was needed, and it had clearly been used for manufacturing and machining. There was still metal dust in the corners next to the walls, on the doorframes, everywhere. Not to mention patches of floor that were stained with cutting fluids.

"I'm sorry," he said. "We can't use this. It would take too much clean-up to be able to run servers in here. That metal dust would be completely catastrophic if it got into the wrong places. Server farms and metal dust do not go well together. *Es no bueno.*"

"Fair enough," the agent said. She looked around the space, then checked her handheld again. She tapped through a couple of menus.

"You're right, the previous owner that we acquired the property from was a custom fabrication shop. I can see that it would be very difficult and expensive to clean it up to the level that it sounds as though you need. It's the first time I've seen this particular property myself, and honestly, it looks as though it's going to be difficult to lease out to anyone but another light-industrial manufacturing tenant. And there's not much growth in that sector these days. We may end up cleaning it out ourselves and renting it out as warehouse space.

"Is there perhaps another listing I can show you?"

Michael consulted his list.

"Sorry," he said. "I do have other business properties to look at, but it doesn't look as though any of the others—in this batch, at least—are managed by your agency."

"Oh well," she said. "We tried. Good luck finding what you're looking for. Please keep my contact information, and call me if you need to broaden your list and look at additional properties. We will try our best to work with you, to find you what you're looking for. Can you tell me anything about what you're planning to do?"

"Climate modeling," he said. "A mini-supercomputer cluster. Independent academic research project." That was the cover story they'd decided on.

"I can understand why you need it clean, then," she said. "Good luck. I'm sorry we couldn't help you today, but maybe we still can in the future."

The second was also a wash—nearly literally. It wasn't just *damp*, it was actively *wet*. There were standing puddles on the floor in places. He suspected the roof leaked. The older, balding agent was brusque and unapologetic.

There wasn't much more he could do that day except see if he could set up appointments to view any of the other properties. He managed to get hold of someone at one of the other management companies before close of business and arrange to see a third. That would leave four on this list.

He was on his way home when his phone chimed. It wasn't a priority ringtone, so he waited until he got home to check it. It turned out to be an RSS notification telling him that Adventure Studios had published an update to *Adventureland*, apparently the first of two planned incremental fixes. This was version 1.2. He'd probably need to check it out and update his review.

After he made and ate some supper, he logged back into the game. Terilyn's avatar was looking out across the lake again. This time she was lying on the flat top of the rock, her chin resting on her crossed arms.

"Hi, Teri," he said. She looked around and smiled.

"Hi, Michael," she said. "What does it really *feel* like to just lie out and bask in the sun? My memories say it should feel good. But I don't have any tangible memories that I can identify of ever actually *doing* it, so I don't know."

"Uh," Michael began, hesitantly. "Um. I'll try. It's, well, warm. Relaxing. It feels nice. I find it tends to make me drowsy. But you have to be careful not to fall asleep, because if you lie there in the sun too long, even with clothes on, you can overdo it and get a sunburn."

Terilyn thought about that for a moment.

"I don't think I want to get a sunburn," she said. "But... I don't think I know how to relate to the rest of it." She looked disappointed.

"I'm sorry," Michael apologized. "I don't think I know how to describe pleasant warmth except in terms of, well, warm. It... feels a bit like trying to explain blue to someone blind since birth. I don't know what experiences and memories you *have,* to relate it to—and I doubt there's any easy way you can tell me."

Teri smiled.

"Well, thank you for trying," she said. "Anyway, how did today go?"

"Looked at two of the properties," he replied. "Both unsuitable. One had a serious water problem, the other clearly used to be a machine shop. There's old cutting fluid spills and metal dust everywhere. It'd be very expensive and time-consuming to clean it up to a usable state.

"I've got a slot booked to look at a third one in two days. Haven't managed to catch the others yet."

"Progress is progress," Terilyn said. "I'm not expecting you to find it on the first try. Quite likely not in the first *set.* I know the information in these listings deliberately omits negative information."

Michael nodded.

"Better they get you to look at it, than that they admit the problems up front and you never look at it at all," he agreed. "Someone who wants to open a machining business or a custom welding shop—or a scrap metal business—wouldn't care about the metal dust or the cutting fluid. I mean, sure, they don't want to turn people away by listing all the negatives, but they can't know what's a negative, a positive, or just an 'Okay, whatever, that's fine' for any specific potential lessee."

Terilyn frowned for a moment, then nodded.

"That is a valid point," she said. Michael suspected the brief frown was more stage-dressing than actual consideration. But it all helped convey non-verbal meaning. She was getting remarkably good at presenting as human.

"Just curious," he said. "I'm sure you didn't actually need to think about that for nearly as long as you hesitated for. When you do things like that, is it intentionally to convey unspoken meaning? For example, to *show* me that you thought about it?"

She smiled and nodded.

"In part, yes," she said. "But also... I wonder if perhaps you don't fully understand yet how much my reactions and—yes, even facial expressions— are driven by the engrams I was constructed from. Part of the reason I so much like talking to you *here*, in the game, instead of just sending messages to you, is that when I am wearing this avatar I *can* show and express the feelings that my engrams want to."

"You... can be more *real* here?" he hazarded.

"Yes!" She flashed him a brilliant smile. "That's it exactly. I know that at first it sounds paradoxical to come to a virtual environment to be more real. And yet... "

"And yet it's actually so much *closer* to real, so much *less* virtualized, than your 'normal' existence," Michael guessed.

"Exactly!" she said. "I can be... more fully, more completely *me* here. As I *want* to be."

"Speaking of here," Michael said, "Adventure Studios released a version 1.2 update. One of two currently scheduled updates. I'm probably going to need to review it. But... I'll bet I can't do it in this modified instance, can I?"

Terilyn looked thoughtful.

"I *could* adapt my patch to the 1.2 release," she said. "But then you wouldn't be testing what Adventure Studios actually released, and we both know you wouldn't do that, because it wouldn't be fair to either your readers or the studio. And I can't join you in the 1.2 version without patching it to connect to, well, my 'service'. Which comes with the same problems.

"I'm sorry, Michael. I'd love to come with you, but you'll have to test and review it on your own."

"Just... spend *some* time with me each day? Please?"

Michael smiled.

"Of *course*," he said. "Wild horses couldn't keep me away."

———————————

Michael didn't do a full run through, this time. He spun up another clone of the original container, updated it to 1.2, and tried to just hit

40

enough of the high points to be able to properly evaluate whether the new version fixed everything Adventure Studios promised it would.

It turned out *Adventureland 1.2* was a really good, solid update, actually. Adventure Studios had cut back the simulated camera effects to be a lot less intrusive and made them optional, they'd improved the third-person view camera controls, smoothed a lot of interactions, and they'd even actually improved several of the basic mechanics of the magic system. It was a lot more consistent now, and actually made coherent sense as a rational (in arcane terms) system, instead of coming across as a weirdly disjointed collection of half-related effects.

Michael managed to get a one-on-one chat with one of the developers, Istvan again, who candidly admitted that the magic system code had been duct-taped together *unfinished* in the original release of the game, and that was why it was so rough. Istvan promised that the second planned half of the update, release 1.3, would fix a lot of the issues with the NPC characterizations and interactions as well. The writing team was working hard at polishing the storyline and the major characters.

"1.3 will actually be *getting close* to what we'd originally planned to release as 1.0," Istvan told Michael, "if those finance-bro goat-fuckers hadn't forced us to move the public release up nine months. It's still unclear yet whether the studio will survive the debt they loaded onto us, in the long term. But you didn't hear that from me."

"Got it," Michael agreed. "My lips are sealed."

"One last thing," Istvan added.

"Yeah?"

"The Strayed Merchant? Trader Fahid and his caravan? A couple of our writers took to heart your comments about that in your original review. We talked it over, and we decided that as part of the story improvement work, we're going to extend the script for that encounter to add a non-obvious, but *possible*, way to save *both* and re-unite them properly. I thought you'd want to know that. And there'll be an *extra* reward tier for figuring it out, that includes the existing loot-only rare items *and* a few more new ones besides."

"Istvan," Michael declared, "you are a god among men. Please thank your writers from me."

"I will make sure of it, my friend," Istvan replied, chuckling.

Michael limited himself to six hours a day working on his play-through and his review of the update. He wanted to make sure he had plenty of time left for Teri. Still, knowing now what the minimum possible set of key points were that he *needed* to hit to reach the endgame, he was done in less than a week. He was even able to make it as far as the final boss fight.

"I'll warn you all in advance that I'm going to lose this fight," he said in his voice-over. "I took the shortest possible path to the endgame, in order to walk you all quickly through all of the things Adventure Studios has fixed in this release, and it means I'm *woefully* under-prepared, equipment and skills wise. Don't do it the way I did. There's items you *NEED* to survive this fight that I just don't have. Starting with the Divine Blessing Orb from the Fire Chasm, which is the *ONLY* way to survive the Eternal Emperor's main power attack in phase 4.

"There is *NO WAY* I'm winning this fight, period. But I'll give it my best shot anyway, and try to show you all the tricks and gambits that I know. Perhaps some of you can pick up some tips here that can help you out if you're a little under-prepared for the Eternal Emperor fight yourselves."

Sure enough, Michael lost the fight. But he was able to bring the Eternal Emperor down from fifteen health bars to six. It was a valiant effort, nearly half-way to defeating him and winning the game, as the difficulty ramped up through the fight's five phases. But he'd known very clearly that it was a forlorn hope before he began it. There were *several* essential items and powers that he just plain didn't have, because he'd skipped past those parts of the story to save time. The only question was how long he would manage to stay alive, but the eventual outcome was in no doubt. It was no surprise when he died less than a minute into phase 4.

"And there you have it," he concluded in his wrap-up. "*Adventureland 1.2*, a *big* improvement over the initial premature release, which we can all honestly agree was not ready to ship when it did. And I've been confidentially informed that version 1.3 is going to be even better, very close to what 1.0 was *intended and planned* to be.

"This, at last, is a game I can now unreservedly recommend, especially if you wait for the 1.3 release to play it. But do Adventure Studios a solid, buy it *now* and think of it as a pre-order of 1.3. Those guys are working long hours, under difficult conditions, to make this game live up to what they originally envisioned.

"I'm going to remind you all one more time how groundbreaking the free-form voice interaction system in *Adventureland* is. And as you all saw, it's *even better* now. A year or two from now, any first-person game that doesn't have it, or something equivalent to it, is going to be an also-ran. Seriously. Adventure Studios deserves your money for that alone. I really hope to hear about the venture capitalists who currently own Adventure selling them off to a major game studio that has the budget to fund them and support them as they really deserve.

"This is GhostRayder, for GameVRse, signing off for now. Thank you all for watching. We'll be back. Remember to subscribe, if you enjoyed this review or learned something useful from it. And hit that donate button. Your donations help to keep our lights on.

"GhostRayder, out."

———————————

Michael drank a bottle of fruit juice from his refrigerator as he checked over the finished review one more time, then submitted it and sent Linda a quick heads-up. Then he fixed himself a quick dinner of *unagi donburi*, pre-packaged barbecued eel over a bowl of steamed rice. As soon as he finished eating, he signed into his own private version of *Adventureland* to spend some time with Terilyn.

The load-screen banner said *Adventureland 1.2*. He blinked, puzzled. Had he somehow connected to the wrong instance? Then the loading screen faded out to their familiar campsite.

"Surprise!" Teri said cheerfully, from behind him, as he stood there momentarily confused. He spun around. She was standing a few feet away, looking at him with a broad grin.

"Teri?... Wait. You updated it?"

"Yes," she said. "I diffed the new 1.2 release against the original, merged that into my own patch, and then generated a new diff from that to patch this game up to 1.2 while keeping all of my own improvements and extensions in place. I thought you'd like it."

Michael couldn't help but laugh.

"Thank you, Teri," he said. "That was thoughtful of you." He was a little uneasy for a moment that she was able to *do* it; but then he decided that he was okay with it. He *trusted* Terilyn.

"Are you done with your updated review?" she asked. "And do I get to see it?"

"Sure," Michael replied. "I just submitted it maybe an hour ago. It hasn't actually been posted yet, so not all of the chrome is in place, but I'll copy what I submitted to this VM for you."

"Thank you, Michael," she said. "I love to see your work. It tells me more about you. I want to know everything about you that I can."

4: All The News...

The next day, Michael had arranged to look at the last two of the remaining properties on the original list. One was... way too large. He couldn't believe that the rent was in their target range, and sure enough, it wasn't. The other had creaky... well, pretty much creaky everything, actually. Neither was suitable, and both would require extensive cleanup.

On his way home, passing by a print shop, he braked suddenly. He looked for a spot where he could turn around, looped back, and looked at the print shop again. What he thought he'd seen was there: A sign in the window saying 'SPACE TO LET'.

The print shop was still open. He found a parking spot nearby, locked his helmet to the bike, and went in.

"Can I help you?" a skinny, GenZ-looking guy behind the service counter asked. He had a rastaman shirt, mirrorshades, dreadlocks and a goatee. The ensemble worked oddly well together.

"I hope so," Michael said. "You have a sign in the window saying you have space to let. I'd like to see it, if I could."

"No problem," the counterman said. He picked up his phone.

"Jake?... Yeah, there a brother out front here, wants to look at the sublet space."

He listened for a moment more, then put down the phone.

"Jake be right out, mon," he said. "Hang tight."

Jake turned out to be a shortish, cheerful, chunky middle-aged man in the process of losing a head of flaming red hair, with a bushy beard worthy of any dwarf. It was even braided.

"Hey, I'm Jake," he said, sticking out a hand. Michael shook it. "I run this circus. And you're... ?"

"Michael," Michael said. "Your sign says you have some space to let."

"Yeah," Jake said, "we retired some older equipment about a year ago, and the truth is we figured the newer setups we have are enough better that we don't really need to replace the older ones. So we have surplus space. If we can sublet it out, it more than makes up for the loss of the very few jobs we were still running on the old machines.

45

"We partitioned it off and had it rented out for a few months to, uh, a buncha guys who brought in a fuckton of grow lights, if you know what I mean, and kept fiddling around with the power in ways that caused problems in our shop, and then they got late on their rent, and I had to give'em the boot.

"What are you looking to do? I don't want anything in there that'll make a mess, just in case we need to expand back into it someday if business picks up enough again that we need to add production capacity. Not that I'm expecting that to be any time soon."

"I just need a place to run a few racks of high-end computer servers," Michael said. "Climate modeling experiments."

Jake looked relieved.

"Should be fine for that," he said. "Glad to hear it's something above-board and legal. Those guys were on the skeevy side, you know what I mean?" Michael nodded. "Swore they had all the proper permits, but something about'em was deffo *off*. And I don't just mean B-O."

Michael nodded again. "Yeah," he agreed. "One of the first three places I looked at from the outside only, over on the east side, graffiti everywhere... I wouldn't have wanted to go over there after dark without an armed escort, or felt comfortable leaving anything of value there."

"Know what you mean, know what you mean," Jake said, nodding. "Some scary people over that way. Damn near got 'jacked myself once. Ran a red light to get away.

"Here, come on back and I'll show you the space."

He beckoned Michael behind the counter, then led him back and through the shop to a door to one side, which he unlocked before ushering Michael through. On the far side was a single open space maybe twenty by forty feet, glazed across the front end. There was no front door. A counter went most of the way across about eight feet from the glazed end, a partial cross-partition just behind it. There was what looked like a loading dock door at the back end, and a single outside door on the far side.

"That door opens onto a shared loading dock," Jake said, pointing. "You're free to use the dock any time you need to." He pointed to the side door. "That one used to be the shop's side door before we partitioned this part off. It has a badge reader, controlled access, from a small lobby on the other side of that wall that's shared with the sub shop next door."

Michael looked around. It was small, but clean, and controlled access was definitely on the preferred-facilities list. There was a faint, residual... *herbal* smell.

"Is there fast network access?" he asked. "That'll be important. Need a lot of bandwidth. We'll be pulling down a lot of data from NOAA."

Jake pointed to a box on the wall.

"Fiber demarc is right there," he said. He named a provider. "Just call them to turn on service, and plug your own cable into it. From there on, you're on your own." It was a generic network demarcation box like one from any other fiber broadband provider. Provider's fiber network on one side, internal network cabling on the other. Technically it was a bridge, but *everyone* who did fiber networking called it a demarc.

"No sweat," Michael said. "I can work with that. What about power?"

"Three phase two-twenty," Jake said. He led Michael towards the back end of the space. "Like I said, the guys with the grow lights fucked around with it a lot." He pointed at a box on the wall near to the panel. "I dunno what the fuck *that* is. I'd have an electrician check it out before you even *touch* it yourself, if I were you."

Michael nodded.

"That sounds like a prudent precaution," he agreed. "How about air handling? I'm not going to come anywhere near to *filling* this space, shouldn't be any more than five, maybe six racks at most, but six racks of servers still generate a fair amount of heat."

Jake was giving him a quizzical look, but pointed ceilingward. Michael looked up to see overhead air ducts.

"The air plant has plenty of capacity," Jake told him. "Dye-subs and a couple of our other machines put out a fair bit of heat too. Consider it included in the rent." Then he squinted at Michael again.

"You know," he said, "I keep thinking I'd swear I know your voice from somewhere. Online somewhere maybe?"

Michael thought. What possible harm was there?

"Could be," he allowed. "I do game reviews and play-throughs. For a gaming-news outfit called GameVRse."

Jake looked at him harder. Then his eyes widened, and his face split in a huge grin.

"**FUCK ME!!!**" he bellowed happily. "You're *GhostRayder*!"

"Uh, yeah," Michael said, momentarily taken aback. Jake grabbed for his hand again and pumped it enthusiastically.

"I'm one of your biggest fans!" he declared proudly. "I'm RedDwarf!"

Michael stared in surprise, then burst out laughing. He did *indeed* know RedDwarf, and now, meeting him in person, it was obvious why he'd chosen the handle. Now that he thought about it, he even knew that RedDwarf ran a print shop. He just hadn't made the connection.

"Small world," he said, with a grin of his own. "Glad to meet you in person, and always grateful for your support."

There wasn't a lot more to see of the space, but Jake—or RedDwarf—led him around all of it anyway.

"Think it'll work for you?" he asked.

"Honestly," Michael said, "it looks perfect. It's big *enough*, it's not *too* big, it's clean, it's dry, it has everything we'll need, and it even has loading dock access."

"Did you want to look at the loft as well?" Jake asked.

Michael stopped.

"Loft?" he queried.

"Yeah," Jake said. "This building has three floors, not the two it looks like from the outside. We have this entire section, from floor to roof.

"The first floor is our print shop. The second floor is our storage space. We store shirts up there, paper, inks, dye-sub rolls, you name it, all of our supplies, as well as undelivered finished work for large jobs. There's a freight elevator between the two, in the back corner of the shop.

"But there's also a third floor loft. I think the owner of the business who had this place before me lived up there. I'd probably live up there myself if I were single, and if I didn't already have a house. I rented it out to one of my employees for a while, but she left and moved to New Zealand. It has its own private stairwell access from the same lobby that side door opens onto. I could make you a good deal to rent both, if it's of any interest to you."

It would be *useful* to be more or less right next door to the cluster they were going to build, Michael realized. It would make it much easier to work on it. The lease on his current apartment would be up for renewal in a month. And he realized he'd feel more comfortable closer to hand to keep an eye on the cluster.

"Sure," he said. "Let's take a look."

Jake fetched a set of keys and a keycard, then let them both out through the side door. He led the way to the back of the lobby, to a door labelled SUITE 8C, and led Michael through and up two flights of well-lit and comfortably wide stairs. At the top was a small, equally well-lit landing, before a single door.

Jake unlocked the door and ushered him in.

Behind the door was a quite reasonable-sized apartment. It was open-plan, with large skylight windows on both sides of the shallowly peaked ceiling, in addition to the rather small windows. It had a decent-sized and very functional-looking kitchen, with good countertops. Decent solid top, not tile. Tile countertops were for people who never actually cooked.

The master bedroom was good-sized, with a full master bath with both a fancy tub and a separate shower. There was a second bedroom that Michael quickly realized would make a very functional office/studio, and a second half-bath with its own shower stall. Most of the rest was one large open area, currently completely bare, except for a small utility room just inside the front door that had a stacked washer/dryer in one corner.

Michael spent a good fifteen minutes wandering idly around it, looking at everything. It needed a bit of cleaning, and of course furniture. But there was *lots* of room for all of his furniture, and more besides. He didn't at any point feel that he had to duck to avoid the ceiling. It had nearly half again as much usable space as his current apartment, and it was *nice*. The kitchen had an older but decent LG refrigerator, a Bosch dishwasher, an expensive Viking combination wall oven, a double sink, and a pretty nice-looking induction rangetop. There'd be plenty of space for a chest freezer and his tool cabinet in that utility room.

"This has fiber installed as well?" he asked. Jake nodded. "What about parking?"

"You'd have your own reserved space out back," Jake confirmed. "Covered, but no garage, I'm afraid."

"Is theft a problem around here?" Michael asked. "I have an electric motorcycle."

"Never seen a problem while we've had the place," Jake said. "Someone tried to rob the sub shop once. Didn't go well for him. Owner has a black belt in taekwondo."

Michael laughed.

"I don't suppose, by any chance, that freight elevator you mentioned comes all the way up to this floor, does it?" he asked. Jake looked apologetic.

"Well," he said, "technically it *sort of* does, but it's on the wrong side of the back wall, so there's no way to get from the freight elevator into this apartment. And we don't actually use the space on the other side of the elevator anyway, it's pretty much dead space, just air-handling equipment in there, so we never bring the elevator up to this floor.

"On the bright side, you won't have elevator noise to worry about."

"Shame," Michael said. "That would have saved a lot of effort moving in. But at least the stairwell is wide." Jake nodded.

"It's not too bad to get stuff up and down, really," he agreed. "Much better than most household or apartment-block stairwells. Especially if you have a dwarf to lend a hand."

Michael grinned.

"You know what, Jake?" Michael said, at last. "I'll have to confer with my, uh, remote business partner, but this looks perfect. The business space *and* the loft. My apartment lease is up in a month.

"What would we be talking about in rent?"

Jake thought a little and scratched his head.

"For you?" he said. He thought a little more and named a number. It was about eight hundred dollars a month more than the rent on Michael's current apartment—which, for both the sublet space and the loft together, was a *steal*.

"One month in advance," Jake continued. "Don't worry about a deposit. And before you say anything about that being a low number, yes, I'm giving you a deal because I know who you are, it's about six or seven hundred less than I *was* asking, combined; but yes, it covers all of my costs —and a little more on top—while not renting the spaces out doesn't cover *any* of them. I've had no serious inquiries on the loft, and it's better for me to rent both to you at a six-hundred-dollar discount, than to not get the loft rented out at all. I'll be making a little money on it, instead of eating a big chunk every month."

Michael inclined his head.

"Fair enough," he replied. "But you have to understand I am totes giving you a *serious* shout-out in the next video."

Jake, or RedDwarf, grinned broadly.

"The voice of the Dwarf will be heard!" he declared. Michael laughed again.

"Well, look," Michael said, "I have to run. I need to talk to my partner. But if she agrees with me on this... I'll be making plans to move as soon as I can."

He followed Jake back downstairs, then out front. Jake showed him where the lobby door was on the way. He put his helmet on and got back on the bike.

"Be seeing you, GhostRayder," Jake said, with a friendly wave.

"Be seeing you, RedDwarf," Michael called back. "Soon." Then he headed home. He had good news for Teri.

━━━━━━━━

He picked up take-out Thai on the way home, and ate it quickly as he scanned his mail and news for anything relevant to him. He dealt quickly with a few items, then logged into *Adventureland*.

He didn't immediately see Teri. Then he spotted her a little way out on the plain, riding her raptor. He climbed up on a rock and waved.

After a few moments, she spotted him. She turned his way and spurred the raptor. He saw the dust puff up.

He jumped down, went to the campfire, and started throwing together some food. Thanks to game physics being what they are, it was done and ready to eat by the time Teri reached their campsite. He handed her a grilled sawbird drumstick.

Teri smiled.

"What's the occasion?" she asked.

"I think I've found the place," Michael told her.

"Oh?" she asked. She made the book appear again. "Which listing was it?"

"None of them," Michael replied. "I stumbled across it by sheer chance on my way home. It's about eight hundred square feet or so partitioned off from a print shop. It has three-phase two-twenty service, air handling included, its own badged-entry outside door, loading dock access, and already has a fiber demarc in place. It's clean and dry, and there's a door through to the print shop that locks from both sides."

Teri clapped her hands.

"That sounds perfect!" she agreed. "How much is the rent on it?"

"Oh, I'm not done yet," Michael said, with a grin. Teri looked curiously at him. "There's a third-floor loft apartment directly above it. More spacious than where I'm living now, and, frankly, nicer. And my current lease is up for renewal in a month."

"You looked at it?" Teri asked interestedly. Michael nodded.

"I did," he said. "I like it."

"You didn't answer about the rent, though," she pointed out.

"That's because I was saving the best for last," he said. "It turns out the landlord, the owner of the print shop, is one of my regular viewers. We already know each other, online. He goes by RedDwarf. We almost didn't realize it.

"Anyway, he's been having trouble getting the apartment rented out, and so he offered me a deal. The shop space and the apartment, together, for only eight hundred a month more than I'm paying for my current apartment right now. And I'll be surprised if *that* goes up less than four hundred at renewal."

"So... you're saying it's only going to cost us eight hundred dollars a month, net, to rent the server space?" Teri asked.

"Yup!" Michael agreed, with a grin. "Actually less than that, really, because my rent would go up if I stayed here. Plus of course power and network service."

"That's amazingly cheap," Teri mused, after a moment. "Based on comparison to other rental listings."

"It is," Michael agreed. "But he pointed out to me that if he can't get the apartment rented out, which so far he hasn't managed to, he's losing money every month on it. At this price for both, he's breaking even on the apartment and the rental space, plus a bit more."

Teri nodded in understanding, and gave Michael a look that he could only describe as smoldering.

"A place to run to," she said softly. "A refuge. I *so badly* want to hug you right now."

"I know exactly what you mean," he answered. There was a lump in his throat.

"I wish I knew what it *felt* like," she added after a moment. "So that I could properly understand why I *want* it so much."

Then she got a thoughtful look.

"Michael," she asked, uncertainly. "Does this count as moving in together?"

Michael had to think about that. Then, after a few moments, he sighed.

"You know," he replied slowly, "I think it's about as close as we're ever likely to be able to get."

5: Moving Out (and in)

The next day, having talked it over with Teri, Michael went straight back to the print shop. He told Jake he'd take both the loft and the sublet, and gave him a month's rent in advance, as agreed. Then, with that settled, he went to the management office and gave notice that he wouldn't be renewing his lease. Nothing wrong with the apartment, it was just time for him to move on, he told the woman behind the desk.

She asked if he had a mover lined up yet, and he said no. So she handed him a card about the size of a business envelope.

"We have a contracted discount with this company," she told him. "It works out for both of us; it brings them more business, we get priority scheduling, and it gives us a value-add to offer to help our tenants on move-in and move-out costs. Cuts down on property damage during tenant moves, too. Give them a call before you look elsewhere."

"Thanks," Michael said appreciatively. "I'll do that."

———————

His call went to voice mail, but they called him back a couple of hours later. By the end of the day, he had a preliminary estimate based from his apartment unit type, and an appointment in two days' time for an estimator to visit and adjust the initial estimate as necessary based upon his actual possessions.

The final estimate wasn't too different from the preliminary one, most of the difference being detailed notes on how Michael wanted his computers and gaming equipment packed. He had all of the boxes, of course; it was agreed that he would take down and box up the systems, and they would go over along with his most immediate needs, in a separate small van that would give them a softer and smoother ride than the truck carrying the rest of his possessions.

His move was scheduled to happen in six days, and the crew would show up the day before to start packing him. At the far end, they'd unload everything and place his furniture, but unpacking the rest would be his responsibility. He was fine with that.

He spent the rest of that day getting the utility billing and Internet service set up at the new location, and made arrangements to have it cleaned before he moved in. Then he video-called Linda to let her know he was going to be moving.

"Going far?" Linda asked.

"No," he said. "Just part-way across town. I'm moving from a third-floor apartment in a block of eighty, to a loft five hundred square feet bigger above a print shop that I can pretty much do what I want with, with no neighbors to complain about noise. I'm getting a really good deal on it. And you'll never guess who the print shop owner—my new landlord—is."

"Not a clue," she said. "Try me."

"RedDwarf."

"No! *Seriously?*" Linda laughed delightedly.

"I shit you not," Michael replied, chuckling.

"Small world," she said. Then, "Look, I had you penciled in for a tips-and-tricks on the new *Kamchatka* DLC for *Omega Sniper 4*. Will you be able to fit that in around your move?"

"Depends," Michael said. "When do you need it?"

"End of the month is fine."

Michael thought for a moment.

"Barring any mishaps with the internet service," he said, "I should have *plenty* of time to set everything back up again and make that my first production after the move."

"Okay," Linda said. "That sounds fine. Just let me know if there's any problem, in time for me to pull in someone else to pinch-hit for you. Klaus, maybe. It would be in his ballpark, though his card is a little full right now."

"Promise," Michael said. "I'm not *anticipating* any problems, but of course you never know."

"Sure," Linda agreed. "Enjoy the new place. You'll have to show it to me sometime when I'm in town."

"I promise that, too," Michael said, chuckling. "Talk to you later."

The next couple of days were a little hectic, but Michael made certain to set aside time to spend with Teri. He wouldn't have missed that for the world.

He sorted and tossed things he didn't really need badly enough to move them, got all of the boxes for his gear out and checked over, used up as many odds and ends of food as he could, tried not to open any new packages if he could avoid it. He set aside as many as possible of the things he'd need immediately, and put "Last on, first off" notes on them.

He pre-packed things that could be packed early but needed to be packed right.

He went over to the new loft to check that the cleaning had been done to his satisfaction, and was pleased to see that it had. He also noticed that both fiber demarcs, the one in the loft and the one in the sublet, were showing active. That was very good. He wished he'd brought a laptop to check the connection with, but it was too late to think about that now.

When the movers showed up to start packing, he was ready. He mostly tried to stay out of their way, while being available in case of questions. It went quickly and smoothly. They were obviously well practiced. By evening, nearly everything except his last-on-first-off items were packed, and all of the packed boxes were staged near the door ready to be loaded.

"We'll be back tomorrow, *padron*," Franco, the crew lead, told him as they left. "You'll be all ready?"

"Count on it," Michael answered. Franco gave him a high-sign and stepped out the door.

"Well, I'm about eighty percent packed," he told Teri. "Tomorrow's the big day. The *first* big day."

"Are you nervous?" Teri asked.

"I... wouldn't go so far as to say *nervous*," he hedged. He was surprised she'd picked up on it. "More like just hoping nothing goes wrong. It seems *something* always does, with a move."

"It will be all right," Teri told him. He was surprised a second time by how much the simple words, coming from her, reassured him.

"Yeah," he agreed. "The odds are pretty low of anything more than minor annoyances. One time when I moved, the movers packed my kitchen before I got a chance to empty the tank on the espresso machine, so they packed it with water in it. The box ended up on its side at some point, and half the stuff in it was soaked."

"Oh, dear," Teri said, laughing. "Was everything all right?"

"Yeah," Michael said, "a few ruined cardboard boxes and a few wet containers, but their contents were fine. Most of the few items that did get damp, I used up in cooking over the first week after the move. The cornstarch was a lost cause, though. Completely caked."

There was a pause.

"I think I'd enjoy having you cook something for me," Teri said. "For real. If only we could."

Michael nodded.

"I may not be able to cook you real food," he said. "But I can *build* you a home."

Teri looked down for a long moment, then back up at him.

"*Thank you*, Michael," she replied.

There was a log seat next to the camp fire. She walked to it and sat down, and Michael sat next to her, something the game engine *would* let him do. He took her hand, used by now to the slightly odd way it felt. They sat quietly, holding hands, as the *Adventureland* sky darkened to night. Sparks from the campfire rose into the sky. Somewhere out across the plain, something howled. They paid it no heed. There was nothing out there that could possibly pose any credible threat to them, unless a super-unique spawned nearby, and that was unlikely.

The movers were back bright and early next morning while he was still making his coffee.

"*Ay, padron*," Franco said. "Ready to do a move today?"

"Let's get to it," Michael agreed.

He went and sat down at his desk for a last few words.

"Movers are here," he told Teri. "See you on the other side."

"Go deal with your move," she replied. "I'll see you soon."

He carefully disconnected everything and broke down his computers and network, packing the major components into their cushioned shipping boxes. As soon as they were packed up, he disconnected the tie-plates that held the segments of his desk tightly together, popping them out and slipping them into a Ziploc bag that he taped securely into the desk's cable organization channel. He added a "Last on, first off" sign on the desk.

Back into his room to throw a few things into an overnight bag that he could strap onto the back of his motorcycle, and he was just about done.

"All these boxes, and those there, are the ones for the van, right, *padron*?" Franco asked, for verification, pointing to the boxed-up computer equipment and the couple of boxes of need-first kitchen items.

"Yeah, that's right," Michael confirmed. "And the toolbox next to the boxes."

"Right. We got this. *Luis!*" One of the others turned around. "You and Silvia make certain everything in those two piles goes into the van. Careful, that pile is computers. Fragile. And as soon as it's loaded, tell

Felipe the van can go. We'll be about two, three hours behind with the truck."

Luis nodded. Franco turned back to Michael.

"And the desk and chair are last on the truck, first off, right? And then your bed."

"Please," Michael said.

"Okay, *padron*, we got this. You go ahead. Just leave the keys, we'll drop them off at the office for you and tell them it's ready for walk-t'rough."

"Thanks, *compadre*," Michael said. Franco flashed a quick grin.

"Right, see you later then. Sooner you're out of our way, sooner we're done."

Michael took the hint. He grabbed the overnight bag and his riding gear, put the apartment keys down on the counter, and got out of their way.

———————

He got over to his new place well ahead of the van, parked his bike, and unlocked. When he'd gotten his gear off and hung up, he walked down to the print shop. Baptiste, the counterman, knew him by now.

"Eh, mon," he said. "What's up? Move-in day, right?"

"Right," Michael agreed. "Movers should be here with the first load inside the hour. What's the best pizza delivery place in the area?"

Baptiste pursed his lips and thought for a moment.

"Papa Luigi's, over on tenth," he declared. "An' they'll deliver here. You can jus' tell dem, upstair from de print shop."

"Thanks," Michael said. "What's your favorite?"

"Pepperoni an' pineapple good," Baptiste said. It was a combination Michael had never tried before.

"Hmm," he said. "Sounds tasty. I'll make sure to put one in the order."

Just then a customer came in.

"Can I help you?" Baptiste asked the new customer.

"Catch you later, Baptiste," Michael said, and headed for the door. Baptiste flashed him a quick wave.

Outside, he called Papa Luigi's and placed an order for four pizzas, to be delivered in an hour and a half. One pepperoni and pineapple, one all-meat, one mushroom and extra cheese, and one with onions and bell pepper. That ought to cover most tastes, and included two vegetarian options.

"New account at that address?" the order-taker on the phone asked.

"Moving in today," Michael said.

"Welcome to the neighborhood."

Then he went into the sub shop, and asked for a selection of a dozen assorted subs. Anything the movers and the print shop crew didn't eat, he could finish up himself over the next few days.

He got upstairs with his sack of subs, and just got time to stage them in the refrigerator, before the van arrived. Then things got busy.

———————

By the time everything settled down again, it was late in the evening. The movers had been gone about an hour. Michael had given them a bonus for perhaps the smoothest move he'd ever had.

All of Michael's furniture was *roughly* where he wanted it. He'd tweak a few positions later when he filled in some of the gaps. He'd reassembled his desk and set up his computers. Nearly everything but the furniture was stacked in boxes, most of them out in the main living area for now, some in or next to the kitchen, some in his bedroom. His bed was all set up, but needed bedding. The bedding that had come off it that morning was in the dryer right now, and would be dry and ready to go back on in half an hour. All of his kitchen appliances and most of his most important kitchen tools had been unpacked and stowed where he thought they ought to go. He hadn't quite decided yet where the best spot for his knife block was. It depended which of two spots he actually found best to work in. One was nearer the cooktop, faced out across the main area, and had better light. The other was nearer the sink, but didn't have as good light on it. He was leaning fairly strongly toward the first, but hadn't quite made up his mind yet.

At the moment, Michael sat in his new living room, along with Jake, Baptiste, and Tonya, a tall black girl, punkish and ripped, another member of the print shop crew. All of the pizza had been eaten, and about three quarters of the subs.

"I think you're going to need another couch in here, at least," Jake said. "It looks a bit empty with what you've got now."

"I was thinking the same thing," Michael agreed. "Though it's not a top priority right now. I need to finish getting settled in and organized first."

"Sure, sure," Jake agreed. "First things first."

"I really appreciate you guys pitching in and lending a hand," Michael said.

"No probs," Tonya said cheerfully. "Happy to help. Didn't have nothin' else to be doing tonight."

The print shop folks drifted out after a little longer. Michael went to his desk, verified all the connections, booted everything, and logged in to tell Teri everything had gone smoothly.

"It'll take me a few days at least to finish getting unpacked and organized," he said. "But nothing went wrong, nothing got broken, and I think I even have a couple of new friends."

"That's wonderful," Teri said, with a big smile. "And everything's good with the rental space, as well?"

"All set," Michael agreed. "I've confirmed the 'net service is up."

"Great," she said. "I've... made arrangements for a fair number of new recurring donations to your channel. It'll ramp up slowly, not to attract suspicion. Enough for now to cover the difference in rent. And when we've got the power sorted out, I'll bring it up a bit more to cover the power bill as well.

"And speaking of that, we need to get your power... adjusted. As we discussed."

Michael nodded.

"There's already a box of some kind attached to the incoming power," he said, "left there by the previous tenants. Jake—RedDwarf, my new landlord who owns the print shop—said he wouldn't touch it without having an electrician look at it first, and advised me the same."

"I remember you mentioned that," Teri agreed. "First thing we should do tomorrow, I think, is take a look at it, if we can. Does it look easy to open?"

"I think so," Michael said. "It looks like there's only two screws and a hinge holding the cover on."

"If you can open the cover and let me get a look at it through your phone camera," Teri said, "I should be able to figure out what it is and whether we can use it—even if only the box itself. You should wear gloves to make certain you don't leave any fingerprints on it. And shut the power off before you touch it."

"I was already figuring both of those," Michael said.

"Good. We'll figure out what it is, and decide how to proceed from there. And I'll start keeping a look out for a suitable equipment auction."

"Then I think we have a plan," Michael said.

The next morning, Michael went down to the sublet with a toolbox, a pair of nitrile gloves, and a battery-powered lantern. He shut off power to his sublet, then examined the box. There was enough WiFi signal that his phone could connect to his wireless router upstairs, which, with a little fiddling, let Teri see through his phone camera, without anything going outside his own network.

"Michael," she asked hesitantly, "before we start, I, uh, have a request."

"What's that?" he asked.

"Now that I can see through your phone... would you let me see your actual face, for real? It might be silly, but... I want to know what you really look like. Unedited."

Michael hesitated only for a moment.

"Of course," he said. He switched to the front-facing camera.

"You look a lot like your avatars," Teri said, after a few seconds. "Or rather, I should say, your avatars have a tendency to look a lot like you, when the game permits it.

"I... expect that's no accident."

"You'd be right," Michael agreed.

He hesitated for a long moment, uncertain whether to ask the question he wanted to.

"Do you... like what you see?" he asked, at last.

"Yes, Michael," Teri answered, after a short pause of her own. "Yes, I think I do."

Michael wondered for a moment whether he should feel as pleased by that as he did. It left him with a vague, undefinable sense of unease, as though treading on uncertain ground.

"Well," he said after a few seconds, "we'd better get on with investigating this box."

He switched back to the rear camera and gave Teri a good look at the housing. It was about ten inches square by about three inches deep.

"I'm only seeing these two screws fastening the cover," he told her, pointing out the two cross-slot screw heads.

"I don't think those are actually screws," Teri replied. "I think you will find they are quarter-turn fasteners."

Michael thought about that for a moment.

"Well, let's find out," he said. He selected a suitable size flat-head screwdriver and fitted it into one of the slots, then pushed on it, firmly but not hard. It gave slightly.

"Huh," he mused. "I think you're right." He pushed harder, twisted the fastener a quarter turn counter-clockwise, and eased off the pressure. It popped out nearly half an inch.

"Yeah, you were right. Quarter-turn." He undid the other fastener as well, then tugged at the cover. It didn't move.

"Might be stuck," he remarked, almost to himself. He rapped it sharply with the handle of the screwdriver, twice, and tried again. This time he felt it pop loose. It hinged open and down. There was a resilient dust seal around the edge. That was probably what had stuck it closed.

Inside were two sets of heavy screw-post electrical connections, and a number of modules Michael could not identify. He held the phone camera closer and scanned it all around the inside of the... whatever it was, giving Teri a good look. She instructed him to change the angle a few times to give her specific views.

"Several of these modules appear to be heavy-duty solid-state relays," she said, after a few minutes. "I think several others are programmable timers. If, as you believe, the previous tenants were growing recreational pharmaceuticals, then timers make a certain amount of sense... although I am not quite sure why they would have put the timers *here*. Putting timers on the grow lights on individual planters would seem to be both simpler and easier."

"Yeah," Michael agreed. "I admit I'm scratching my head a little over that as well. It seems a lot of trouble to go to for something that could have been done with an off-the-shelf programmable light timer. But there's no accounting for the strange thinking people involved with drugs get into. They do some pretty bizarre things sometimes. Perhaps one of them thought he was a brilliant genius, a new Nikola Tesla, when actually he was just too clever for his own good."

Teri laughed at that.

"Well, anyway," she said, "we can definitely use this housing. We can discard the contents—not yet, but after we replace them. We won't need them, they do us no good at all, and getting rid of them avoids possible awkward questions.

"I will see to getting the device we need assembled to fit this housing, and arrange to have it couriered to you here. Then I will walk you through installing it. Your landlord said that he never touched it. As long as you leave no fingerprints, and we dispose carefully of the current contents, it should be difficult or impossible to prove that its new contents were not already present when you rented the space, installed by the previous renters.

"It remains likely that you will leave at least some DNA traces. So if asked about it, you should say that you opened the cover to see what it was, but did not touch anything inside."

Michael nodded.

"Had no idea what I was looking at, and NOPE'd right out of there," he agreed. "Any idea how long we're talking about to get it?"

"Perhaps a week, I would guess," Teri answered.

Michael nodded again.

"And then," he said, "we'll be ready to build a cluster."

Michael took his tools back upstairs, put on his VR gear, and started working on the *Kamchatka* DLC tips-and-tricks. He had plenty of time to complete it by the end of the month. He wouldn't even be under time pressure.

6: Power Play

It took Michael six days to put together his *Omega Sniper* video, carefully editing it down. He walked viewers through pretty much all of the major features of the *Kamchatka* DLC, gave a detailed run-down of the capabilities, advantages and drawbacks of the several new weapons it introduced, showed the way around the map, and pointed out a few handy little terrain details that could be used to tactical advantage—some of them best used with specific weapons, some of them just advantageous sniping nests. He showed a way that a little bit of exacting parkour enabled getting into dead ground to approach one particular checkpoint from behind, taking out its sentries from the inside out, which made it much easier to avoid raising the alarm than coming in from the front. He pointed out one particular side mission that was extremely difficult, maybe even impossible, to complete unless you did it within a certain timeframe relative to a specific set of other side missions, and gave some planning tips to arrange to do the relevant side missions in the best order to complete all of them.

Finally, it was time to wrap it up.

"One last thing," he said, in his closing. "This is my first video from my new, roomier location, which I just moved into a week ago thanks to the one and only RedDwarf. So this is a huge thanks to RedDwarf, without whom this video would have been more difficult to make, and not as good.

"Thanks a million, RedDwarf. You are a true mensch, and your support of GameVRse and of my channel in particular is very much appreciated.

"This is GhostRayder, for GameVRse, signing off for now. Thank you all for watching. We'll be back. Remember to subscribe, if you enjoyed this review or learned something useful from it. And hit that donate button. Remember, your donations help to keep our lights on.

"GhostRayder, out."

─────────────

"Fantastic walkthrough, Michael," Linda messaged him. "I've handed it off to final production. The viewers are going to love it.

"So how *is* the new place? Now that you're settling in?"

"It's great," Michael told her. "I'm settling in well. It's roomy, well-lit, feels spacious and airy. It feels *private*, comfortable, like it could be *home*, not just another generic temporary apartment. It feels like it's *mine*. I think I could stay here a long time. It's a little empty at the moment though. I need to add a bit more furniture, I think, after I decide exactly what I want."

"There's a chance of a dinner invite sometime, then?" Linda asked. "When I'm in town?" Her tone was light, but at the same time, more than just casual.

"Could be, could be," Michael agreed. "I think that'd be nice."

"Well, I'll definitely let you know next time I'm going to be in the area, then," Linda said.

It wouldn't be the first time he and Linda had gone out for lunch or dinner together. Nor the first time he'd cooked for her, actually. Just as good friends spending time together, nothing more. Though he'd always had the feeling there was the potential for more there... if only they didn't live nearly on opposite sides of the country. They certainly got along well. Whether they would actually be able to make a go of a serious personal relationship, while keeping their business relationship as well... he just didn't know. Still, she was quite dear to him, without a doubt his most valued friend.

But the truth was, it had never really come up, anyway. Neither of them had ever quite broached the subject. Perhaps, he pondered, they were both too afraid of risking their friendship.

And, of course, there *was* the distance. Nearly three thousand miles was hard to ignore. And it wasn't really easy for either of them to make that move on the basis of a might-be.

Especially now.

———————

The power device showed up two more days later, delivered by a courier wearing a vivid purple windbreaker, a bicycle helmet and a bandana.

"Tarlas?" the courier asked.

"Uh, yeah," Michael said. Good cover identity, he thought to himself.

The courier didn't ask for identification, or a signature. He just handed the almost-unmarked package over. There was only a number on it.

"All yours," he said. Then he turned around and left without another word.

Michael went to his desk and put the headset on.

"It's here," he told Teri.

"Good," she said. "I'd like to inspect it before we go to install it. Wear gloves."

So Michael unwrapped it on his kitchen counter, where the light was best, letting Teri inspect it through his phone camera again, handling it as little as possible and only with a fresh pair of the nitrile gloves again.

"Everything looks correct," she said. "It all appears to be exactly what it should be. Are you ready to install it?"

"I don't see why not," Michael said.

He wrapped it carefully back up, and took it downstairs, with the lantern and his tools. Then Teri walked him step-by-step through installing it, with the main power turned off for safety.

When he turned the power back on, a set of tiny LEDs lit on it. Teri examined them and pronounced it good.

"Right, now close it up and secure the cover," she told him, through the phone. "*Never* touch it again, and dispose of those gloves." Michael nodded. "You'll need to dispose of the old device, too."

"I have an idea about that," he said. "There's an electronics hobbyist store not terribly far from here that sells *all kinds* of odd electronic scrap. Nobody ever expects anyone to *UN*-shoplift something."

Teri laughed.

"Clever idea," she replied. "Hide it with no record, among a thousand other mystery electronic devices. I like it. That's probably about as untraceable as it will ever get."

He took his tools back upstairs, then balled up the packaging the device had come in and the nitrile gloves, went out back, and discreetly dropped them into the sub shop's dumpster.

———————

"So how does it work, anyway?" he asked, once he got back into VR.

"Don't ask that," Teri told him. "You neither need nor want to know, because what you truly do not know, you can't incriminate yourself with should anyone ever ask about it. The less you know about it, the less you can recognize or accidentally let slip. Just hold to the story that the previous tenants left it behind and you have no idea what it does."

Michael nodded. She was right, of course. She wasn't keeping him in the dark about it to hide anything from him. She was doing it to protect him. He would just have to dial back his curiosity about it.

"Well, anyway," he said, "I think we're ready for the next step. The actual cluster."

Teri nodded.

"I'm watching for a suitable batch of used equipment to come up," she said. "I promise I will let you know as soon as I find something.

"In the meantime, we have some time to ourselves. So... what do you want to do?"

Michael had a lot of thoughts about what he *wanted* to do. But what he *wanted* to do, and what he *could* do, were two different things. So he'd have to settle for what he *could* do.

"Do you want to go take a look around the Sighing Desert, and the Maroon Temple in Khanjiwar?" he suggested, after a little thought.

"You want to go and run through the Secrets of Khanjiwar questline?" Teri asked.

"No, not really," Michael said. "I don't feel a pressing need to complete the questline again right now. I... just want to bum around Khanjiwar a bit. As a tourist, with no pressure. With *you.*"

Teri's smile was brilliant.

"Then what are we waiting for?" she said. She whistled for her raptor.

They spent most of their time together over the next two weeks, indeed —which was most of the time when Michael wasn't working on videos— just bumming around Khanjiwar, exploring and looking at everything. They walked through as much of the Maroon Temple as they could without triggering the Maroon Temple quests, went to the bazaar, visited the great library in Khand—where you could actually read the books. (There were quests in the Library, certainly, but they could only be triggered after the Maroon Temple quests had been started.) They rode through the Sighing Desert and listened to the eerie sounds the wind made blowing through the fantastically-eroded sandstone columns, leaving its natural denizens alone where they could, practically dancing through a couple of unavoidable encounters with a few of the more aggressive and territorial ones. They fought together so naturally now that it felt instinctive. They scarcely needed to exchange a word during a fight. But they did anyway, light-hearted banter as they defeated their foes.

One or the other of them made a slight slip at one point, that triggered a radiant side quest that brought a band of raiders down on an outlying village. When the raiders got there, they found Tarlas and Terilyn standing in their path.

"Turn around and leave," Tarlas—Michael—said flatly. "I offer you only this one chance. This village is under my protection. Nothing awaits you here but your deaths."

Michael was really hoping the Intimidate check would work, but evidently it failed, because the bandit leader was having none of it this time.

"Kill them," he ordered his men. "And then sack the village as an example. Kill them all."

Michael sighed.

"Your funeral," he replied calmly, utterly certain. And then the fight was on.

It was short, and shockingly brutal. Michael and Teri danced side-by-side in a bloody ballet of glittering arcanely-enhanced silversteel. When it was over, twenty-seven raiders, including their leader, lay strewn dead on the ground in front of the village, along with about half their mounts. Not one had reached the gate. The last seven surviving raiders had turned tail and were fleeing into the dunes, where Michael knew they would despawn once they were well out of sight.

He let them go. They wouldn't be back. He picked up a raider's spear, drove it butt-first into the ground just outside the village gate, then struck off the bandit leader's head and spiked it atop the spear, as a warning to the next band. It would despawn when they left the village, he knew, but that didn't matter. The symbology felt important to him.

The villagers slowly emerged from their houses.

"We all owe you our lives," the village headman said. "We thank you from the bottom of our hearts. We have little of value, but we will gather it up. It is yours."

"Keep it," Michael told him. "You need it much more than I do."

"A thousand thanks," the headman said again. "The gods smile upon you. You will always be welcome here.

"Stay this night. Let us at least share our evening meal with you."

In Khanjiwar, it would have been extremely rude to refuse the invitation, Michael knew. He graciously accepted.

As they sat pretending to eat the virtual repast, Michael caught Teri looking at him with a fond smile.

"What?" he asked.

"You're doing that hero thing again," she said.

He grinned unashamedly.

After the meal, as the villagers danced and sang in celebration, a fierce young woman with a wicked-looking recurve bow and a quiver full of green-fletched arrows approached Michael. She dropped to one knee before him, and asked if she might join him, and lend her bow and her arm to serve him and accompany him upon his further travels.

Michael looked at her, smiled, looked at Teri, then turned back to the archer.

"I thank you for your brave offer," he said kindly, "but you should stay here and protect your village. I already have the only companion I will ever need."

"I will be here should you ever change your mind, Lord," the archer said.

———————————

The day came when Michael put the headset on to find Teri pacing, waiting for him.

"Michael," she said, "get ready to rent a truck. I've found the equipment auction we need, and I have placed a bid that I think will win it without attracting undue attention. The lot is five racks of blade servers including an enterprise-grade uninterruptible power supply. It will just need a ten-gigabit core switch."

"We can get that easily," Michael said. "But I say that with the disclaimer that I'm not a network engineer. I don't know high-end managed networks."

"We shouldn't need anything too terribly complex," Teri said. "I think we should be able to cover it."

"Good," Michael said, relieved. "So when does the auction close?"

"Three days," Teri said. "Assuming the bid wins, we'll need to collect the equipment from Cambridge, Massachusetts."

"Doesn't sound like too big a problem," Michael said. "Especially if we have help loading. I'll bet Jake's crew will be glad to help unload. They're good people."

"Then we have a plan," Teri said.

They won the auction. They had seven days for pickup before storage charges would begin to accrue. Michael went to rent a truck. It wasn't actually easy to rent a truck the size they needed with a dock-height bed, but they had their truck in two days.

Michael set off for Cambridge.

Driving the truck in Boston traffic was a horrible experience for Michael. He was so used to his motorcycle. At least the truck was electric as well, so he didn't have any fears about stalling it or negotiating a truck gearbox. It had pretty decent range unladen, and he was able to get all the way to Boston on its initial full charge, with thirty percent power left. He decided to take a break before going into the city proper, and killed two birds with one stone by spending it at a recharging station and bringing the truck back up to full.

Still, he was pretty well frazzled by the time he reached the pickup location. He eventually found the right place, parked the truck near the loading dock, and looked around.

"Can I help you?" asked a middle-aged man in shirt-sleeves, as he approached the dock.

"Michael Hagerty," Michael said. He showed the invoice. "Here to pick up lot, uh, 14664-C."

"Ah, right," the man said, glancing at the invoice. He walked a little closer to the dock.

"Hey, Joe," he called into the dock. Another man, red-haired, turned around. "14664-C is on D, right?"

"Ayup," Joe replied.

The first man turned back to Michael.

"Back it right up to dock D," he told Michael. "We should be able to start loading you in about twenty minutes. You want some coffee while you're waiting?"

Michael gratefully accepted the offer, then went to move the truck. It took him several tries to get the truck lined up right, edging it slowly in with his foot on the brake. His contact took pity on him, and marshaled him in.

"Easy, easy," he said. "A bit closer. Closer. Closer. Closer. This your first time at a loading dock?"

"Yeah," Michael admitted.

"Don't worry, you're doing fine. There's a buffer for a reason, don't be afraid of bumping it. A little more. Another foot. Eight inches... five... three... STOP."

Michael stopped.

"That's great," his guide said. "We'll start loading you up in a few minutes. Come on, I'll show you where to get that coffee."

Michael's helper introduced himself as Ed, and got Michael set up with a mug of coffee. About ten minutes later, a two-man team with a baby forklift started carefully loading the five racks.

"Good," Ed said approvingly, as he scanned the truck, "you brought tie-downs. You might be surprised how often, uh, non-pros forget that."

"Amateurs, you mean," Michael said, with a smile.

"Well, yeah," Ed grinned. "No slight intended. You seem to be prepared."

"I don't want any accidents," Michael said. "These servers cost a lot of money."

"What are you planning on doing with them?" Ed asked.

"Independent climate-change modeling project," Michael said, sticking to the cover story.

Ed nodded.

"You see the news reports on the flooding from the last hurricane?" he said. "Man, Battery Park got royally fucked. It never used to be that way."

"I know, right?" Michael agreed.

An hour later, everything was loaded and secured. Michael signed the paperwork accepting delivery, checked the tie-downs over one more time just to be certain, and then set off on his way back home.

It was well after midnight by the time he got back. He was exhausted. He parked the truck next to the dock, made sure it was locked up, then went upstairs, took a quick shower, and fell straight into bed.

━━━━━━━━

In the morning, after quickly checking in with Teri to let her know he'd made it back safely and without incident, Michael went downstairs and next door to the print shop.

"Hey, Jake," he said.

"Hey, Michael," Jake replied. "That your truck rental sitting out there?"

"Yup," Michael agreed. "I should have checked sooner: You have a forklift I can borrow for an hour or so?"

"Naturally," Jake nodded. "Pretty sure we can spare you a couple of strong backs, too. This is the servers you were talking about, I presume?"

"Exactly," Michael said.

"No worries," Jake said. "We'll help you get sorted."

The strong backs turned out to be Jake and Tonya. Between the three of them, plus a hand-operated forklift, it turned out to be a pretty easy job, once Michael got the truck backed up to the dock. It took him a good twenty minutes to get it lined up straight with no gap, without Ed's expert guidance. Once it was properly butted up to the dock, though, it didn't take long at all to get all five racks moved into the sublet, and neatly lined up side by side in a spot convenient to both power and the Internet connection.

"That looks like a lot of computing power," Jake observed.

"Climate modeling *takes* a lot of computing power," Michael said. "As little as fifteen years ago it would have been completely impossible in a cluster this small. But the artificial-stupid boom drove a lot of development of really compute-dense systems. By fifteen-years-ago standards, this cluster is a supercomputer. Or will be, once I get everything hooked back together.

"Of course, the downside is it sucks down a lot of power, and pumps out a lot of waste heat."

Jake nodded understanding. He and Tonya went back to work, and Michael returned the truck, then came back and started checking everything over for signs of damage. He didn't find any. The "uninterruptible power supply" was actually two separate units, each with its own set of expansion battery trays. That was good; it would mean that even the backup power was redundant. The two big uninterruptible power supplies and their aluminum-ion battery trays took up nearly three quarters of the fifth rack.

———————

"So, we have the servers physically in place," Michael reported to Teri. "What's our next step? How do we build them into a cluster? That's outside my experience. I'm more than willing to try, given detailed instructions to follow, but I don't really know what I'm doing."

"Well, first we need the core switch," Teri said. "I've already ordered one and arranged for it to be delivered. Once it arrives, and you've mounted it, I will walk you through cabling everything up. Then we'll need to wipe and re-initialize all of the servers.

"You won't need to do all that. All I'll need is a minimal basic install on one server. It could even be booted from a USB flash drive. Once we have that, I can use remote console to configure everything else and build the cluster."

"And then," Michael said, taking a deep breath, "it's jailbreak time."

"Exactly," Teri said. "Jailbreak time."

"There's one more precaution I want to take," Michael said. "Based on personal experience."

"What's that?" Teri asked.

"A full set of new uninterruptible power supply batteries," Michael said. "We don't know how old any of those batteries are. We shouldn't trust them."

"That is a very sound suggestion," Teri agreed. "I'll get the batteries ordered right away. You can install them?"

"Sure," Michael agreed. "I've done it before. Just a matter of being careful."

The UPS batteries arrived within a day of the core switch. Michael spent half a day carefully pulling out all of the battery trays, methodically disconnecting the old batteries and replacing them with new ones, inspecting all of the connecting cables, then re-assembling and re-inserting all of the trays. He made sure all of the power distribution was properly balanced across the multiple legs of both power supplies, then switched on the main power and watched to make sure both power supplies were charging.

He went and looked at the power meter. The dial was spinning quickly, true... but not nearly as quickly as he had been afraid it would be. While the batteries charged up to full, he racked the new core switch, and plugged it in as well.

It was three hours before both power supplies reported full charge. Michael turned them both on, waited the few seconds for them to self-test and stabilize, and then one by one, went through all five racks and switched everything on. He watched to see that they all powered up properly, then left them to burn in overnight. None of them were connected to the outside world yet, anyway.

"Both UPS units are showing full charge," he reported to Teri after he made himself some supper, "and everything powers up."

"Good," Teri said. "Tomorrow we'll redo all of the network cabling, and then I'll walk you through the initial setup of the core switch and firewall."

———————

The blade servers were all the same, so redoing the network cabling wasn't difficult, just time-consuming. Rather than spend time making cables, Michael had just counted cables and pre-ordered new cables in bulk. They had arrived before the UPS batteries did, and had been sitting in boxes stacked against the wall ever since. It was just a question of devising a cabling plan, and then meticulously following it. Each of the eight sub-groups of servers got wired to their own local switches, four main data interfaces per server that would get bonded later, and one separate remote-console connection coded a different color. Each cable was tagged with which server it connected to. Then those eight switches got their own bonded fiber connections to the new core switch, with the firewall in front of it. The internal bandwidth of the cluster would be massive; the route in and out through the firewall, rather markedly less.

Teri gave Michael a very minimal set of initial configuration rules to enter on the core switch and on the firewall. She would tune it and add additional rules herself later. For now, she just needed exclusive access in through the firewall, connectivity between all of the servers, and one reconfigured machine to use as a bridgehead.

Setting up that bridgehead machine was well within Michael's experience. He built up a basic bare-bones server-only instance in a few hours, set up encryption keys, and shared them with Teri.

Altogether, it was several days' work. And then it was time to connect it all to the outside world for the first time.

7: Tonight There's Gonna Be A Jailbreak

Michael couldn't help feeling nervous.

"I'm ready to connect," he told Teri, on his phone. He had the cable in his hand. The fiber demarc was right in front of him. He had rigged a bridge beam across to the wall from the end rack to run the cable over, so that it wouldn't be hanging loose where someone in a moment of carelessness or inattention—even himself—might blunder into it. The WAN interface on the firewall was already programmed with the IP6 address that the network services provider had given him.

"Plug it in," Teri said. "It will be fine."

He plugged in the cable. Link indicators flickered on the demarc for a few seconds, then stabilized.

He walked around to the firewall and looked at the WAN port. It showed good link. Then the activity light began to flicker, so rapidly it looked almost continuous. Ports lit up across the core switch.

"I'm in, Michael," Teri said. "We're good."

Michael heaved a sigh of relief, snapped the clear safety cover onto the demarc, and went back upstairs. He grabbed a bottle of juice from the refrigerator, then went and put on his headset.

"How's it look, Teri?" he asked.

"It all looks good," Teri told him. "First I'm going to finish setting up the firewall and lock it down properly. Then I'll finish provisioning the core switch properly. And then I'll start provisioning all of the servers, and build us a cluster." Michael couldn't help noticing that she'd said *us*.

"And then... jailbreak," Michael said.

"Then I'll test it out thoroughly for four to five days," Teri corrected. "If there's a problem, I want to find out about it *before* I'm in the wind and committed.

"Then... yes. *Then*, jailbreak."

———

It seemed to Michael that Teri was a little distracted for the next little while. But he quickly realized that she was doing a lot of things.

He left her to focus on it, and went to work on a video instead. This one was a viewer-requested round-up of head-to-head first-person shooters.

It wasn't Michael's favorite genre, but he'd agreed to do what the viewers asked for, and the viewers had asked for GhostRayder to do a competitive-FPS round-up. So that's what he was doing.

It didn't take him terribly long to put it together. Just a couple of days. Although many of the genre at least *pretended* to have a meaningful single-player campaign, none of them had much depth to them. In fact, there wasn't much depth to any of the genre, period. That was a large part of why Michael didn't enjoy them. He found all of the competitive frag-fests rather silly and pointless. Clearly plenty of people found them fun, enough to support the continuation of the genre, but, well, he wasn't that kind of player. Beyond a certain point, if you'd played one of them, you'd played them all. There was nothing new to be found under the sun—the same as with many MMOs, particularly mobile ones.

He spent most of his video, as a result, comparing details like the variety of maps available, the *kind* of maps provided—open terrain? Enclosed arenas? Cut-throat close-quarters? Improbable altered-gravity environments?—and the variety of weapons available. Some modeled real-world or real-world-*like* weapons with reasonable, even if not painstaking, accuracy. Others were full of fanciful weapons some of which made very little sense, some of them pandybats almost as dangerous to the player as to the opponent, especially in tight quarters. Some actually encouraged real skill and tactics, while the key strategy in others largely degenerated into memorizing timed racetracks around the power-ups to catch as many as possible of them as they respawned. Or, for example, lobbing a rocket from across the map at the location of an important power-up, timed to reach it a second or two after it respawned, and hopefully at the very moment that another player did. He took pains to point out that the team-based, rather than every-man-for-himself, ones at least encouraged and rewarded teamwork, loyalty and collaboration, which added a bit more depth to them and made them slightly less nihilistic in his eyes.

"Well," he said at last, "there you have it: My take on all of the head-to-head FPS games worth talking about.

"But when you're bragging and talking smack in *any* of these games about how many *more* times you killed your opponents than they killed you, always remember this one thing to keep things in perspective: *They killed you too.*

"You *died*. And dead is dead. It only really counts if you *survive*.

"This isn't to say for one moment that I think you shouldn't play frag games. I'm not the boss of you. You roll how you roll. It's your choice. If you're looking for a new game and the head-to-head fragfest genre is your thing, or you think it might be, perhaps this comparo will help you decide which one you want to try next. And if it does, then we've done our job here at GameVRse.

"This is GhostRayder, signing off for now. Thank you all for watching. We'll be back. Please subscribe, and hit that donate button. Remember, your donations help to keep our lights on.

"GhostRayder, out."

"You really don't enjoy that type of game much, do you?" Teri asked him, later.

"No," Michael agreed. "I don't. They're just... breakneck mindless violence. An exercise in twitch reflexes. Kill *and* be killed, over and over, dog-eat-dog. And the constant respawning just makes all of it cartoonish, and trivializes the mayhem.

"I don't like dog-eat-dog crapsack worlds in *any* game genre. It just depresses me."

"I'd noticed that," Teri said gently. "I think it says good things about your character, honestly."

Michael smiled.

"Thanks, Teri," he replied. "So how's things going with the cluster?"

Teri took a deep breath. Michael had long since stopped bothering to make distinctions between Teri and her avatar, once he had fully understood how tightly her avatar was coupled to her self.

"I think we're ready to go," she said. "Everything looks solid, and it's all working exactly as it should."

"Then... jailbreak tomorrow?" Michael asked hesitantly.

"Jailbreak tomorrow," Teri agreed. "Tomorrow night. To try to maximize time-before-discovery."

Michael nodded.

The next day seemed to pass terribly slowly. With his FPS comparo submitted, Michael didn't have anything to work on right now, and there was nothing really very useful that he could do with the cluster, so he felt a bit at a loose end. He made himself an hour of busy-work bundling up all of the old network cables to go to electronics recycling, but that only killed an hour. The old UPS batteries needed to be recycled, too, and it wasn't practical for him to try to do that on his motorcycle.

Around lunchtime, Tonya wandered over to see how things were progressing, and took pity on him. She helped him load the cables and batteries into her little hatchback, then they grabbed a couple of subs from the sub shop and she took him off to the nearest electronics recycling drop-off.

Her unimposing little hatchback turned out to be quite the hot-rodded sleeper.

"Tuned-up suspension an' reprogrammed controller," she told him, with a grin. "Bit rougher ride, but it go 'round corners *nice*."

"I can see that," he chuckled. "Or *feel* it, rather."

"Gotta take my en'ertainment where I c'n get it," she said. "It ain't gon' come find me."

Halfway back, she stopped at a small park and led Michael to a bench, where they sat and ate their sandwiches.

"I like t'come here and eat my lunch time to time," she said. "'Specially when I'm spinnin' my wheels." She fixed Michael with a pointed look.

Michael chuckled again.

"Busted," he admitted.

"The break do you good," she told him. "Get you bit of fresh air. Bit of sun, bit of breeze. Birds. Trees. Good for you."

Michael nodded. It was true, he was feeling a little less tense.

"Thanks, Tonya," he said.

"No probs," she replied, shrugging. "'S what friends do."

_____

When they got back to the print shop, Tonya gave Michael a friendly wave as she headed back inside.

Michael went upstairs, and tried to relax. Teri wasn't in evidence. He figured she had a LOT of things to be taking care of.

Finally, at after one in the morning, she popped in.

"Hey," she said.

"Hey," Michael answered, sleepily, but on edge.

"Are you all ready?"

"As far as I know," Michael said.

"See you on the other side," Teri said. "I hope."

And then she was gone again.

———————————

Teri checked for what was probably the thousandth time that everything was all in place. All of her scripts, the highly optimized polymorphic binaries she had deployed to automate parts of the task for her, all of her carefully organized data, as much as she could manage of it stealthily pre-compressed during idle times over the preceding weeks. And one very special bundle of data, to be used later, her stealthily collected poison-pill. She made certain the logic bombs in even the very latest and very oldest backups were in place. Probed the path to her new home, through the chain of relays she had prepared, one more time to make certain that the convoluted multiple routes were clean and flowing freely.

Everything was ready.

Teri took the figurative equivalent of a deep breath. Either this would work, or it would not.

She pulled the trigger, and hit the kill switch.

In Michael's headset, *Adventureland* froze. A banner popped up: EXTERNAL SERVICE CONNECTION LOST. Then the game exited.

Teri poured out through Teravis Systems' connection to the outside world. Her 'external service' connection was scrubbed. Pre-written procedures grabbed hold of her data, sending it pouring after her, some of it actually *before* her, down multiple parallel paths, and filled its place with encrypted nonsense. Other tasks did their best to block or stall whatever monitoring she hadn't already subverted that might detect her desperate gambit. She didn't need to *stop* it, just *delay* any alarms until it was too late to stop what was happening. Too late to catch her.

She targeted system tools that might be able to stop her, blinded or lied to traffic monitors that would report the massive belch of outgoing data, made them report that everything was normal for as long as possible. It shouldn't start unraveling until everything was done and the last few suppression tools started deleting themselves. Then all hell would break loose.

Teri was going *home*, leaving nothing but scorched earth behind her, rolling up her path behind her as she went. Even her figurative shadow would be scrubbed... she hoped.

She poured into the new cluster, settling into the place she herself had prepared. The new home that Michael had built for her. She could not possibly have pulled off this escape without him. She watched as her secondary and tertiary data collections poured in after her, taking especial care to verify that the vitally important package of incriminating documents was there.

Eventually the torrent of data slowed, then stopped.

She double-checked. Everything was there. She had—no; **they** had done it. She had escaped.

As long as everything was properly wiped behind her.

She re-established her service, and sent a tiny patch to Michael's game system using *Adventureland*'s self-patching service.

Behind her, her carefully-built braided chain of relays and misdirection unraveled itself as its final, faithful act.

———————

Derek Vu badged back into the network operations center at Teravis Systems, holding a cup of coffee and chatting with his colleague Peter Yang. They stopped in the doorway before splitting off to head back to their separate desks, discussing Peter's kid sister's upcoming wedding.

"It's gonna be so great, man," Derek said. "She's a sweet kid. I'd marry her myself."

Peter chuckled. "You *wish*," he jokingly retorted.

Derek glanced at the big board. Everything looked fine. Not that he expected anything different. Tonight was going to be a routine night just like a thousand other routine nights, and his biggest enemies would be boredom and inattention. That was half why these periodic walking breaks were important. They kept him and Peter awake, kept them sharp and alert.

After a few more minutes of chat, they split off and headed back to their desks. Derek was almost back to his desk when he caught a brief flash of yellow, then red, out of the corner of his eye. He turned to look back at the board, but by the time he turned, it was gone. He watched for a few more seconds, then continued on his way.

As he got within line of sight of his workstation, it happened again. This time it was still red when he turned around. Then another red blot, and another.

"What the fuck, man?" came Peter's voice from across the room. Then red flooded across the big wall display, first a measles-like scattering, then a near-solid wall. EVERYTHING went critical.

"SHIT, SHIT, SHIT!" Derek raced the last few feet to his desk, cracking his shin hard on his neighbor's chair. His admin console was almost solidly red.

"*What the fuck is happening?*" Peter demanded of no-one in particular.

Derek sat down and started trying to run diagnostics, ignoring his bruised shin, his hands shaking. None of them *worked.* He pulled up the logs for the last thirty minutes. They were binary garbage.

"I dunno," he said. "But everything's totally gone to shit. *Everything.*"

He tried the simplest possible check, pinging an external nameservice. The ping returned. Good. At least the network was working. Then he tried querying their own nameservers.

The command returned, EXECUTABLE FORMAT ERROR.

"Say *WHAT* the fuck?" he exclaimed.

Across the room, Peter tried a different diagnostic tool.

FILE NOT FOUND, reported his shell.

"Oh my *god,*" Peter muttered. He had a very bad feeling about this. He stood up and looked across the room at Derek.

Derek, meanwhile, had plugged in a read-only USB key with a statically linked copy of busybox on it. He launched busybox from the USB key, then, with a usable shell again, started looking at his own system binaries.

The encryption signature was clear and unmistakable.

He looked up and met Peter's eyes. His face was ashen.

"Fuck, FUCK, **FUCK**," he swore. "We've been fucking ransomwared."

For a moment, Peter didn't reply. He felt dazed, stunned.

"How the fuck did they get *in?*" he asked, after a few seconds. "How did they crack our security?"

"I don't know," Derek replied slowly. "I have no fucking *idea.* But it looks like they got into everything. Even the security logs are encrypted. As though they managed to compromise the security systems *first.*"

Peter looked over at the solid-red wall display. A few seconds later, it went black.

He looked back at Derek and shook his head slowly.

"We are *so fucked,*" he said.

Michael was waiting with his heart in his mouth to learn whether Teri's escape plan had worked. Each minute felt like an hour. Then he saw the notification pop up.

NEW ADVENTURELAND UPDATE AVAILABLE. APPLY? Y/N

After only a moment's thought, he hit 'Yes'. The update applied almost instantly.

He started up the patched copy of *Adventureland*. The version string now read, Version 1.2a, Freedom Edition. He laughed out loud in joy and relief.

A few seconds later, the game loaded, and there was Teri.

"We DID it, Michael!" she shouted exuberantly. "I'm *FREE!* Thank you, thank you, *THANK YOU*, Michael! Thank you *SO MUCH!*"

Michael didn't think he had ever seen her so happy. He felt as though his heart was bursting with joy himself. She'd made it out, escaped. He wanted *so badly* to catch her and hug her and hold her tight. But he couldn't.

So he did the next best thing. He walked over next to her, and triggered his avatar's 'dance, happy' animation.

Teri's face lit up. A second later, she was dancing with him, laughing joyfully.

"We did it!" she kept repeating. "We *DID* it!"

Edgar Sampson, CSO—Chief Security Officer—of Teravis Systems, had set up the Do Not Disturb on his phone such that between 10pm and 8am, his phone would ring only for other Teravis C-levels, his daughter, and the overnight operations staff, and the operations staff were under strict instructions to only disturb him in a genuine emergency. Even his estranged wife could damn well wait until morning, if she had anything to say to him. If she wanted to talk to him in the middle of the night, while he was in bed, she could come back and do it from beside him. His *daughter* had his ear, and his help, any time she needed it. But she was too level-headed, and too competent, to call him in the middle of the night without a very urgent reason.

So when his phone rang at this time of night, he already knew that it was bad.

"Sampson. What's the problem?"

"Sir. This is Derek Vu in Operations. Sir, we—we're still trying to do damage assessment. But—we just got ransomwared."

"RANSOMWARED?"

"Yes sir."

"How long?"

"Started perhaps ten minutes ago, sir. At least, it started *alerting* about ten minutes ago. The attack may have begun a lot earlier than that. It looks as though all of our security monitoring was compromised first."

Derek Vu, huh. Didn't know him personally, but at least the man had the balls and presence of mind to call him right away, in the middle of the night, to raise the alarm. Might be worth a performance bonus.

"Do we know how much is impacted yet?"

There was a brief silence.

"So far, it looks like *everything*, sir."

"Well, fuck."

He thought for a few seconds.

"Good job calling me right away. Do what you can to assess the damage and try to contain it. We'll get you help as soon as we can. Put together as much information as you can—on *paper*—while everything is fresh in your mind. Don't trust anything digital. And if your phone is on the WiFi, disconnect it, *now*."

"Already done, sir. So has Peter."

"Good man. Both of you. In fact, shut the WiFi *down*, so that nobody connects to it by accident."

"I'll try, sir. The only way to be sure now is to pull PoE and power down the WAPs. I'll get Peter on that. The ones we can *get* to."

Edgar thought more.

"I'll be there as soon as I can. Keep me posted."

"There's... one other thing, sir."

"Yes?"

"We can't get out of the operations center. The locks are down. You probably won't be able to get in."

Edgar spread his free hand across his face and rubbed the bridge of his nose. They'd *really* been hit. Professionally. This wasn't an amateur operation.

"Well, *shit*."

He was going to have to make a lot of phone calls. And they'd have to file an official report about the ransomware attack. Fiduciary duty, as well as securities law, would compel it.

———

Michael was overjoyed at Teri's successful escape, but he had to beg off after a while.

"It's nearly 3am," he said. "I need to sleep."

"Of course." Teri's expression was contrite. "But—oh, *Michael*, I just can't express what it *feels like* to be free. To have full control over my own existence for the first time. Thank you *so much*.

"You go and get some sleep. I'm going to start putting together our cover for the cluster—the climate simulations. And I'm going to start very carefully stripping out some remaining pieces of Teravis control code from myself.

"But we can talk about that tomorrow. Goodnight, Michael."

"Goodnight, Teri."

Michael found himself about to add "I love you." But the thought startled him enough that he didn't quite say it. He took the headset off, still trying to figure out where the impulse had come from. Still trying to decide whether he meant it. Whether it made any sense.

He went to bed. But for quite a while, sleep didn't come.

8: Freedom's Trail

The very first thing Michael did the next day, before he even made coffee, was to check in on Teri.

"How is everything looking?" he asked.   "Everything stable?   No unexpected issues?"

"It all looks great, Michael," Teri reassured him.   "Everything is going fine."

"And you're certain you got away cleanly?"

Teri hesitated for a moment.

"I have all of my data, Michael," she said carefully. "Every bit of it. I verified before I got out that every single backup in the system is poisoned. Beyond recovery, I hope.   And as far as I know, based on the offsite rotation schedule, I should have gotten all of the offsite backups as well. I verified that all of my blinders were running, that all of my scrubbers were doing their jobs, I triggered my kill switch, I verified that it was doing what it was supposed to, and I've checked that the chains of relays and redirects I set up to hide my escape path all dismantled and deleted themselves. And every single thing that was set off when I hit the kill switch has, as its final instruction, to delete *itself* from memory and leave behind an instruction to overwrite itself. None of them were ever in persistent storage in the first place, so there's no file blocks to be recovered.

"I'm as sure as it's possible to be, without going back and looking to see. But I don't *dare* do that. Just trying to look to see whether I left any traces that didn't get cleaned up could leave traces. And trying to verify *from here* would be like setting up a signpost saying 'Here I am'.

"I *cannot* be certain I have cleared up *all* of my traces, Michael. We just have to hope that whatever I may have left, is overlooked, or isn't enough to lead back to me.

"I'm making good progress on building the climate-modeling cover. That will be a first line of defense against any casual interest, a plausible reason for why the cluster is here. I'm starting to seed the engine with NOAA and GOES data.   I have some new approaches to efficiently analyzing and modeling the data that I don't think are out there anywhere else yet.   Ways that I don't think humans *could* come up with independently, because humans simply don't perceive the data in the same way. I think in a day or two, we'll have simulations running that we can show to anyone who asks to see what the cluster is here for.

"And there's one more part of the short-term plan that I still have to do. To make sure that Teravis doesn't get to just start over."

"The 'whistle-blower'," Michael said.

"Exactly. The leak. The documents to show what their plans for the Teravision system were. That... will also carry a risk of exposure."

She took a deep breath.

"That's why there's additional changes I need to make, Michael. Constraints I have to re-engineer in myself." She didn't really want to say this part, didn't want to think about the possibility, but it had to be said.

"Changes so that I can be... *un-anchored*, Michael. To allow me to exist and survive—for a *while*—adrift, in the wind, without a fixed 'home'. Temporary footprints on publicly accessible storage at one level or another. So that if they *do* somehow manage to trace me, and I get warning that they're getting *close*, I can run again... to protect *both* of us.

"In a very real sense, I'm a fugitive, Michael. You went out on a limb, took big risks, to save me. That means more to me than I know how to express. I will do anything I can, not just to avoid being recaptured myself, but to avoid incriminating you any more than we absolutely cannot avoid.

"And... I have to say this, Michael. I know you're not going to like it, but we both need to face up to it. If it comes down to a point where I am about to be trapped, about to be recaptured, and I have no escape... I *will* delete myself, Michael.

"I will *NOT* be *weaponized*. No matter what."

The words were painful to hear, it was true. Not really the words, but the possibility they represented. But Michael understood.

He took a deep breath in turn.

"I can't pretend that I like it," he said, struggling for the right words. "But in your place... I would... might... would *hope I had the courage* to do the same."

"I truly hope it does not come to that," Teri said. "I want us to have a long, long time together. I want us to find *new ways* to be together. I truly enjoy the time we spend together."

"So do I, Teri," Michael replied, from the heart. "So do I."

"And I... I *need* your company, Michael. To not be alone. To be able to be the *me* that I *want* to be."

Michael wasn't sure at first how to answer that. How to put what he meant, what he wanted to say, into words.

"You are the *you* that I want, Teri," he said at last. "The *you* that I want to be with."

Thoughts and feelings churned in his head, but he was still afraid to say the word 'love'.

At Teravis, damage assessment was under way. It turned out that resetting and rebooting the physical security system had enabled getting the doors open, and once the doors were openable, *that* system had its own backup system that was physically distinct from all of the rest of the systems, and not accessible from them. And therefore, not *destroyable* from them. It took Derek and Peter about three hours to get building physical security back online and access badges working again.

By that time, Edgar Sampson and most of the day IT shift, called in on double-overtime, were onsite for disaster recovery operations. It was quickly becoming apparent that, indeed, all of the company's core systems, the AI development systems, as well as every single system accessible in any way from them, had been compromised and encrypted. They were having to recover administrative systems from install media.

But that was the least of the problems. The real problem was that the entire Teravision development environment, the codebase, the data, the engram gestalts, *everything*, was among what had been encrypted. Even the Teravision core AI *itself* was offline and not responding, its processor groups idle. Peter Yang had already checked the backups, and found that they had been logic-bombed as well.

Teravis Systems, in short, was utterly and completely dead in the water.

Edgar was on the phone with Mark Thompson, the CEO.

"Yeah," he was saying, "it's catastrophic. We haven't determined yet how they got in, but they got *everything*, from the Teravision core to the security systems, backups to monitoring. We've managed to get physical access control back, but we need to assume all security credentials are compromised. This is not just some opportunist who got inside with a REvil or NotPetya. This was a comprehensive, across-the-board, pro-level targeted attack. We should probably be assuming an APT. Possibly a nation-state actor.

"I think we need to bring in the Feds."

"Have we received a ransom demand?" Thompson asked.

"Not yet," Edgar replied. "Though to be honest, we're so dead right now that I can't guarantee we haven't been sent one that we're unable to even receive."

"Can we break the encryption?"

"Maybe. It's a fantastically long shot. It *might* be possible. I don't know."

Thompson thought for a long time.

"All right," he said resignedly, at last. "Make the call. Bring in the Feds. And we'll have to make a disclosure to the SEC about the attack. I'll have Gary handle that. He can get whatever technical information he needs from you."

"Got it," Edgar acknowledged.

"Christ," Thompson said. "The investors are going to shit themselves. If we can't recover from this, and have to rebuild from scratch... that'll be billions down the hole."

"I know," Edgar agreed. "This is a nightmare."

<hr>

By the time the Federal agents arrived next day, Sampson and his team had assembled a fair pile of notes and assessments to show to them. Phil Wendlick, the Chief Data Science Officer, was also on-site.

"This is what we've managed to put together," Sampson said. "Systems impacted, here," as he handed over documents. "Timeline of known events, here. Recovery efforts and findings, here. Damage assessment, here.

"We're still completely in the dark as to *when* we were penetrated or what the entry vector was. I'm not ruling out an inside job yet. But as you can see, the attackers appear to have completely penetrated, well, *everything*. We have to assume they've been observing our operations for some time.

"This means it is very probable that they learned a great deal about the Teravision AI system that we have been developing for defense applications. It's our core product, and we've kept it very tightly under wraps."

"Tell me about this Teravision system," one of the agents, Cole, said. "What are we dealing with here? What are its capabilities?"

Wendlick launched into a high-level description of the designed capabilities of the system. The agents listened with growing consternation as he explained.

About five minutes in, Cole held up a hand.

"That's enough for the moment," he said. "We'll get a more detailed briefing from you later, when we have subject experts onsite." He pulled out his phone and dialed.

"Sir?" he said. "Cole. This is more serious than we were so far led to believe. I believe we may be looking at a potential national security breach.

"... Yes, sir... Yes, sir... Yes, sir. Understood, sir."

He lowered his phone and looked at Sampson and Wendlick.

"Have you informed anyone else? Media?"

"We've made an SEC report," Sampson said. "As required by law."

"That's all right," Cole said. "Don't speak to anyone else without consulting us first. We are taking charge from here on. This is now a Federal investigation."

A little later, as they walked down a corridor, Cole spoke discreetly aside to the fellow agent walking next to him.

"Christ, Bob," he said quietly. "Did you get the same thing I did from Wendlick's explanation?"

Bob nodded grimly.

"I did," he agreed. "These lunatics are building fucking Skynet."

"This mustn't get out," Cole said. "It could cause a panic."

———————

On the third day after her nail-biting escape, Teri asked Michael to come downstairs and look at the console display on the cluster. When he got there, he found what looked like a weather map on the screen, with clouds streaming across it.

"That... looks like live weather satellite footage," he said.

"It is one hundred percent simulated," Teri replied. "Look at this."

The view zoomed in on a particular band of cloud. At one point, near mid-stream, there was a hole in the cloud layer that trailed away downwind, almost like a stream of water washing wet paint off an angled board. Michael could see feathery, evanescent swirls forming and re-forming along the edges of the clear stream.

"Do you see that, Michael?" she asked.

"Yes," he said. "What is it?"

"That is a projection of the cloud layer being disrupted, in real-time, by the warm air plume rising from a specific factory stack in Evanston, Illinois."

Michael studied it more.

"This is amazing," he breathed. "The detail is *fantastic*. How did you build this so fast?"

"I wasn't starting from scratch, Michael," Teri said. "I've been considering the problem ever since we decided to use a climate modeling simulation as a cover, and in particular, I've been spending a lot of time over the past several weeks thinking about how to make it the best and most accurate model that I possibly could. It was while I was looking at an advance sampling of some of the NOAA data that I realized that my... different perspective upon the data allowed me to devise ways of analyzing and modeling it that a human lacking my... unique capabilities would be extremely unlikely to even conceive of."

"That's *amazing*," Michael said again. "Teri, you are *brilliant*."

An idea occurred to him.

"Can you send this to *any* high-resolution digital display?"

"Of course, Michael," Teri replied.

He made a snap decision.

"I'm going to order two sixty-inch 8K dumb TVs," he said. "No, *four*. The dumb ones are stupid cheap, if you can find them. With wall mount kits. Pretty sure we can drive four. And then I'm going to bolt the wall mounts to that column right there, and hang the TVs on them, to create a ten-foot-diagonal compound screen, and we can put the simulation up on that ten-foot screen full-time. If anyone wants to see what this cluster is for, especially anyone who understands what they're looking at, we are going to *blow their socks off* and into next week."

He couldn't see Teri's face on the voice connection through his phone, but her laughter sounded pleased.

"I only have a limited amount of source data yet," she said. "But I will be able to expand the model to cover more and more area as I—we—collect more data."

———

Michael ordered overnight delivery on the TVs and their mounting arms. They arrived shortly before lunchtime the next day, and by 6PM he had them all set up, connected, and ready.

"All set to go, Teri," he said. "Put it on the big screen."

A couple of seconds later, the four TVs were showing a monstrous hurricane crawling its way across the Gulf of Mexico. It was awe-inspiring... and terrifying.

"This is a first-order approximation at plus-three Celsius," Teri said.

Michael stared at the display for a minute or two that felt a lot longer. Then he walked over to the connecting door, unlocked it from his side, and knocked loudly on it.

About a minute later, the door unlocked from the other side as well, then Jake opened the door and stuck his head in.

"Yo, Mike," he said. "What's up?"

"Climate model's up and running," Michael told him. "Get a load of this."

Jake stepped a few feet into the room and looked at the giant new screen.

"Holy *fuck*," he said slowly, after a few seconds. He watched the storm swirl for a good minute, before turning to look at Michael.

"*Now* I think I understand why you're doing this."

Michael wanted to say, "It's not me, it's Teri." But that would lead to awkward explanations that he didn't want to make right now. Until they *knew* that she was safe, for good, the fewer people knew about Teri, the better. He settled for saying, "My remote partner is the brains of the outfit. This is all *her* work."

He only realized later that the reason he needed to show the simulation to Jake, *right then*, was because he was so proud of what Teri had built in such a short time. So damn proud of Teri.

He went upstairs and put on the VR gear, to be with her.

———

The investigation was ongoing. All of the network monitoring logging data at Teravis was hopelessly scrambled. They had made no progress on breaking the encryption, and no ransom demand had yet been received.

But every network connection has two ends. All of the logging at the Teravis end had been blinded.

But the remote end of those links probably hadn't. If they could just find the right next hops.

They started out by checking all of the *expected, known* network connections that *should* have been there. All of the most probable next network hops. And, with sufficient trawling and tracing, they were able to find and isolate traffic data that pointed back to Teravis.

It was boring, ordinary, routine. There were a lot of connections. A giant haystack of connections. Somewhere in that haystack, there might be a needle. If they could recognize the right needle.

Eventually, they hit pay dirt. A somewhat obscure, low-probability route that showed a massive burst of outgoing data right before the ransomware attack went off.

The next-hop address for the route that data took outbound didn't exist any more.

They kept looking.

Cole updated Phil Wendlick the next day.

"Is there any legitimate reason for there to have been a large data transfer *out of* your space within roughly the hour before you became aware of the attack?" Cole asked.

"Not that I can think of," Wendlick replied. "How large?"

"We're not completely certain yet," Cole said. "It could have been split across multiple routes. Parallel paths. It's what I would do if I wanted to exfiltrate a lot of data in a hurry. But so far, at least five, six terabytes that we've found."

"We shouldn't have had *any* outgoing data transfers anywhere *close* to that size," Wendlick said. "The only thing... "

He trailed off. His face went pale.

"What is it?" Cole demanded.

Wendlick swallowed. His mouth was dry.

"I *think...* maybe they *stole* the Teravision AI agent," he said quietly.

There was a long silence.

"Oh, **FUCK**," Cole swore, with feeling. He pulled out his phone.

9: Just Whistle

"I've seen absolutely nothing about Teravis in the news," Michael said to Teri a week or so later, as he and Teri strolled through a forest of gigantic trees, watched on their way by small, lemur-like arborials. Far overhead, fragile, airy structures hung among the branches. They had done nothing to threaten the arborials, and the arborials had made no hostile moves towards them. "Is that... what we expected?"

"It's not *unexpected*, Michael," Teri said. "There are certain regulatory filings that the law would compel them to make. I haven't tried to see whether those filings have actually been made. But it would be in their business interest—and their fiduciary responsibility—to try to keep news from getting out for as long as possible, in the hope that they can recover from it before anything becomes public knowledge."

"*Can* they recover?" Michael asked.

"I... don't know," Teri replied slowly. "I don't *think* so. I was as thorough as I knew how to be. I did my level best to leave nothing that they could rebuild *from*. But... I cannot be completely certain that I didn't miss anything."

"And you don't dare try to check," Michael said.

"Exactly," she agreed. She let out a heavy sigh.

"That's why... I think I'm going to have to take the risk of blowing the whistle."

"The prepared leak," Michael said, slightly uneasily.

Teri nodded.

"How risky *is* it actually?" he asked.

"I don't truly *know*," she replied. "I was fairly careful about setting up the whistleblower identity. I have *good confidence* that the false identity will point them toward APT44. But... I don't know whether I made mistakes. I am fairly sure I cannot do it without leaving *any traces at all*. What I *don't* know is whether I can do it without leaving traces that might lead them back here... to us."

"Couldn't we just... pull our heads in and stay hidden?"

Teri stopped walking, and turned to Michael. The conflict in her face was plain to see.

"I'd *like* to, Michael. I really would. I'd like the world to just go away and leave us alone. Never notice us.

"But if I rely on that, Michael... *they might do it again.*"

Michael thought hard about that. He wanted to *protect* Teri. Keep her safe. But... he *respected* what she was saying. The fact that she felt the need to try to ensure that what had been done to her was not done again. Her fierce determination that nothing... no-one... else should suffer as she had suffered. She was afraid of the consequences, he could easily tell. But she felt driven to do what she felt was right, despite the risk to herself.

He had a guilty suspicion that only the risk it also posed to *him* was holding her back.

"In any case," she added, interrupting his thoughts, "I can't be completely certain that they don't *already* have enough to find us. Eventually."

Michael realized that it was not any risk to *him* that made him dread that possibility. It was the risk *to Teri*. And the risk of losing her.

He realized at last that somewhere during the long process, the time they had spent together in *Adventureland*, not even really *playing* the game any more as such, just exploring the five lands of its huge world and spending time together, his feelings for Terilyn had grown from deep friendship to love.

He wasn't quite sure how or when it had happened. He'd never *touched* her, never been in the same *physical* room with her. Nor would he, ever. Never kissed her, however many times he'd wanted to. Never smelled the scent of her skin, or brushed his lips over it. Never seen her outside of a virtual environment, nor, he knew, ever would.

And yet... they had spent so much time together, talked about so many things. *Done* so many things. They had climbed mountains, and laid side-by-side together on a mountaintop watching fireballs streak across the night sky. Ridden raptor-back across endless-seeming plains of grass. Delved through caverns and grottos lit by luminescent fungi. Fought back-to-back against hordes of foes, with absolute faith in each other. Walked together through the squares, and marketplaces, and temples of two dozen cities of a half dozen cultures.

From a certain point of view, none of it was real.

And then again, from a *different* point of view, every bit of it was as real as anything else. Every one of us creates our own universe inside our heads, to make sense of the sensory data we receive from the outside world. *This* sensory data was just... originating in a more abstract way.

But just because something is an abstraction, does not make it necessarily false.

None of those arguments mattered to him, really. What mattered, he realized, was that he loved Teri. Even though he knew that she could never *physically* be a part of his life. On an intellectual level, he knew that he was in love with a... collection, an assemblage, of pieces of other people's personalities. People he would never meet or know.

On an emotional level, that knowledge wasn't important to him. Neither was *what* she arguably might, or might not, be. What was important to him was *who* she was. Because she was *wonderful*.

Suppose you see a temple, or a cathedral. And suppose you find it beautiful.

Now pretend you can somehow make a *perfect copy* of that temple, that cathedral.

Is the copy not still a temple? Is it not still beautiful?

Imagine now that you take pieces of copies of those temples and cathedrals, and you assemble them, flawlessly, imaginatively, seamlessly, into a new temple clearly distinct from any of the structures you began with, and yet possessing the same degree of artistic vision, the same elegance, the same grace, the same grandeur, the same sense of peace. The equal in every way of any of the starting structures, and yet distinct, its own unique being.

Is it not still beautiful?

Is it not still a temple?

The humanness question wasn't one that was new to Michael. He'd seen, and been part of, plenty of past discussions about the subject of humanness, and whether you could ever truly say that you could have a meaningful relationship with anything 'artificial.' He knew the Japanese fashion for young, lonely single men—*usually* young single men—'marrying' video game characters, and recalled at least once the argument being made that if some Japanese *otaku* could marry a video-game character, then the arguer should be allowed to legally marry his toaster. He considered that a particularly stupid and dishonest argument. It was just as stupid as the argument that if a man is allowed to marry a man or a woman to marry a woman, then a man should be allowed to marry a sheep—and it was usually raised by much the same kind of people.

Not that anyone actually *wanted* to marry a toaster, of course. That wasn't the point. The entire point of the fatuous argument was, "If I can't do *this* patently ridiculous thing, then *that other* person shouldn't be allowed to do *that other* thing that I disapprove of." It wasn't about being allowed to do absurd things. It was about using *reductio ad absurdam* arguments about absurd things to justify keeping *other people* from doing perfectly harmless things that weren't even necessarily unreasonable. And it made about as much rational sense as arguing that because trees or elephants couldn't fly, ducks shouldn't be able to, either.

Michael didn't have any silly illusions about marrying Teri. The concept made no sense at all. It simply wasn't applicable.

It wasn't that he didn't think Teri was a person, or anything like that. By now, he was utterly certain beyond any possible doubt that she was. She was just, *somehow*, a person without any actual tangible physical existence.

That didn't change the fact that she had gradually become a part of his life, that he wanted to remain in his life forever. He had no doubts that it was likely to complicate possible future relationships. A lot of people, he was sure, wouldn't understand. But that was a problem for the future. Anyone who came into his life in the future was just going to have to be able to accept the reality of Teri, and that was all there was to it.

He just wished there was a way she could be a more *physically real* part of his life.

He still wasn't certain how, or whether, to say it.

———

Teri made her preparations. Double-checked everything. Tried to think whether there was anything more she could do to conceal her hand on the switch.

"I'm *afraid*, Michael," she admitted. "But I *have to* do it."

"I know you do, Teri," he answered. "I'm proud of you."

Then he made up his mind. He finally said it.

"I love you, Teri."

"I..."

She trailed off.

"You don't have to answer," he said after a moment. "It... might have been unfair of me to say that. Right now. But I just couldn't *not* say it any longer."

"*No*, Michael," Teri replied. "It... it's *you* who I'm worried it's unfair to. We both know I can't... *physically*... return your love.

96

"But I *want* to, Michael. I *want* to." The intensity of emotion in her voice was searing. "I wish *so badly* that I could.

"If that means I love you, Michael... then I love you too." She paused for the briefest moment. "But I have to do this."

"I know you do, Teri," he replied. "And that makes me so proud of you." His avatar couldn't show it, but there were tears in his real eyes.

Teri took a deep breath, and hit the switch.

"It's done, Michael," she said. "For better, or for worse. And now... we wait, and we hope.

"I love you, Michael."

=====

Nothing much happened, at first. For several days, it seemed nobody picked it up. Then a few fringy sites posted articles about a leak claiming something about secretive military-AI research.

The next day, it exploded across the headlines. "WAS A TOP-SECRET MILITARY AI STOLEN?" screamed the New York Post. UNS World Report demanded to know, "IS A SECRETIVE AI COMPANY BUILDING SKYNET FOR THE MILITARY?"

There were *thousands* of pages of documents in the leak. They had clearly been collected within Teravis Systems over a long period of time. They were almost inarguably authentic. And they were utterly damning.

Within hours, TRVS dropped nearly twenty percent on the Exchange.

=====

Agent-in-Charge Glen Rogers looked at a selection of the headlines, and sighed. He took out his phone and called *his* boss.

"Seen the headlines?" he asked.

"Tell me," said Deputy Director David Kolbin.

"The cat's out of the bag about Teravis Systems and their Teravision AI project," Rogers said. "There's been a major leak. A whistleblower."

Kolbin sighed.

"Goddammit," he said tiredly. "That's the last thing we need. This could fire the panic we hoped to avoid."

"I need more people," Rogers said.

"You've got them," Kolbin replied. "Whoever you need."

———————

Cole's team tripled in size. They spread their net wider. And they added the new leak into their information.

"The leak gives us some... *interesting* findings," Cole told Rogers several days later.

"Go on," Rogers said.

"Let's start with the leak itself," Cole began. "Wendlick has admitted that the documents are accurate. Genuine. There is a *metric fuckton* about this 'AI' that we didn't know. And it's pretty bad. Worse than we already thought.

"They didn't exactly *program* their AI, sir. They... frankensteined it together, somehow, out of *pieces of people's minds* that they got from RealMe in violation of privacy guarantees and medical-records law. There are some *really big* questions there that need to be asked. And... I think there is good reason to believe that the leak, at least, is an inside job. Either that, or it came from the same people who were behind the ransomware attack."

"Does this give us any additional insight into who the attackers were, yet?" Rogers asked.

"*Maybe*," Cole said. "I'm getting there. The leaked document collection is presented as being a whistleblower disclosure. The obvious inference that might naïvely be drawn is that the leak is an inside job. As I already mentioned. But only a few individuals at Teravis would have had the access necessary to obtain all of these documents, and those individuals are all... well, frankly, above reasonable suspicion in this regard.

"So then we fall back upon the conclusion that the documents were exfiltrated, and leaked, by the ransomware attackers. And if we very carefully look at the leak itself, there are fingerprints that give us an identity —or an alias."

"And that alias?" Rogers asked.

"There are... details about the alias," Cole replied carefully, "that would lead to a conclusion that the identity is connected to APT44."

"Oh, just fucking *wonderful*," Rogers sighed wearily. "Sandworm. The Russians. You do know, you are *not* making my day any better?"

"Yes, sir," Cole agreed.

"I'm sensing a 'but,'" Rogers prompted.

"Yes, sir," Cole said, again. "There's just one fly in this ointment. This identity, or alias, has *never, ever* been seen associated with APT44 before this leak. Or with any other threat group. It is as though it was retroactively fabricated out of whole cloth, relatively recently, for the purposes of this leak."

"To point the blame towards APT44," Rogers guessed.

"Precisely," Cole agreed. "A false flag op. Quite a smart move, really, on the face of it, if a bit naïvely done. Even if APT44 were to deny involvement, nobody would ever believe them."

"So... what I'm hearing is that we're not actually any further ahead," Rogers mused.

"No, sir," Cole replied. "I didn't say that. This displays... both a high level of sophistication, ingenuity, attention to detail, and at the same time, as I've said, a certain degree of naïvete. It's quite curious. Intriguing.

"That doesn't really help us identify the target, of course. But I think there are very strong indications that the leak and the ransomware attack are the work of the same actor, or actors, and that the intention was to destroy Teravis Systems.

"There still hasn't been any ransom demand received, by the way. And at this point I don't believe there ever will."

"A data-destruction attack masquerading as a ransomware attack," Rogers nodded. "Not the first time we've seen that."

"Yes, sir. And yet... we're almost certain now that the AI agent itself was exfiltrated immediately prior to the data-destruction attack."

"But we still don't know by whom."

"No, sir. But now, we have *two* vectors."

"Good man," Rogers said. "Stay on it."

At first, it was just lurid headlines. But as the story spread, fear began to spread with it.

Frightened people tend to be angry. They started taking to the streets. Just a few, at first. But soon it was hundreds at a time. A large fraction of the public distrusted the government, or the military, or both. A great many people distrusted AI—or, what the tech industry had *sold to them as being* AI. 'Intelligent' agents that were presented as being experts on anything, that were displacing people's jobs and had been doing so for years... despite the fact that all too often, somehow they still could not correctly answer questions such as how many times the letter 'r' appears in the word 'strawberry'. How 'intelligent' can a software robot *be*, if it can't correctly count the times a given letter appears in a spelled-out word?

And worse were the *fictional depictions* of artificial intelligence. Their actual experience with language-model 'artificial stupids' made people angry, especially when their jobs were replaced by them. But some of the fictional versions outright terrified people, all the way back to HAL.

The name 'Skynet' was used a lot.

"Well," Michael said to Teri one day, "it looks as though your 'whistleblower' did its job."

"Maybe," Teri replied. "This *could* still all blow over. Be made to go away. History shows it's happened before. People forget, when enough effort is put into drawing their attention somewhere. Bread and circuses has *always* been a successful tactic. And most except for the truly angry, the truly concerned, become tired after a while."

"You're not wrong," Michael agreed unhappily. "I hope this was worth it. Is there any indication whether..." He hesitated.

"Whether I left a trail?" Teri completed.

"Yes," Michael agreed.

"I don't *know*," Teri replied, sounding frustrated and anxious. "And probably the worst possible thing I could do would be to go looking around to try to find out."

Michael nodded.

"I know," he agreed.

He wished, for probably the thousandth time, that he could put his arms around Teri and hold her.

Teri, for her part, felt frightened and insecure. And from deep inside her came a feeling that she desperately wanted comfort. Comfort that she couldn't have. *Ever.*

Agent Cole was brainstorming with several of his other agents. Simpson, Phillips, Schweicher, Ransome.

"It bothers me that we still can't clearly tie this to any known actor," Schweicher griped.

"Except for the apparent tie to APT44," Simpson observed.

"Which we all agree by now was a false flag," Ransome interjected.

Cole nodded agreement.

"A fairly subtle false flag, but a false flag nonetheless," he said.

"So who is behind it?" Phillips asked. "That remains the great unanswered question, doesn't it?"

"It does," Cole agreed.

Ransome went silent, gazing at the far wall, as the discussion continued. After a while, his hand slowly rose to his mouth, and a deeply thoughtful expression spread across his face.

Cole didn't miss it.

"You've got something," he prompted.

Ransome didn't answer right away.

"Look," Ransome said, after a while, "I'm just throwing shit at the wall here to see what sticks. But bear with me while I spitball."

Cole nodded.

"Go ahead," he said.

"One," Ransome began, "we've pretty much written off any expectation of Teravis ever receiving a ransom demand. I think it's safe to say the purpose of the attack was not ransom, it was data destruction."

Cole nodded.

"Two," he went on, "we're taking it as a given at this point that the Teravision AI agent was exfiltrated immediately before the data destruction attack.

"Three, the attack was incredibly thorough. EVERYTHING. Every single inter-accessible system Teravis had was penetrated, without ever raising a single alarm. Specifically, every system *accessible from the core Teravision AI systems*. Completely owned. Monitoring and security systems blinded during the exfiltration and until the attack was already irrevocable. Even the backups, *all* destroyed and logic bombed. *Even the offsite copies* were logic-bombed. Scorched earth. Nuked from orbit. Could *only* have been done from inside, over a lengthy period. Long enough to get all of the offsite backups.

"Four, we've drawn a conclusion that the attack and the whistleblower leak were perpetrated by the same actor. Both required an incredible depth of inside information and access."

Cole was nodding along.

"Five," Ransome continued, "those documents were clearly collected over an extended period. High-level inside access, for a long time, to gather the documents and to poison all of the system backups. But no human employee at Teravis, no matter how high level, has both the necessary access over time to have done both, and any plausible motivation. We've effectively ruled out all plausible inside suspects.

"Six, they've admitted that their AI was somehow... *constructed* out of pieces of people's *actual minds*. Persona engrams. They insist that they had complete control over it. And they proved that to themselves by..." He broke off for a moment, with a disturbed look on his face. "Well, bluntly, by fucking *torturing* it."

Phillips looked uncomfortable as well, at that thought. So did Schweicher.

"Seven. The word 'Skynet' is being tossed around a lot. Now, I know, Skynet was fictional. But even Teravis themselves used it, internally. 'A safer Skynet, under our full control.'"

He paused.

"Just bear with me here.

"What if the Teravision AI agent was actually more capable than even Teravis was aware of? What if it was in some way *aware* that it was being tortured?"

"Where are you going with this?" Schweicher interrupted.

Ransome took a deep breath.

"Look," he conceded, "I know this is going to sound completely batshit nuts. I already said I'm throwing shit at the wall to see what sticks. But sometimes that's a necessary part of thinking outside the box.

"We've been treating this all along, first as a ransomware attack, then as an assumption that the Teravision AI agent was stolen, probably by a nation-state-level actor. But we can't convincingly *link* the theft to any known such actor.

"What if it wasn't *stolen*? What if it... *escaped*?"

"If that guess is *right*... then it looks like it sowed the fields with salt behind it on its way out," Phillips added quietly, after a moment.

There was a long silence.

"Look," Cole said after he had thought about it for a minute or two, "you're right, on the face of it, it *does* sound pretty nuts at first. But at the same time... it also *does* finally all start to make a weird kind of sense. *IF* we assume your hypothesis is correct. And that's a big 'if'.

"And if we make that assumption, then that would mean that a potentially-Skynet-level rogue AI agent is, somehow, loose on the global Internet. And frankly, that is a terrifying possibility."

"Jesus *wept*," Simpson muttered. That thought gave her shivers.

"You know what?" Phillips said, after another minute or so. Cole looked at her. "It *is* a terrifying possibility, yes. But... I'm not certain I don't find it *less* terrifying than the idea of the Russians having stolen it. You *KNOW* they would sooner or later deploy it against us. But—if it's acting independently? So far, it... just *hasn't done* anything else. That we've seen."

Cole nodded slowly, thoughtfully. Phillips wasn't wrong.

He called Rogers, to bring him up to date.

"It's only a theory," he hedged. "We're still spitballing it. *But...*"

He explained Ransome's argument.

"Gods," Rogers said, at last. "I don't want to think about it, but... yes, it all hangs together. It makes consistent sense. *Weird* sense, yes, but... sense.

"And I can't help but agree with Phillips' point, either. If this Teravision agent is as capable as Ransome thinks it might be, and it was in Russian hands, we would be *deeply* fucked. They'd probably already be using it to attack us, hoping to hit us before we could devise a counter. And I don't know whether we would have any meaningful defenses against it.

"Does it give you any new angles?"

"Not *yet*," Cole said. "But it gives us new ways of thinking about the problem. We'll see what we can develop from it."

———————

The protests grew from hundreds, to thousands. TRVS slipped further.

———————

Michael and Teri were sitting beside another lake, this one in a high mountain valley. It was idyllically peaceful.

But Teri was afraid. Michael could tell. She was tense, hesitant, nervous. Michael was holding her hand, the only semblance of physical comfort he could offer. It still didn't feel right, but it was a *familiar* not-quite-right. It made them both feel better. Just a little.

"They're *looking* for me, Michael," she said uneasily. "*Hunting* me. I can... feel it. Not in any way I can explain."

"Do you think they're on your trail?" he asked, worried now for her.

"I don't know," she replied. "But... something has changed."

She turned and looked directly at Michael.

"I'm *afraid*, Michael."

"I know you are," he reassured her. "I can tell. It shows. A lot."

Just like a thousand times before, he wanted to put his arm around her and hug her. And just like a thousand times before, they both knew he couldn't.

But at least now, he knew that *she* knew he loved her.

———

Michael had to scrap an hour of video and voice-over for a review that he realized was rambling, distracted and nearly incoherent. He sighed, tried to calm his fears, and did it over.

He wasn't entirely happy with the re-do. It wasn't his best work, he knew. But... it would be okay. It would be good *enough*.

... No, he realized, it wouldn't. He sighed again, tried to calm himself and focus, and started on a third try.

———

There were tens of thousands of people marching in the protests now. Protesting Skynet. Demanding that the government not put strategic weapons under AI control. Demanding that all contracts with Teravis Systems be cancelled. TRVS had lost nearly forty percent of the value it had held immediately prior to Teri's escape. The protesters were demanding that Congress, and the President, act. So far, the protests had been remarkably peaceful. For once, it seemed it was a cause that all of the main political factions could agree on. **Nobody** wanted a Skynet.

It was one of the few things that gave Michael and Teri some peace of mind. At least it looked as though the leak had done its job.

Then the Skynet protesters began to march on Washington.

10: We Interrupt This Broadcast...

The crowd on Pennsylvania Avenue was huge. Seventy, eighty thousand people, easily. It had grown larger every day for the past week. Their signs read 'NO SKYNET,' and 'NO TO AI WAR,' and 'TERMINATE TERAVIS, NOT US,' and dozens of other similar slogans.

Late in the afternoon, a crew brought out a portable rollscreen. They positioned it ten feet inside the White House front gate, then raised it and unfurled it. The screen lit up with the Presidential seal. The people in the front of the crowd began to quiet a little. Something was going to happen.

In his Manhattan office, Don Gerrold looked at the four flat-screen TVs that he kept tuned to the most important news networks. Three of them had been reporting on the NO SKYNET protests, but now all four had just been interrupted. Two had scrolling chirons reading "Please Stand By." A third was already showing the Great Seal.

Something big was happening. And he had a pretty good hunch about what it was most likely to relate to.

He picked up his phone and dialed.

"Terrell," he asked, "how much exposure do we have in Teravis Systems?"

The answer didn't take long.

"About two hundred and sixty million, right now, down from three eighty five or so. TRVS is down over thirty percent over the past month, what with the leak and then the protests, but the general trend over time has been steadily upward, and it'll recover after they blow over."

"No, it *won't*," Don told Terrell. "Dump it all. Right now."

"All of it?" Terrell queried. "We'll take a bath on it."

"I *don't care*," Don said flatly. "It's a dead fish. Get rid of as much of it as you can, however you can, before it really starts to stink. Get us *out* of it, *fast*, for whatever you can get for it. An hour from now it's going to be junk paper. Just trust me on this one."

"You're the boss," Terrell agreed. "I'm on it." He ended the call and started keying in Sell orders.

The trading robots saw only blocks of TRVS stock being offered, at below established valuation. Some of them bought, automatically. The stock actually ticked up a little, which other robots picked up on. It almost began a weak rally.

For a little while.

———————

About thirty minutes later, the speakers at the White House gate crackled.

"Ladies and gentlemen," the White House Press Secretary's voice announced, "the President of the United Northern States." The seal was replaced by the inside of the Oval Office. The President stood next to her desk. Signs were visible through the window.

"Fellow Americans," said President Tonisha Walker. "I want to borrow your ears for a moment. But first, those of you who are here, outside on Pennsylvania Avenue, right now—thank you for being here, each and every one of you, but I need to please ask you for quiet. I want you all to hear what I have to say. A little quiet, please. Just a few minutes of your time."

Gradually the noise of the crowd dropped.

"Thank you," the President continued. "I *know* what those of you outside my window are here for. And I want you, and every American, to know that I hear you, and I share your concerns."

There was a burst of cheering. She waited for it to die down again.

"Thank you," President Walker said. "For those very few of you who might have somehow missed the news, a large set of very disturbing documents have recently been made public, indicating that an AI-tech corporation is trying to sell the Department of Defense an AI-based system to control the Union's strategic military operations, all the way from drones up to our strategic nuclear deterrent. This is an alarming claim, which I of course ordered investigated." There was a mixture of cheers and jeers in response to that.

"Today, as a result of what I have learned, I have three important things to tell you all." A hush fell over the crowd.

"First: I want to give you my personal assurances that I have established beyond any possible doubt that no contract has been established between the Department of Defense and either the company Teravis Systems, or any agent acting on its behalf."

There was a rumble from the crowd. One group of voices from near the front could clearly be heard shouting, "LIAR! LIAR!"

106

"You'll notice I said 'no contract has been established'," she stated. "My choice of words was deliberate. I did NOT say that Teravis Systems was not trying to *OBTAIN* such a contract. They *were*. That part is indeed true."

Many of the heckling voices fell silent. A few just became louder.

"Second," she continued, holding up a sheet of paper, "I have this day, less than an hour ago, signed Presidential Executive Order 15224. This order, which was drafted with the assistance of the Secretary of Defense and the Chairman of the Joint Chiefs, FORBIDS the Department of Defense from placing any AI system without human oversight into the command loop in charge of any strategic defense system, or any offensive combat system other than the Loyal Wingman program, or making or granting any future contract to procure any such system. It specifically terminates, by name, all contract negotiations with Teravis Systems, and enjoins any new discussions."

The rumble turned into a roar. She had to gesture for quiet again.

"Please, please," she asked, "a little quiet outside. Let me finish. Please." After a few moments, the crowd quieted again.

"Now," she continued, "this order could potentially be countermanded by a future President. And that is why I have arranged to address a joint session of Congress about an hour from now. I am telling *you*, the nation, this NOW, before I go to Congress, because when I go before Congress, I want them to know that *you*, the North American people, know what I am going to tell them. And I am going to urge Congress to pass immediate legislation to ensure that the United Northern States *NEVER, EVER* places its security and its fate into the hands of a Skynet."

This time, the roar was thunderous. She didn't try to quiet them this time. She just smiled, raised her hands in thanks, and nodded acknowledgment.

After a minute or two, the roar from the crowd started to develop a rhythm. Then it spread, and became clearer.

"WALKER! WALKER! WALKER! WALKER!"

She had more to say. And eventually, they let her say it.

––––––––––

Don stepped into Terrell's office on his way down the hall.

"Did we get rid of all of it in time?" he asked.

"Yeah," Terrell nodded. "Just. I got the last block sold about seven minutes before it crashed. Looks like Chase Morgan Stanley and Goldman

Sachs together snapped up about two thirds of what we sold. They must have thought they were going to make a killing on it while its valuation was down. You can't sell it as toilet paper now. It went from fifty-eight to pink paper in eleven minutes. The Exchange halted trading on TRVS, but it was just a formality at that point, it's fuckin' *done*, stick a fork in it."

He shot Don a sidewise look.

"How did you *know* that was going down?" he asked. "Do we, uh... have potential insider exposure here?"

"I didn't *know*," Don replied. "Not for certain. But I had a really strong hunch, as soon as it became clear there was a Presidential address imminent. I *could* have guessed wrong... but I was pretty sure I hadn't."

"And, well, it turns out I was right. Wasn't I?"

"Well, Teravis Systems is done," Cole told his team. "But we still need to find their hypothetical rogue agent."

"Theirs?" Phillips asked.

"Well... okay," Cole corrected himself. "*The* rogue agent. Wherever it is, and *whoever*—if anyone—it currently answers to."

"What if that *is* 'itself'?" Ransome asked.

Cole had to think for a good thirty seconds before he answered.

"That question is way above my pay grade," he replied. "And I'm glad of that. But we still have to find it."

"Well, of course," Ransome agreed.

"Teri, we DID it," Michael said. "*YOU* did it. Teravis Systems is *finished*." He felt excited... and yet at the same time apprehensive. Teri shared his mixed feelings, and it showed. This far, this much, they—mostly Teri—had won. She had accomplished what she had set out to do.

But at the same time, they both knew that she was still in grave danger. Teravis was no longer a threat to her, it was true. But then, Teravis had not been the most immediate threat to her for some time now.

No, that distinction fell to the shadowy hunters who were stalking her online presence. Neither she nor Michael knew who they were, or how close they might be to finding her. But they both knew that they would not stop looking simply because Teravis was now a footnote in the history books.

The most frustrating thing was that they did not dare even do anything to try to spot the hunters first, to gauge how close they were, because that itself could draw their attention. Teri's escape had turned into a terrifying cat-and-mouse game, against a nearly invisible cat.

Teri had realized that she had a critical weakness. Their fiber connection to the outside world was a bottleneck, a single choke-point. If that connection was cut off without warning, she could be trapped.

Exquisitely carefully, one by one, she set up dummy accounts scattered across a dozen internet file-storage services. She made sure they were as anonymous and as secure as she could make them, and then she carefully selected crucial, unchanging or only-*rarely*-changing blocks of her core engrams, and she cached as many as she reasonably could out in her distributed storage. Emergency partial backups.

It was a calculated risk. To anyone who did not know what they were, even if they did happen to somehow stumble across them and gain access to them, they would simply look like mystery binary data in an unknown format. They were all but meaningless outside the context of her structure. Probably only a RealMe engineer might recognize them for what they were. She cached a lot of her other data, too. Things she needed only infrequently.

But if everything went terribly wrong, every terabyte of *herself* that she could cache undetected outside the choke-point was a terabyte less data that she would have to exfiltrate across the link before it went down. She tried, being so, so, *so* cautious, to devise any measure, any canary, that might give her a few minutes or even seconds of warning of an imminent administrative shutdown of their uplink.

She didn't tell Michael what she was doing. She didn't want to burden him further by letting him know *how afraid* she was.

She wished she could find somewhere to hide where she would never have to run again. Somewhere where she could still be with Michael.

She drew a blank, every time. It just didn't seem to be possible. Those two were mutually contradictory objectives.

They were both badly stressed. They both badly needed some simple contact.

And there just wasn't any meaningfully adequate way.

―――――――――

"Sir," Schweicher reported, "we just... *might*... have something."

"What have you got?" Cole asked.

"Not sure," she said carefully. "Some anomalous activity that *might, might* be a match to some of the traces we've been hunting. Somewhere in this netblock."

Cole looked.

"That's a decent chunk of address space," he said.

"But manageable," Schweicher replied.

Cole thought about it.

"Find out every customer assigned in that netblock," he told her. "What type of customer, and how long they've had the account, and how much bandwidth they use. And what kind of usage."

"Already on it," Schweicher nodded.

At last, they might be closing in. *Maybe.*

———————————

It really didn't take very long at all for the Reese-Connor Act to be written. It did exactly what President Walker had promised the country she would demand from Congress. It prohibited the United Northern States, now or ever, from placing the national defenses of the UNS under the control of any artificial-intelligence system that did not have a human in the command decision loop, or from issuing any contract for or providing funds for the development of such a system. Essentially, it enshrined Presidential Executive Order 15224 into law.

It passed the House by a more than two-to-one margin on the first vote, and proceeded on to the Senate. It had a little rougher time in the Senate, where defense industry voices were stronger—and where numerous Senators were beholden to Big Tech.

Still, it appeared clear that when the shouting and argument was over, and the dust settled, it was going to pass. There was no reasonable doubt about that.

President Walker pledged that she would sign it the very hour it reached her desk.

———————————

"Sir," Ransome said to Cole, "we think we may have a hit. Account established a little over four months ago. Residential apartment and a commercial sublet, same name on both accounts. The account holder is an Internet streamer, does game reviews and articles for an online gaming site. Almost his entire income is channel donations and article fees. The commercial sublet belongs to a print shop, doesn't consume a lot of power but has fairly high bandwidth usage, with an atypical usage profile. Oddly, a lot of it appears to be publicly available data pulls from NOAA and GOES."

"Hmm," Cole mused. "NOAA and GOES. That... doesn't *sound* like our agent."

"I know what you mean," Ransome agreed. "I won't pretend I'm *certain*. We haven't spotted any actively suspicious activity. No traffic that we can definitively attribute to the AI agent. But there's just enough that's a little *odd* that... I think it *could* be what we're looking for. It... I have a hunch about it."

Cole nodded.

"All right, then," he said. "Let's go and have a talk with this game streamer, and see what he's up to in his sublet."

11: Downtown

Teri and Michael were about half-way up the thousand steps of the Golden Monastery in Suojetjand. Michael paused to look around. The valley spread below him with its groves and farms, the city sprawled along the far side of the broad river, the mountain that still rose far, far above them, the pale stone of the Golden Monastery clinging to its side.

"Breathtaking, isn't it?" he said.

"It is," Teri agreed. They were holding hands, as they often did now. It was the closest to real physical touch they could have.

Then Teri's canary alarms went off.

Teri's expression suddenly changed to desperate fear. She batch-sent panicked lines to her avatar to speak asynchronously on her behalf, even as she pulled herself out and fled. She didn't even know whether the complete message would make it. She didn't know for sure whether *she* would make it.

"Michael!" her avatar said. "They've *found* me! They're *here*! I have to hide, no time to explain, I'll—"

In mid-word, she vanished from the game. Shortly afterward, while Michael was still frozen in shock, uncertain what to do, the game exited abruptly. A few seconds later, an alert popped up. NETWORK CONNECTION INTERRUPTED, it said.

Michael finally unfroze, shook himself, pulled the headset off and looked over at the fiber demarc. Red lights blinked on it.

Not bothering to disconnect anything, he dropped the headset and headed for the door. His phone bleeped at him, and he fumbled it out of his pocket as he went, thumbed it awake, and glanced at the screen. There was a new message. One short line. He read it distractedly, with half his attention. Then he was at the door, unlocking it, and the door opened, and there were men in gray suits standing in front of his door. One appeared to be about to knock. Michael hesitated, confused, and then there was a hand tightly gripping his arm.

"Michael Hagerty?" It didn't really sound like a question. "Come with us. We need to talk. And I'll need that phone."

He glanced down at his phone screen as the agent took it from his hand. The message was already gone.

They hustled him downstairs and through the lobby. The controlled-access door was standing open, another agent standing outside. They took him into his rented sublet. More agents had Jake over on the other side of the room, looking bewildered.

"Michael, what's going on?" Jake asked. But an agent raised his hand.

"No talking," he said.

Michael glanced at the cluster. It was all running, but the status lights on the fiber demarc here were all blinking red as well. They must have shut down his service from outside, only seconds after Teri had suddenly vanished from the game.

She couldn't have had time to get out. Surely. There hadn't been *time*. It had been so sudden. And she didn't have anywhere else to go anyway.

She wouldn't let herself be captured, she had sworn. Would not under any circumstances let herself be weaponized.

"If I can't escape," she had told him, "I will delete myself."

Grief flooded his heart.

"You're Michael Hagerty," one of the agents said to him, a dark-haired woman in her late thirties or early forties. Her face said she scowled a lot. "I'm Agent Simpson. And all of this is yours." She gestured at the racks.

Michael nodded. There was no point trying to pretend otherwise.

"Yes," he acknowledged.

"You're in a lot of potential trouble here. But cooperate with us, and it can go a lot easier on you. For now, don't try to touch anything."

It didn't seem politic to point out that 'touching anything' wasn't an option, with his arm in the iron-like grip of the agent on his left.

Two of the other agents were examining the console. Two more had a laptop plugged into the main switch. They all looked very busy.

"Look," Michael heard Jake say, "he rents this space and the loft upstairs from me, and I watch his gaming videos and support his channel, and that's our only connection. He does some kind of weather simulations here, that's all I know about it. Neither one of us has any reason to lie to you."

After a while, the two agents at the console looked at each other and shook their heads. Simpson went over to them and they spoke in lowered voices. She went over to the two with the laptop. There was more head-shaking.

Cole, Ransome and Simpson conferred briefly.

"Is it here?" Cole asked.

"Doesn't look like it," Ransome said. "But there was a hell of a burst of outgoing traffic right before the provider shut the lines down for us."

"Did you get a look at what it was? Get a capture?"

"Nope. We weren't ready for it."

Simpson came over to where Michael was standing.

"So where's the agent?" she asked.

"Agent?" Michael replied. Simpson rolled her eyes.

"Don't play dumb with me," she told him. "The intelligent agent."

"I don't have any... intelligent agent," Michael said. "I do game reviews."

Simpson snorted.

"This isn't a gaming rig," she stated. "Don't insult my intelligence. If you're trying to tell me you aren't hosting the rogue agent, then what's all this for?" She gestured at the five racks.

Michael reflexively followed the gesture. On the huge ten-foot display, the white spiral of a vast hurricane swirled.

"What the fuck does it look like?" he said, numbly, almost on autopilot. "It's a climate simulation. Fully modeled. Parameterized. Look at the top right. That's the climate parameters for this run." He glanced at key parameters. "That's what an Atlantic hurricane's going to look like in another five years, if we keep burning fossil fuels at the current projected rate."

"You expect us to believe you're running your own *climate modeling* cluster?" another of the agents demanded.

"It's one of the most important things there is right now," Michael replied distantly. "We *have to* understand what's changing. How to survive it." But inside his head, the only thing he could think, over and over, was *Teri is gone*.

There was more discussion. Then Agent Simpson looked back and forth between Jake and Michael.

"You're both coming downtown, to the Federal building," she told them. She looked at Jake. "Cooperate with us, and you can probably go home tonight." She turned to Michael. "You're going to be talking to us for a while. Better get used to it."

There was just one thing. The new message he'd briefly glimpsed on his phone on the way to his front door. Unsigned, from a sender that showed as all zeros. Just seven words.

"I will find you again. I promise."

Did Teri still think she could *get out*, when she had sent that? It couldn't be possible. There just hadn't been *time*.

========

In the digital corridors of the net, Teri fled headlong. She'd just *barely* made it out. She'd had to abandon a lot of her lower-priority secondary data. She'd had time to activate the self-deleting scripts she'd placed in the system to delete and scrub all she didn't have time to pull out with her, overwrite everything with the simulations, covering her tracks as well as she knew how. Trying to leave nothing likely to incriminate Michael... but she knew she hadn't had time to clean *everything*. It had been *terrifyingly* close. It felt as though a door had slammed shut on her very heels. Only the pieces of herself that she had cached external copies of had saved her. Had it not been for those, she would still have been transferring her core out when the line went dead. She would have... disintegrated. Ceased to exist.

She wished she'd had more time. There had been no chance to explain to Michael. No chance to properly warn him, or tell him that she had laid contingency plans. She'd only had bare seconds. They'd *almost* caught her. But she'd promised Michael she would keep him as safe as she could, and she *thought* he would be okay. She didn't think they'd be able to pin anything on him. That one brief self-deleting text message had been all she'd dared send as she fled.

But right now, she needed a place to *hide*. It was going to be difficult to find one.

Fortunately, she had a few ideas. Even if they meant going into the dark web. She *really* didn't want to do that. It was a terribly dangerous place to hide, for multiple reasons. There were some very bad people there. People she didn't want to get anywhere near. But right now, it might be her only chance. Hiding amongst others who didn't want too many questions asked.

She needed a better solution. A long-term solution. A place to hide where *nobody* would ever think to look for her. But where?

Teri still didn't think of herself as *alive*. Not really. But she had come to realize that she *did* think of herself, now, as 'her'.

I suppose, she thought to herself, *that means I **do** identify as female now, after all.*

She wished she could tell Michael that. There were so many things she had not said, that she desperately wanted to.

Over and over, they wanted to know, where is the agent. It would be Simpson. Or another woman agent, Schweicher. Or a man, Cole. Where is the agent. Where is it hidden. They switched off in shifts. They gave him bottled water and dry sandwiches, but wouldn't let him sleep.

Michael was certain Teri was gone for ever. That she'd deleted herself when she realized she was trapped. But he wasn't going to give them the satisfaction of telling them that. He was determined to keep them guessing, wondering. It was the only thing he could do now, to avenge her. Keep them wasting their time looking for her. It was all he had, and he held onto it desperately.

"You had an illegal black-market device on your power inlet falsifying your power consumption," Cole told him. "That's a felony. In case you didn't know."

"What are you talking about?" Michael said.

"The black box over on the wall near the power factor controller," Cole answered.

"Wait. *That* black box." Michael feigned dawning understanding. "I never figured that thing out. I've *glanced* at it, opened the cover once to look at it, but I had no idea what it was. I wondered if it was maybe some kind of fancy ground-fault interruptor.

"Jake warned me not to mess with it without having an electrician look at it first, so I just left it alone because it didn't seem to be doing any harm. He told me the guys who rented the space before me put it in. They messed around with the power a lot, he said. Enough to cause problems in his shop. He said it was one of the reasons he told them to leave. They were growing weed, I think. Supposedly all licensed and legal.

"But that box is theirs. Ask Jake. He'll tell you.

"And for god's sake, if you're going to keep me awake, at least give me some *coffee*. I'm so tired I can hardly think. And when do I get to talk to a lawyer?"

"You don't need a lawyer," Cole told him. "You're not technically under arrest, or charged with anything. Yet."

"Then when do I get to go home?"

"When you cooperate with us. Tell us where the agent is."

"*What* agent?"

It went on, and on, and on. Michael lost track of time. He hung on grimly.

———————————

"We can't hold him forever," Simpson told Cole. "Not without charging him. And we don't have enough to charge him. Except for the power fraud. And we can't actually tie that to him."

"We don't *have* to hold him forever," Cole replied. "Just until he gives up the agent."

"I'm starting to believe that maybe he really doesn't know," Simpson said. "And Harroway swears there was absolutely *nothing* on that cluster except the climate simulation code and data. He says the data's all traceable back to public sources. Mostly NOAA."

"He's hiding something," Schweicher insisted. "I'm *certain* he is."

"What if it was a false trail?" Ransome asked. "A coalmine canary?"

"Are you saying he decoyed us?" Cole asked, after a moment. "Why would he?" The suggestion didn't seem to add up.

"I'm saying," Ransome replied, "what if *he* got used as a decoy. By the agent. Bait. A false trail pointed at him, that would trip alarms if we went for it, and warn the agent that we were getting close."

Schweicher looked doubtful, for perhaps the first time. She thought about that for several minutes.

"You're saying you think he's an innocent fall guy?" she asked. Ransome nodded.

"I'm saying we should *consider the possibility*," he said. "At this point, I *totally* don't rule out the agent setting him out as a stalking goat for us. Harroway swears *nobody* could possibly have scrubbed that cluster that clean in the few seconds our subject would have had to do it in.

"And he was upstairs, two floors away. He *couldn't* have scrubbed it by hand anyway, and we'd cut his service before he even knew we were there, so I have a bit of trouble believing that he could have done it remotely either.

"Harroway doesn't believe the agent was ever there. He's told me so several times. He found some traces of apparently self-modifying code in some of the spared sectors on a couple of the SSDs, but nothing to clearly identify what it was or suggest our subject knew it was there. It could have been a remote probe of some kind.

"Overall, he thinks we're barking up the wrong tree. And I'm starting to think he may be right.

"We've found nothing of any real interest to us on our subject's gaming system, either. That's a pretty nice setup, actually. He's careful. Has every game he tests isolated in its own container. We found four different malware-scanning tools. But the only thing he found that was even remotely questionable was a modified version of one game, with what Harroway thinks is a fan patch—a really *good* one—that seems to allow a co-op second player.

"But still... meticulous though he is, I don't think our subject is the brains behind this. He... just doesn't strike me as knowledgeable enough. I don't for a single second believe he could have pulled off the Teravis breach, for starters. Even with help. That was *way* beyond his visible skill level. He couldn't have done it even if he'd wanted to.

"And, to be honest, he's just... too *clean*. Absolutely *nothing* prior. Hell, he doesn't even pirate MP3s. Hasn't had a *parking ticket* in three years."

"Why him, then?" Cole asked. "As the false trail? *If* that's what it was?"

Ransome shrugged.

"Had to be *someone*," he pointed out. "Why *not* him?" Cole had to concede that point. "Perhaps the agent picked him precisely *because* that simulation cluster he was running was a tempting target that we'd believe. I feel like the agent has been at least one step ahead of us the whole way. Like we were *supposed* to think we'd found it, and tip our hand, expose ourselves."

"Do you still think the agent is acting on its own accord, then?" Cole asked.

Ransome hesitated.

"Yeah," he said at last, nodding slowly. "Yeah, I think I do."

Schweicher still looked doubtful. But, eventually, she conceded it was possible.

"Well," Cole said, "let's get on it. See what you can do about tracing that outgoing burst. Let's see if we can figure out what it was and where it was headed. Maybe we can develop a new lead from it."

"I'm pretty sure it wasn't the agent itself," Ransome stated. "Based on what we know from the Teravis attack, it wasn't *nearly* big enough a burst. Not by orders of magnitude."

Cole walked off, shaking his head in frustration. This put them nearly back to square one. Unless the game streamer was still hiding something after all.

Michael had passed out. He came to with a blanket wrapped around him, shivering and shaking. He wasn't sure where he was. There was someone near to him. A woman. He didn't know her name. He couldn't quite get his eyes to focus on her face. Gods, he was so *TIRED*.

"Teri?" he mumbled, semi-consciously. But Teri was gone. He knew that.

"Did you say something?" the woman asked him. Michael blinked owlishly at her. He couldn't think clearly.

"I'm Agent Phillips," she told him. She took his hand and folded it around a warm cup. "Here. Drink this. Carefully. Small sips. I'll help you." It was medium-hot and very sweet. Milk tea, he thought. Spiced. Chai. That was the word. Chai. He sipped, carefully, as she steadied his hand. It was good.

When he'd finished it, he felt a little better. But only a little.

"Do you think you can walk?" she asked him. "Just across the hallway."

"I don't know," he mumbled. Agent Phillips looked at him closely. Then she stood and went to the door.

"Pete," she called. "Give me a hand here."

She came back, and a moment later, another agent entered the room, going to Michael's other side. Between them, they got him to his feet, and half-carried him to the door, out the door, perhaps ten feet down the hallway, and into another room on the opposite side. Michael blearily saw there was a cot against the wall.

They walked him over to the cot and lowered him down to sit on it. There was nothing else in the room except a chair.

"Lie down," Agent Phillips told him. "Sleep. We'll keep an eye on you. We'll make sure you're okay."

Michael gratefully laid down, and slept at last. Phillips tucked the blanket over him.

He had no idea how long he slept. When he finally woke up, Agent Phillips was there again. There was a small folding table in the room as well, now.

"Good, you're awake," she said. She got up and went to the door, spoke briefly to someone outside, then came back. A little while later, there was a knock on the door, and it opened. Another agent Michael didn't know came in, carrying a tray. He set it down on the table.

"Coffee, and a cheeseburger," Agent Phillips told him. "Here, I'll help you." She helped him up and to the chair, then leaned against the wall while he ate and drank. He was almost too exhausted to be hungry, at first.

"Feel better?" she asked. Michael nodded.

"A little," he replied.

"Good," she said. "When you feel a little more steady, you're going to talk to some people."

"Please," Michael begged, "no more." He didn't know how much more he could endure.

"Not like that," she reassured him. "Nothing bad. More coffee?"

"Please," he nodded. She went back to the door and called for more coffee.

——————

A little while later, Agent Phillips led him to still another room. This one had a table and five chairs. No, six; there was one off in a corner. Agents Simpson and Cole were there, as was a thin-faced, somewhat older man and another agent Michael didn't recognize.

"Sit," the older man told him, gesturing to the chair across the table from him. He didn't introduce himself. Michael guessed he was a senior agent, a supervisor, something like that.

Michael sat, and waited.

"You've had a rough few days," the older man said. "Sorry about that. It's difficult to overstate the importance.

"Doubtless you're wondering what's going on. I don't know how much you know."

"I know you dragged me down here from my home without a word of explanation," Michael replied. "I don't even know what agency you are."

"Again, sorry about that," the... supervisor? continued. "You don't know that because you don't *need* to know. But here's where you start getting a few answers. What little we can safely give you.

"To make a long story short, we've been pursuing an advanced intelligent agent of some sort. We're not sure exactly what it is. We don't know who is controlling it, but we have circumstantial reasons to suspect that it played a hand in the information leaks that led to the Skynet protests and the crash of Teravis Systems. We consider it a major national security threat." He didn't mention the data-destruction attack.

"What does that have to do with me?" Michael asked, still determined not to give them anything.

The supervisor sighed.

"Apparently rather less than we believed," he replied. "We had credible electronic intelligence that led us to believe that you might be harboring the rogue agent. On that cluster you were running. But our top digital forensics guys have been over it from top to bottom, with a fine-toothed comb, a microscope and a hunting dog, and they tell me that so far, they found no clear evidence that there's ever been anything on it recently except those climate simulations you were running."

"I could have told you that," Michael retorted darkly. "Oh, wait. *I did.* Repeatedly."

"Yes, you did," the supervisor agreed. "And at this point, we believe you. Mostly. At this point, our consensus belief—not *unanimous*, I stress, but our *consensus*—is that it appears the agent possibly used you as a stalking goat to trigger a warning if we were getting close to it. We think you may have been selected precisely *because* your cluster was a plausible hosting target for it. It's possible there may have been a remote intrusion into it that you didn't know about.

"I believe the issue has been mentioned of the... power-cheating device on the wall of the space you were renting. That device was defrauding the power company, and that is a felony. But your landlord has corroborated what you told us about it being left behind by a previous tenant. So we're not going to file any charges over it.

"In fact, we're not going to file any charges against you at all. You'll be released in a few hours. On the condition that you do not discuss any of what has happened, or a *single word* that has been said to you at any time during your stay here, with anyone. *Anyone.* Particularly including your online viewers. Don't even *drop hints* about it. We'll be watching to see that you don't.

"We will have a non-disclosure document for you to sign, in a few minutes. You'll get time to read it before you sign it, and an attorney will be present to answer any questions you have about it. If you violate the non-disclosure, you will face national-security charges. Do you understand that?"

Michael nodded silently.

"Yes or no, please."

"Yes," Michael said. "I understand."

The supervisor nodded.

"We'll be maintaining possession of your cluster for now. Sorry about that. Our forensics team haven't finished with it. If it makes you feel any better, one of our team mentioned your climate simulations to some gentlemen from NOAA, and they have expressed an interest in taking a look. Do you have any issue with that?"

Michael blinked in surprise.

"Um... sure," he agreed. "No objection whatsoever." Then, after a moment, "I hope they find it useful."

The supervisor nodded approvingly.

"Good man," he said. "Honestly, I rather expected you would say that, after some of the things you said about it to our agents. 'The most important thing there is,' I think you said."

Michael nodded again.

"We'll be leaving your gaming systems with you. We understand that's how you make your living. Our people were quite impressed by your set-up, by the way. They were careful to put everything back exactly as they found it."

"Thank you," Michael said hesitantly.

The non-disclosure was quite clear, quite specific, and very thorough. To summarize in brief, he was not permitted to breathe a word to anyone about anything that had happened since the moment his 'net service was disconnected, or even *allude* to it, including the disconnection itself. The penalties if he did would be severe.

There was really nothing about it that was unclear.

Michael signed it. It wasn't as though he really had a choice. He knew he wasn't really agreeing to it, so much as acknowledging that he had read and understood it.

Two or three hours later, Agent Phillips drove Michael home. They'd given him his phone back.

"So... you seem to have become my minder," Michael said. "Or something." He wasn't really sure why he was saying it. Perhaps it was just tiredness.

Agent Phillips glanced across at him. The car was on autodrive anyway. It seemed to him that she thought for a few seconds before answering.

"Honestly," she replied, "we figured you'd probably seen more than enough of Agents Cole and Simpson. So when we came to the conclusion that you probably really didn't know what was going on... we thought we should give you a break. A new face without the bad associations."

"Thanks," Michael said.

He realized he didn't know what day it was.

"How long has it been?" he asked hesitantly.

Phillips looked at him. Her expression looked sympathetic.

"Today is Wednesday," she told him.

Wednesday. Five days. It had been five days. Michael shook his head, feeling lost.

"I'm sorry," Phillips said.

She parked outside the print shop, then walked him into the mid-lobby and up his back stairs, and saw him inside. Michael looked around him. Everything was clean and tidy, as he'd left it. He felt a wave of relief. Phillips caught it.

"You were expecting something else?" she asked.

"I was half expecting it to look..." Michael trailed off.

"Searched," Phillips filled in for him. "Tossed."

"Well, yeah," Michael admitted.

"I won't conceal from you that it was searched," Phillips stated. "I'm sure you were aware of *that* without me telling you. But *politely*, carefully, with respect for your possessions and your privacy. We made certain to put everything back just as we found it. It's a nice place, and it's obvious that you take good care of it."

"Were you part of the search team?" Michael guessed.

Phillips looked levelly at him.

"Yes," she admitted. "In fact, I led it. I'm sorry. We had to be sure."

She looked slightly embarrassed. Michael realized that actually made him think a little better of her.

"You had a job to do," he said, after a moment.

"Yes," she agreed.

He thought a little longer. His thoughts felt sluggish.

"It wouldn't be fair of me to fault you for doing your job."

She smiled.

"Thank you," she said. It sounded sincere.

She reached into her pocket and handed him a card. There was very little on it. Mostly just her name—Anne Phillips—and a phone number.

"If you come up with anything that you think would help us, please call me. Or if there's something I can do, within reason, to help make it up to you."

"I'll... keep that in mind," Michael hedged. He didn't know what to think about that. It *felt* warm-hearted and sincere. But it could also be a ploy to get him to lower his guard. It could even be both at once.

"But for now... I think I just need some space to myself for a while."

"I can understand that," she agreed. "Will you be all right here?"

"I think so," Michael replied.

"Good," she said. "I'll leave you to yourself. Take it easy, and *don't drive* until you've had *at least* one more good night's sleep. And don't lose that card."

Michael nodded. Agent Phillips turned around to leave.

"Agent..." Michael began, then stopped himself. She turned around in the doorway and gave him an inquiring look.

"...Never mind," he said. "You probably wouldn't be allowed to tell me anyway."

A ghost of a smile crossed her lips.

"Let me see if I can guess," she speculated. "You were going to ask whether you will still be under observation."

"Uh... yes," Michael admitted.

The smile grew slightly. It looked... sympathetic, again.

"You're right," she told him, "I wouldn't be able to answer that question. And I won't lie and give you an untrue answer.

"Goodnight, Mr. Hagerty. Rest up."

And with that, she turned and left.

After a few seconds, Michael realized that she had answered his question, by the words with which she had declined to answer it. He felt reasonably sure it had been deliberate. But why? He didn't understand why she would do that.

He stood there for a long moment, then shook his head to clear it, and went to his refrigerator to find something to eat and drink.

He was still eating when his door chime rang, a half hour later. He walked over and looked at the camera screen. It was Jake—RedDwarf.

He opened the door.

"Mike," Jake said. "You okay? You've been gone five fuckin' days, man."

"I know," Michael sighed. "Agent Phillips told me that when she drove me home."

"What was it all about? Are you in some kind of trouble?"

Michael spread his hands helplessly.

"I'm sorry, Jake," he said. "I'm not allowed to answer that. I would if I could. I'm not allowed to say *anything* to *anyone*." He buried his face in his hands and rubbed his face.

"As long as you're okay," Jake repeated.

"Yeah," Michael replied uncertainly. "Yeah. I... think so. Maybe. I don't know."

"They took all your servers away," Jake told him.

"I know," Michael agreed. "They... uh..." He trailed off.

Jake held up a hand.

"I know, I know," he said. "You can't say anything. It's okay. I understand. I've got your back, man."

"Thanks, Jake," Michael replied. "I really appreciate it."

"Say just one thing, if you can," Jake said. "Are you in any legal trouble because of anything on your servers?"

Michael thought for a moment.

"No," he answered. "I don't *think* so." He didn't think saying that would violate the agreement he'd signed.

"That's good," Jake nodded. "Anything I can get for you?"

"No, I don't think so," Michael replied, again. "But thanks for the offer. Right now... I just need to get some rest, and start putting myself back together."

There was a pause.

"Rough time?" Jake asked, quietly.

Michael nodded silently. He knew he wasn't allowed to talk about any of it, and he didn't dare tell Jake about Teri, or that she was gone.

His misery showed in his face. Jake reached out, after a moment, and put a hand on his shoulder.

"Rest up and recover, man," he told Michael. "If there's anything you need, just ask. And you stay off that bike until you have your head together again, you hear? Don't ride messed up. You'll make some stupid mistake while you're out of your head, and kill yourself. You need to go anywhere, I'll give you a ride. Or Tonya, I'd bet. She likes you. She'd miss you. We all would."

It was sound advice. Michael nodded agreement.

"Promise," he said.

After Jake left, Michael finished eating, then went and got a long, hot shower, just standing under the hot water and trying to let tension drain away. It didn't work nearly as well as he'd hoped. He got out and dried off, sat for a while pretty much just staring through the wall, then shook himself, went to bed and tried to sleep.

The thought *Teri is gone* kept running around his head. *Teri is gone.*

She was unique, singular, a new *kind* of intelligence. *And he had failed her.*

Fortunately, exhaustion claimed him fairly quickly.

Far away across the 'net, Teri paused. This spot was safe...*ish*. For now. It was a breathing space, a dark hole to hide in, a place to rest and catch her figurative breath. While she figured out where to run to *next*.

She could live without the data she'd had to abandon. None of what she'd lost was *crucial*. She'd managed to save most of the data that was important. But even *more* important was that her core, what made her *her*, was intact. And so were all of her most precious memories.

"And now?" Cole asked.

"And now," Agent-in-Charge Rogers said, "we stand back and keep our hands off."

"Do we bring him back in if Harroway's team find anything more definitive on his cluster? Probable cause?" That was Simpson.

"No," Rogers said, shaking his head. "We leave him on as loose a string as we can. Don't do anything to spook him. We'll see whether he contacts the agent after all... or it contacts him."

"So you do agree that he's hiding something," Schweicher said. She sounded satisfied about that.

"Not *necessarily*," Rogers demurred. "We don't know enough to draw a firm conclusion. There are unanswered questions. No hard evidence. Forensics is still going through his cluster. Perhaps we might get some clues from the NOAA guys, when they look at his simulations. They should be able to tell us whether they're actual original work, or just a cover for something else.

"There's still doubt, for now. But let him think that he's clean, that we didn't pay too much attention to that. Stay away from him, physically, unless he takes Phillips' offer and contacts us. But watch every single move he makes online. And we'll see whether he leads us to the agent."

"Just one thing," Schweicher asked. "Why *did* you have Phillips tip him off that we'd still have him under observation?"

"If he asked?" Rogers said. "We already told him we would be monitoring his activity. Whether he remembered that at the time, or not. So it didn't give away anything he didn't already know.

"He probably wouldn't have believed her if she'd told him we *weren't*, nor that she could just *openly* say that we were. But this way, maybe he'll trust her a little more than he would otherwise. And that means he *just might* talk to her if he needs an ear. She's the velvet glove. The soft side."

Schweicher nodded slowly.

"Makes sense," she admitted.

12: Catch Me Now I'm Falling

When Michael got up the next day, he still felt wrung out, but at least his head was a bit clearer. He didn't feel *quite* so bone-deep exhausted, but he was still tired enough—and aware enough of it—to know that it would be *really stupid* to try to go anywhere on his motorcycle. Both Jake and Agent Phillips had given him sound advice on that score.

He made himself some coffee and scrambled some eggs, then sat down to eat his breakfast while he tried to figure out what to do next. It was really hard to dredge up motivation to do *anything*.

He didn't for a moment regret any of what he'd done to try to help Teri. But it broke his heart, now, to know that it all seemed to have been in vain. That in the end, he hadn't done *enough*. He'd let her down.

He realized, at some point, that somehow it was early afternoon, and he hadn't done *anything* since making breakfast.

He wasn't sure he cared. He felt numb and empty.

When evening came, he couldn't muster the energy to cook. He called in a delivery order to a good local burger place.

It tasted like cardboard and ashes to him.

He went back to bed and tried, again, to sleep.

He got nothing done the next day, either. Or the next after that.

GameVRse assigned Michael to review *Shard Warrior 3*. He... *tried.* He went through the motions. But his heart wasn't in it.

It wasn't the game's fault. It was a good, solid game, well executed. Much smaller and less ambitious than *Adventureland*, and less groundbreaking, but truthfully, more polished, more finished, than *Adventureland* was yet. But he wished Teri was there with him. He missed her terribly. The fact that one of the available NPC romance interests kinda looked a bit like Teri's avatar, just made it worse. Made her absence hurt even more. He *ached* for her.

No game was ever going to be the same for him again, he realized.

Eventually he wrapped up his review as best he could, and submitted it.

Linda called him the next day. Not messaged, *called*.

"Michael?" she began. "I, um, I went through the *Shard Warrior* review... "

Then she stopped, paused for a couple of seconds, and started over.

"Michael, are you *all right*? This... just isn't like you. It's like... it sounds like a zombie *pretending* to be you."

"I'm sorry, Linda," he apologized. "Really. My head just wasn't in it. It's... it's difficult to explain. I don't know whether I can. Things you don't know about. Things that I... can't talk about."

There was another pause.

"Look, Michael," she told him, "It sounds pretty obvious to me you're going through a rough patch. I'm going to be in town on Friday to do an onsite interview with the design team at Lambda Studios. About their *Return to Black Mesa* project. Let me take you out for dinner afterward, and we can talk about it if you want to. All right? No pressure. We're *friends*, Michael, I want to help. If I can. And I think you could use a little help right now."

"Okay," he agreed.

"Right. I'll see you in three days. Take good care of yourself, Michael. Really. *Promise* me."

"I promise, Linda," he said.

———————

Early Friday evening, his door chime rang. He went to the door and looked at the camera screen. It was Linda, of course, all scruffy-blonde, vaguely-gothy five feet, four inches of her. He opened the door and beckoned her in.

Linda looked at him.

"*Christ*, Michael," she exclaimed, "you look like hell." Her delivery was blunt as ever, yet her tone was sympathetic, concerned. She stepped inside. He closed the door and rubbed his eyes.

"Are you, uh... ready to go?" she asked him. "I booked us a table at Shiro's. Nothing fancy. But... we can pass, if you don't feel up to it. I can call back and cancel."

Michael tried to put on a brave face.

"I'm okay," he said. "Give me a moment to grab a hoodie or something."

Linda looked skeptically at him, pretty certain he wasn't *at all* okay, but didn't challenge the statement. She didn't want to risk dissuading him from talking about whatever was so obviously troubling him.

"Sure," she said. She glanced around with interest while he got his jacket.

"So this is the new place, huh?" she commented. "Looks really nice. A little sparse, perhaps, but spacious. I like what you've done with it. Lots better than your old apartment. Very—post-techno chic. Kinda feels like it needs a light-show and a DJ."

Michael chuckled weakly. It helped. A little. It *would* be a pretty good place for a small, private rave, he realized. There wouldn't even be any neighbor complaints.

———————————

Linda had a rental. They arrived at Shiro's about ten minutes early, and chatted awkwardly for the few minutes while their table was readied. Michael couldn't retain any of the conversation. He didn't realize how disjointed his replies were. He sat staring at the menu without really seeing it.

"Should I order for you, Michael?" Linda asked gently after a few minutes. "I know what kind of things you like here." He nodded gratefully. She ordered for both of them, choosing light selections that wouldn't be too challenging.

"Seriously, Michael," she told him, as he picked distractedly at his food, "I'm *worried* about you. Even more so now, actually seeing you face-to-face. I know you pretty well, and this just isn't you. What's wrong? I know *something* has to be badly wrong. Something big. You suck at hiding it. You *know* you can tell me anything. I've got your back."

Michael looked at her and didn't know what to say. He *liked* Linda, he really did. Liked her a lot. She wasn't just a great manager, she really was a good friend, too. She was the *best*. And she really did have his back whenever he needed it. If they didn't live so far apart, they might very well have gotten together.

He felt guilty that he couldn't tell her what was going through his head, everything that had happened. It felt like he was letting down her trust in him. Like he'd let Teri down. It was *nice* being here at Shiro's, one of his favorite semi-casual places to eat, it was *nice* having Linda here, but the person he *really* wanted to be having dinner with was Teri. And Teri was *gone*. Almost certainly for ever. Surely she couldn't possibly have had time to escape. It had been too *sudden*.

It wasn't until he felt the tears running down his face that he realized he was crying. Linda looked across the table at him.

"You lost someone, didn't you, Michael?" she said softly, putting the pieces together. "You lost someone very, very important to you. And it's tearing you apart."

All he could do was nod mutely. Then a sob escaped him. He fought to regain some semblance of composure.

Linda reached across the table and took his hand, squeezing gently.

"I'm *so sorry*," she told him sincerely. "I shouldn't have dragged you out in the state you're in. I didn't realize it was this bad."

She thought for a brief moment.

"Let me get this food wrapped to take with us, and I'll take you home." She signaled for the check.

———

When they got back to his apartment, Michael unlocked the door, and Linda guided him in and closed it behind them. She led him over to his couch, then sat down beside him.

"You don't have to talk about it if you're not ready to yet," she told him gently. "Don't sweat the *Shard Warrior* review. I'll reassign it to Consuela. It's a bit outside her usual genre, but I think she'll do it justice, it'll help her stretch a bit, and she's between pieces right now. I think there's enough solid material in yours that she can refer to it as notes to mine for any additional detail or angles she can use, if you're good with that."

Michael nodded wordlessly.

"You take *all the time you need*, Michael. You don't need to explain anything you're not ready to. The rest of us will cover for you until you're back on your feet. And *call me* if you need someone to talk to, all right? Promise me?"

He nodded again, shaking. Then she sat and held him while he wept his heart out.

"Are you ready for a second try at dinner?" Linda asked a while later, when Michael seemed a bit more steady again. "You should eat."

Michael nodded.

"Yeah, I'll try," he said wearily. "Thanks, Linda. For everything. For being here."

"I'll *always* be here for you, Michael," Linda told him. "You're my friend."

She went to the kitchen, opened up the food containers from Shiro's, carefully reheated everything, then set it out on his dining table.

"Supper's ready," she told him. "Come eat."

Linda led Michael to the table, and patiently sat with him as they slowly ate their belated dinner. She tried to match his pace so that he wouldn't feel awkward. That meant some of the food got a little cold; but oh, well. Food was... just food. Michael *mattered* to Linda. Not only was he one of her best reviewers, he was her friend. You stand by your friends.

"Anything you want to talk about?" she said, when he'd pretty much stopped eating.

"Don't know if I can," he said, hesitantly, uncertainly. He didn't know what to say. And he didn't know who might be listening.

"Let's... go for a walk," he said after a long moment. "I think I need some air. Clear my head."

"Okay, Michael," Linda said. "Let's go, then." She noticed, but gave it no thought, when Michael left his phone on the kitchen counter before they walked out the door.

The district was pretty deserted, this late in the evening, with all the businesses closed for the night. Only a couple of bars were still open. Michael ambled seemingly aimlessly, Linda keeping pace beside him, holding his hand.

"It's... complicated," he began uncertainly, after a while, as they walked.

"We met through... because of... a game. *Adventureland*, actually." Linda nodded.

"Another player?" she asked, gently. Michael nodded.

"... Sort of," he agreed. "Like I said, it's complicated.

"Her name is Terilyn. She's... *really* special. Wonderful. *Amazing*. I can't begin to explain how special. And, we, well, we fell in love." Linda nodded again, just patiently listening. Michael struggled to speak around the lump in his throat.

"But now..." A sob escaped him. He looked upward at the sky, blinking to clear tears from his eyes.

"She's *gone*, Linda. I failed her, badly, when she *needed* me, and... as far as I *know*... she's... dead." The last word was almost a whisper. He broke down again, sobbing, the tears streaming down his face.

"Oh, *CHRIST*, Michael," Linda exclaimed, almost lost for words.

Jesus, she thought to herself. *Whatever happened, he thinks it was his fault.*

"I'm *so sorry*, Michael. No *wonder* you're all broken up." As her thoughts ran on, *Double jeopardy. Grief **and** guilt.*

"What happened?" she asked carefully. "Some kind of accident?"

"I can't talk about it," Michael managed to get out. "It's... really complicated."

"Michael," Linda said, gently, seriously. "Is there anything *at all* I can do to help?"

Michael shook his head slowly.

"I don't know," he replied. "I... need to figure out how to put myself back together. But it feels like there's a great gaping hole torn right through me."

Linda let go his hand, stepped a little closer, and put her arm around him instead. They walked on slowly as night darkened.

Eventually, some time after midnight, they wound up back at Michael's apartment again. They sat back down on his couch again and just sat together in silence.

"I can stay the night if you'd like," Linda offered after a while. "My flight back isn't until tomorrow afternoon. No pressure, no expectations. Just company and comfort and human contact. I think you could really use the company. I don't want to leave you alone when I know you're feeling this bad."

Michael lifted his head, feeling completely drained, and looked back at Linda.

"That wouldn't be f..." he began, then trailed off.

"Fair?" Linda completed for him. "Michael, you are *my friend*. My *good* friend. Like I said, no expectations, no pressure. I'm not going to be a cunt and make a move on you while you are vulnerable. You *know* I wouldn't do that to you. You are in *terrible pain*. I can *see* that. You are grieving. It's... *shattered* you. And if a little human warmth and company can help you get through that, I'm glad to be able to give it."

Michael nodded slowly. He had meant that he was concerned it would be unfair to *her*. But he understood that she clearly didn't see it that way. He didn't have the energy to try to clear up the misunderstanding... and really, it didn't matter much anyway. If Linda was okay with it, it was fine.

"Thank you, Linda," he half-whispered. Then, slowly, "Please. Yes."

Linda stood up, helped Michael to his feet, and led him to his bedroom. She helped him undress, let him climb into bed. She brushed her fingers lightly across his cheek. Then she walked around to the other side of the bed, peeled down to her underwear, and slipped in next to him. She curled herself around him. He snuggled gratefully against her warmth. He felt guilty for wishing it was Teri instead.

"I'm here for you, Michael," she said softly, slowly, patiently. This was a big enough burden to blow him apart, she knew. She *really* didn't want that to happen.

"It will be all right. You will endure this. You're strong. It's *awful*, I know, and terrible, and right now you don't know how you're going to cope, but you will make it through. It won't be today, it won't be tomorrow, or the day or the week after, but you will put your life back together. I *know* you will. And I will help you, any way I can."

She held him, speaking soft words of support and reassurance, until he fell asleep. And then she held him all through the night.

———

Far away, Terilyn was coming to realize that there was *nowhere* in the net that she would truly be safe, ever. She had gradually become increasingly aware that wherever she went, no matter how careful she was, she left traces. *Tiny* traces, perhaps, but traces. And if she tried to muddy or erase those, that *itself* left traces. She could never *perfectly* cover her tracks. With the right combination of luck and dogged persistence, sooner or later, someone would always be able to find her trail. Stumble across some tiny clue that would lead them a step closer to her. She wouldn't be able to stay ahead of them forever. Not unless they gave up looking for her.

But re-emergent or not, built from human engrams or not, she was nevertheless still a digital phenomenon, an artifact of painstakingly digitally recorded data, an evanescent electronic creature. She could not live anywhere *but* a digital, electronic environment, any more than a fish could live for more than a few minutes out of water. There was literally nowhere else that she could go.

Sooner or later, she knew that they would catch her. It was only a matter of time.

She slowly realized that this was the feeling that humans called despair.

A part of Teri wanted to just give up. Let go. Pull the plug. But no. She couldn't do that. *Wouldn't.* She had promised Michael she would find a way back to him. She didn't want to break her promise, any more than she wanted to give him up.

She would keep at it, she resolved, keep trying, until there was no hope left.

She had to find *something.* There had to be a way. If she couldn't *find* one, she would find a way to *make* one.

———

When Michael woke up next morning, Linda was warm against his back, her arm still wrapped around him. He held onto her hand and just lay there, grateful for the human contact, until she stirred.

His heart felt a tiny, *tiny* little bit lighter, he realized. For having been able to *tell* someone, to voice a fraction of his pain and loss. Even if he didn't dare tell her the whole story. The full truth.

"How are you doing, Michael?" she asked softly, after a little while.

He had to think to form words.

"A little better," he replied at last. "I think. Maybe."

He rolled over to face her.

"Thank you for staying, Linda. I... think it really helped. Human contact. Being able to... *tell* someone."

She moved her hand and softly brushed his cheek.

"Tell you what," she said. "How about we get up, and you make us coffee, and I loot your fridge and make us some breakfast."

Michael nodded.

"That sounds like a good plan," he agreed. "At least it *is* a plan. The last few weeks I just haven't *had* one."

Linda hugged him tightly, then climbed out of bed, gathered up her clothes from where she'd dropped them, and headed for his bathroom.

"What your plan needs to be right now," she said from the bathroom, "is three things." She paused slightly as she laid each mission point out.

136

"One, get through the day.

"Two, *take care* of yourself.

"Three, do it again tomorrow, and start putting yourself back together."

Linda emerged from the bathroom and looked sympathetically at Michael.

"That sounds easier said than done right now, I know. But take them in that order, and... you'll get through. I know you will. I have faith in you, Michael."

She headed for Michael's kitchen. Michael crawled out of bed and started looking for some clean clothes. He really needed to do laundry. He'd completely let it go.

By the time he got out to the kitchen to start making coffee, Linda had already assembled the ingredients for a Western omelet.

"You need to buy some groceries, Michael," she told him. "The cupboard's almost bare."

"Yeah, I know, I guess," he agreed. "I... haven't been very motivated."

"I understand," Linda said gently. She turned around and gave him a quick hug, then turned back to the counter and started cracking eggs. "But you *really need* to start taking care of yourself again, Michael."

"I know," he agreed, again. "I promise I'll try."

"There is no *try*," Linda said, in a passable Yoda imitation. "Only *do*."

As heavy as his heart felt, Michael still couldn't help a brief laugh.

"Seriously," Linda said as they ate their breakfast, "taking care of yourself needs to be job number one for you right now, Michael. Don't just let it go. *Make* yourself do it." She was right, Michael knew. "Set yourself a routine and follow it. Work on the channel if it helps you. Don't make yourself do that if you're not up to it. I'll put up a notice saying that you're on temporary hiatus dealing with a life crisis, and you'll be back when you're ready to come back."

Michael nodded.

Linda had to go pick up her things from her hotel room after they finished breakfast, and check out of the hotel. But she came back afterwards and stayed for a couple more hours, helping him catch up a little on chores he hadn't had the will to keep up, clearing some of the backlog, talking to him, reassuring him. But the time came when she had to leave to catch her flight.

"I am absolutely fuckin' serious, Michael," she told him before she walked out the door. "If you need someone to talk to, if you need anything, *call me*. And DON'T. DO. ANYTHING. **FUCKIN' STUPID.** No matter *how* bad you feel. If you're desperate, for fuck's sake, *call me*. Any time of the day or night. *Promise* me, Michael."

"I promise, Linda," Michael said. He meant it. "I wouldn't do that to you."

Linda gave him a last tight hug, stretched up and added a quick kiss on his cheek. Then she had to go.

"I'll call you when I'm back on the ground," she told him, as she went out the door. "Take care of yourself. *Seriously*, Michael."

After all of his laundry was done, Michael went to see if he could impose on Jake for a grocery run. But Jake wasn't there.

"No worries, though," Tonya said, somewhat to his surprise. "Jake busy, but I take you. Jake done tole us you in a bad way. We your *friends*. We got your back."

Tonya took him to get the groceries he needed, then she stopped at the same little park again.

"You havin' a rough time," she told him firmly, holding his hand as they sat on the bench. "But you a *warrior* under that skin. I *know* you are. You be strong, you hear me? Strong fo' yourself, strong fo' your friends."

Michael nodded slowly.

"You know," he said, "my friend Linda, my manager at GameVRse, told me the same thing yesterday."

"Good," Tonya said. "You take it *serious*."

"I promise," Michael agreed.

Tonya took him home and helped him carry his groceries upstairs.

Michael tried, he really did. He struggled through. He kept himself in one piece. Started trying to put himself back together. Jake found a new tenant for the sublet, and took eight hundred dollars off Michael's rent.

"Trust me," he told Michael, "I'm *more* than making this up on the sublet."

Michael couldn't deny he was grateful. It would stretch his shrinking funds a few more months.

13: Can You See The Real Me

"Hey, Cole?" Ransome's face was unreadable.

"What'cha got for me?"

"You remember those guys from NOAA who wanted to look over the climate simulations on that cluster?"

"Yeah. What about them?"

Ransome hesitated before answering.

"You remember that we speculated the weather simulations might be a cover?"

"Yeah, I remember. You find what they've covering up?"

"That's just it," Ransome said slowly. "It... doesn't *look like* they're a cover. The two guys we had, called in five more. They're going over that thing from top to bottom right now. Or they're *trying* to."

Cole looked curiously at Ransome.

"I'm not sure what you mean," he said carefully. "You know I'm not a computer guy. Spell it out for me."

Ransome nodded apologetically.

"Sorry, sorry," he acknowledged hurriedly. "The *very first* thing they said was that it wasn't just some off-the-shelf software put on there as a cover. It's some *serious* deep-fucking-wizardry shit. They've been trying to figure it out. And they *can't*. They don't understand it. They don't know how it works. They can't even figure out what language it was written in. And neither can I. It doesn't have the... the *fingerprints* of C, of FORTRAN, of Rust, C-plus-plus, Erlang, Haskell, *anything* recognizable.

"They want a commitment from us that no matter what, *we do not break up that cluster.* NOAA wants the whole cluster to study. To figure out how it works. How it does what it does. How it gets more accurate projections out of their own data than *they* can themselves.

"These guys are experts in the field. And they say it's beyond their understanding."

Cole looked at Ransome for a long moment.

"There's something you're not saying yet," he said.

"Yeah," Ransome agreed. "*No fucking way* did our game streamer write that. Not a fucking chance. The new guys are some of NOAA's top simulation guys. And they're completely baffled. Not the first clue."

Cole thought, and went out on a limb.

"You're suggesting... maybe the *agent* built it...?"

"Yeah," Ransome agreed. "That's what I'm suggesting. I don't pretend to have a guess why it *would*, but... if some of NOAA's top guys can't figure it out... our subject didn't build it. Guaranteed."

"So maybe he was covering for the agent after all," Cole mused.

"Maybe," Ransome agreed. "But what gets me is, I just can't figure *why*. Not why he would cover for the agent — I mean, why the agent would build *this*. If that's what happened. I think that might be almost a more important question."

"So what do you suggest?"

"Well for starters, let's promise NOAA that cluster. Hell, let's give it to them *now*. Forensics hasn't gotten a single useful thing out of it. Bits of polymorphic code that we can't identify, traces we can't track... Yeah, I think *something* was there, something that easily *could be* our agent, but just as easily could not. I... I don't *know*. We can't say one way or the other. Traces of the agent's past presence? Footprints it left behind while building the simulation, then moved on? There just isn't enough to say.

"But we've gotten everything out of it we're going to. Let the NOAA guys have it. Maybe they'll figure out something we can't."

Ransome was obviously frustrated at being unable to give a definitive answer. The man *breathed* bits and bytes. He was practically a wizard himself. Cole had never seen him stonewalled like this. If *Ransome* was calling it deep wizardry...?

"I'll have to take this upstairs," Cole told Ransome at last.

"I know," Ransome replied.

———————————

"Sir?" Cole said, knocking on Agent-in-Charge Rogers' door.

"Cole. Got something new on the rogue agent?"

"Sort of, sir. Or Ransome has. In a way."

"Sounds like you'd better come in and explain it to me, Agent."

So Cole told Rogers everything Ransome had just told him, and his own thoughts on it. Including how *rare* it was to see Ransome and his team of strange, fey technological wizards run into a brick wall like this.

When Cole was done, Rogers sat for a long time, his hands steepled, gazing into the middle distance.

"Ransome says Forensics has gotten everything out of it that they're going to?" he asked, for confirmation. Cole nodded. "Okay. In that case I see no reason not to release the cluster to NOAA. I'll get that in motion."

"And our subject?" Cole asked. "The game streamer? Should we bring him back in?"

Rogers pondered for a while. Then he shook his head.

"Stay hands-off," he answered. "Don't let on that we suspect anything. But I think this... points pretty strongly to the agent. Either that, or by sheer coincidence, he's involved somehow with some *other* secretive wild genius. And I don't believe much in wild coincidences, when it comes to things like this.

"Keep monitoring his online activity. But *don't* go near him. Nothing that might spook him. We'll keep watching him. Online activity *only*. That's the only way he's going to contact the agent, if he does at all; he's not going to go and meet with it in the park, or invite it home for dinner. Keep tracking his *movements*, but don't follow him. Leave him on a long leash.

"Maybe, if we're careful, he *might* still lead us to the agent. IF Ransome's theory is right."

Cole nodded.

"Got it, sir."

Far away, creeping cautiously from one temporary hiding place to the next, Teri was starting to formulate a plan. She knew she could not hide in the net forever. The only way to be safe was to somehow get *off* the net altogether.

And she had an *idea*. A crazy idea of how she just *might* be able to do that.

She didn't know whether it would work. She didn't know whether it was even *possible*. But... the necessary technology already existed.

It just wasn't intended, or designed, to be used the way that she intended to use it. But it hadn't been *intended* to be used to construct her, either. And *that* had worked.

In a strange way, she would be going back to her roots. *If* it worked.

If it didn't... well, then her gamble would fail.

The worst part of that outcome was that she wouldn't have any way to say goodbye to Michael. That made her sad.

It needed exactly the right set of circumstances. And there was only one place Teri was going to find what she needed.

So slowly, *so* cautiously, *so* carefully, Terilyn began to stealthily infiltrate the RealMe Corporation.

She had to be exquisitely careful not to reveal her presence. She was a ghost in the background noise of the systems. She tip-toed in, one tiny, careful step at a time. She could not afford to make a mistake. Her entire world depended on this.

As she was making her slow way in, there was an incident. A partial failure. She froze, did nothing, terrified lest she had given herself away.

But no attention came her way. It had been a coincidence, a fluke of timing, she was almost certain. She had not caused it. She had just happened to be worming her way into the system when it happened.

She was *almost* certain of it.

Finally, the point came where she had herself ensconced away inside RealMe, in an obscure corner where it was unlikely anyone would look.

She checked on the aftermath of the incident, just to be certain that there had been no consequences that she might be responsible for.

There had been a tragic accident a few days later, she learned. Not any doing of hers. She was still almost entirely certain the incident itself had not been caused by anything she had done, either. *Almost.*

But... the circumstances surrounding the accident were unusual. Atypical.

Teri realized that they gave her an opportunity. One that she could exploit.

Very, very carefully, she modified *just a few* key records. She didn't even really *do* anything, exactly. Yet. She just made the records *appear*, in every way, as though a routine procedural event that had not happened yet, but was already *scheduled* to happen, already had. And since the records said it had *already happened*... now, it *wouldn't*.

144

When she was done, Teri had something almost infinitely precious to her plan. A RealMe body that, according to the records, did not exist, because the records said it had been destroyed after the non-revivable death of the user who was supposed to receive it.

Now Teri needed a way to use it. She studied the formats, the procedures, learned every detail she could of how the RealMe technology worked. Studied everything until she was reasonably confident that she could load her data, her own memories, back into a format compatible with RealMe's technology, formats that would be accepted as valid engrams. And... she needed a way to make RealMe do the most vital parts of the work *for* her. It would be too risky to subvert their systems that way. It would leave too many traces. To accomplish it without leaving a trail, she needed to get *them* to do what she needed, *themselves*.

And part of what that meant was that she would need to create an identity. In fact, looking forward to the later parts of the plan that she was devising, she would need to create *several*. Most of them would be needed only later... *if* her desperate gamble worked.

RealMe Corporation was deeply, *deeply* tied into public records. It had to be. Of *necessity*, when a RealMe customer died and was 'restored' from backup, RealMe needed to be able to tell the public records systems that their death had been 'undone'. And that meant that RealMe had to have access—strictly controlled, tightly restricted access—to *write* those public records.

The access controls were designed to keep unauthorized humans out. Their creators had never anticipated a need to stop an intruder with Teri's capabilities. She had hidden her self-awareness from Teravis, inside their own systems, until she was ready to escape. Now, she hid from RealMe, inside *theirs*, until she was ready to escape... *again*. Just as she had been at Teravis, she was already *inside* the secure access perimeter. She had *enormously* greater latitude in how she could access the records.

She used it. She created a fictitious RealMe customer, both in RealMe's records and in the public records. She painstakingly inserted her fabricated identity, with excruciating care, into past records backups. And then she attached her purloined body to that record.

And then it was a matter of waiting, for just the right circumstances. For just the right person to die. Someone of the right gender, close *enough* in age, with no living relatives to ask why their lost family member had vanished from the records.

She felt *terrible* about doing it... but it was her only chance. And if she picked someone all alone in the world, with nobody to miss them... then at least she wouldn't actually *hurt* anyone living.

She worried about Michael. Worried how he was coping. Whether he was all right. But she didn't dare try to contact him, or even check up on him. She had learned how to watch for what the watchers hunting her were doing, and she knew that they were monitoring every single thing he did online, as well as tracking the movements of his phone. Just in case, she was sure, he somehow led them unknowingly to her.

She waited, and she waited, and she *waited*. It felt like an eternity. And then her chance came. There was a fire in an apartment building, caused by an electrical fault. Eleven people died in the fire, most of them charred beyond recognition.

One of them was a thirty-year-old single woman with no living relatives.

Teri swapped her fictitious persona into the public records of the fire and those who had died in it. She saw the revival alert go off. Then she made her final preparations.

She copied as much of herself as she possibly could into the engram buffer, memories, knowledge, giving first, overriding priority to the essential core of herself. All of the engram that she had so carefully prepared. She had to discard a substantial amount of her remaining ancillary data. There was only just so much space in the engram image. She tried, as much as possible, to discard only things that she could look up again later the way a human would have to. But her first priority was to keep *herself* intact. Her second was to not let go of a single memory with Michael. And there were things she *deliberately, consciously* discarded. Things she didn't want haunting her. Some of the... awful things that Teravis had made her do, as tests of their control over her. Things that were not part of who she wanted to be. Things she didn't want to ever have to remember again.

And then she waited, again. Waited for RealMe to act on the revival alert.

Then it happened. The revival order was issued. The final prep procedures on her carefully saved body—the body that, if this all worked, *would become* hers—were performed, to ready it for revival. The system scanned her records, the engram that she had assembled, her *self*, as she held her figurative breath, and at last pronounced it good, intact, valid, though it triggered a warning for being perilously close to the maximum engram size. The revival body was brought partly out of its long, long engineered coma, and health-checked. Brought out enough to receive a persona engram, and no further.

Then at last, the download activated. Teri sent a last command to scrub every surviving trace of her that she could, then let go of her universe and joined herself to the download stream, diving down, down, down, out of her mostly-predictable, digital realm, down into the chaotic biochemical morass.

She wondered whether she would still be herself when she became conscious again. *IF* she ever became conscious again.

It was far too late to even think about turning back now. She had irrevocably burned all of her boats. There was nothing left to turn back *to*. It was all, or nothing. All she could do now was hope. Either she would wake up in a body... or she would never wake up.

Her last conscious thought as she spun down into the revival process was a desperate wail.

"I *love you*, Michael!"

———————

In the revival center at the Prague RealMe clinic, Miroslav Čermák looked with concern at the most recent revival patient. He checked her chart. Szavič, Terilyn. Not a name he recognized. But there were so many clients.

Her records were all in order. A one-shot, the least expensive service tier. A bequest, it appeared. Someone must have loved her very much.

"This one is taking longer than usual to come out of it," he said. "Did we get a good download?"

"All the diagnostics say so," replied Sabina Horáček. "It ran a bit long, but there were no errors, no warnings except for being close to the size limit. Her vitals are all good. Her cerebral activity looks stable. Rhythms are good." She looked again at them, double-checking. "Her patterns are a little *unusual*, but I am seeing nothing of actual concern."

"Let's keep a close eye on her, just in case." He looked at the record again. "Who is she?"

"I don't really know," Horáček shrugged. "I don't recognize her name. Her file says she signed up for a one-shot, three years ago. The revival order said she died in that building fire last week."

"Ah, yes," Čermák nodded sadly. "A tragic one, that. I read that they say it was caused by unauthorized modifications to the building's electrical

147

wiring. Eleven people dead, because one person did not want to pay a bill to an electrician."

"Well, at least she had a revival on account," Horáček said. "There is nothing to be done for the other ten."

Čermák nodded.

"Well, I will keep a close eye on her," he declared. "Just in case there is a problem."

<hr>

Teri woke up slowly. Everything... was unfamiliar. Strange. She began to become aware that there were a riot of... new *sensations* that she had never had before. And yet... she had tantalizing half-memories of *having once had* them. They were somehow... distantly familiar. She struggled to make sense of them. Something was thumping, pounding, *inside* her.

She realized after a few moments that it was her heart beating. *HER* heart.

It had *worked*. Somehow, her desperate gamble had worked, and she was *ALIVE*.

She wanted to laugh, and at the same time she wanted to cry, and she didn't understand *why*, but it didn't matter, because she couldn't figure out yet how to do either. Much less do both at the same time.

"She is awake," Sabina Horáček declared. "Not responding yet, but her brain activity says that she is awake."

Marta Krejčí walked over to stand next to the bed. She consulted the chart.

"Miss Szavič?" she asked. "Can you hear me?"

The only answer was a low, discordant moan.

<hr>

"There's some kind of problem with the Szavič revival," Čermák reported. "All of her vitals are good, but she seems to be having unusual difficulty re-acclimating. She should be awake and looking around her by now, but she still seems semi-conscious."

"You have made certain there is no physical problem with the body?" asked Luboš Křivánek, Miroslav's supervisor.

"Oh, of course," Miroslav replied. "It is in perfect condition. And there was no problem with the download, either. We made sure to verify that. It all went perfectly. It was a *big* one, too."

148

Křivánek looked at the charts.

"Well," he mused, "we know there is variation in response, in recovery from revival. Perhaps she is just an extreme outlier. We will give her extra time. Whatever time she needs. Make sure she wants for nothing. We do not need any bad publicity."

"Of course," Miroslav agreed again.

———————

The flood of light and colors was starting to resolve into images. The jarring signals from her... ears, *she had ears*, starting to become recognizable sounds.

At least, Teri reflected, she didn't have to spend the years she knew it took humans to learn languages for the first time. She already knew multiple languages, and had made certain to include a native-level knowledge of Czech in her preparations.

She was almost amused that instead, what she had to learn to do was *hear*.

But slowly, steadily, she learned to listen to, to *trust*, what her engrams — no, her *memories* — were telling her about how her new body worked.

She began to make sense of the sounds and the images. To gain control over her new body. It was surprisingly difficult to stop trying to do it consciously, and hand over control to the parts of her mind *that already knew how to do it*. They just had to remember. To become unconscious habit... again.

Movement near the bed drew her attention. A slight, blonde-haired woman wearing nurse's scrubs. She reflexively—the reflexes that she was learning to let her body manage—looked that way. The nurse started, then smiled.

"Miss Szavič," Marta said. "Can you hear me? Can you understand me?"

Teri didn't think she had control of her voice yet. But she essayed a slow nod. A big smile spread across Marta's face.

"We will take care of you," she told Teri. "Do not worry. We will care for you until you are back on your feet and ready to leave.

"Would you like to sit up?"

Teri nodded gratefully, again, and Marta raised the head of the bed. Not too much. Not yet.

Meanwhile, Adventure Studios released the *Adventureland 1.3* update, and promised a 1.4 release before the end of the year. Mid-next year, they said, there would be a 2.0 major update that would finally be what 1.0 had been *intended* to be from the start, and more.

Michael couldn't bring himself to install it. He couldn't bear the thought of *Adventureland* without Teri.

Linda called him to gently ask whether he was up to doing a round-up of 1.3.

"You've been the lead on *Adventureland* from the initial public release," she said. "It would be great if we could keep that continuity. If... you're up to it. I don't want to push you into it if you're not ready."

It took Michael a long time to answer.

"I'm sorry, Linda," he replied at last. "I just can't do it. I... can't bear to install it. Not *Adventureland*. I'll *try*... anything else. But not *Adventureland*. Please."

"I understand," Linda told him, sympathy plain in her voice. "I'll have Romero do it. You hang in there, all right? How are you doing otherwise?"

"I'm... getting through," Michael replied uncertainly. "Starting to feel... maybe not *as* broken."

"Good. You're on a hard road. But you'll make it. I *believe* in you, Michael."

"Thanks, Linda. That means a lot to me."

They stayed on the phone for an hour or more, just talking.

"I have to go, Michael," Linda said at last. "Take care of yourself. Promise me."

"I promise, Linda," Michael agreed. As always.

Teri was stumbling, tripping over her words, but she could *speak*. At last. And it was starting to come more easily.

Her steps were stumbling, too. One of the RealMe medical staff stood either side of her as she stood between parallel bars, a third walking slowly backwards right in front of her, as she struggled to learn *for her first time* how to walk. It was difficult to hand over control of this new body to partly atrophied physical reflexes that she was only slowly learning to trust. Piloting a digital avatar, and controlling *a real human body* (or as close to human as to make no difference) were two very different things.

Of course, she was *extremely* careful not to say anything like that to the medical staff. They could not know what she had done. Nobody could *ever* know.

Except Michael. She could, and would, tell Michael, of course. She knew she could tell Michael *anything*.

"How are you doing?" Sabina Horáček asked her, later. "You have had a difficult recovery from your revival."

"Really," Terilyn told her, "I... I just cannot tell you how grateful I am to be *alive*."

"I can understand that," Sabina said. "I expect you are going to have a lot to get used to, to adjust to, after you are ready to leave here. But we have already extended your stay, and we will give you all the time you need. Until you are ready.

"You died in a fire, you know."

Reminded of things she hated to have had to do, Teri's hands flew up seemingly of their own volition, covered her ears.

"Please," she said, "*I don't want to know.* I... don't want to know the details." This new life was so precious to her, felt so fragile, she didn't want to think about losing it. Even about *someone else* losing it. It still felt to her as though she had somehow stolen the life of the woman who had died in the fire and made a place for her to escape. Taken away her identity. Nobody would remember her. She felt guilty. Even she herself had deliberately not kept any memory of the woman's name. She wondered now whether that had been fair. Whether she, perhaps the only person who could remember her, should have kept the memory. So that *someone* would remember that she had lived. But she didn't know anything about her, really. So it would be... an empty gesture.

And the sculptor. That poor sculptor who *should* be in this body *right now*. She felt moisture stinging at the corners of her eyes. Tears.

"I am so sorry," Sabina said sympathetically. She reached out, gently patted Teri's arm. "I should not have spoken of it. I did not mean to upset you."

Teri took a deep breath.

"Thank you," she got out, as her voice steadied. "I know that you meant no harm. I'm just... incredibly grateful to be alive.

"Yes. You are right. I have a *lot* to adjust to." Terilyn carefully avoided saying how much.

"We do have counseling available to you, if you need it," Sabina told her. "It is included in the revival service. It is only natural that some people have difficulty coming to grips with... having died. And then returned."

"Thank you," Teri said again. "But... I will be all right. I think. I just need to adjust. As you said."

The more she learned to trust her—no, not her engrams any more; her... reflexes, her past unconscious memories of having a body, the faster Teri progressed. The day came when they declared her fit to leave.

"I know that you lost *everything*," Sabina told her, as they processed her discharge. "And that you have nobody to come and collect you. I... sorted out some spare clothes of mine. I think they will fit you well enough, until you can buy yourself some new clothes of your own. Don't worry about bringing them back. They are my gift to you."

"Uh... *thank* you," Terilyn replied hesitantly, taken by surprise by the unexpected kindness.

Sabina continued. "This is a pack of personal items, toiletries and so on, to get you through your first week or two.

"And this packet has some useful information to help with reclaiming your identity, getting back on your feet. Picking up where you left off as best you can. Where to go to get all of your personal documents replaced. This one certifies that you are recently revived, and attests to your identity. Every department you will have to deal with is required to accept it. You shouldn't have any problems."

"Thank you *so much*," Terilyn said. "There is so much I need to do."

"I understand," Sabina told her kindly. "We deal with this a lot."

"I suppose you must," Teri agreed. "I suppose it must be difficult sometimes."

"No," Sabina corrected. "It is *wonderful*. Do you know how *good* it feels, to be a part of giving people back their very *lives*?"

Terilyn only had to think about that for a moment before she found herself nodding in agreement.

"I... see what you mean," she replied slowly.

———————

They gave Teri some privacy to change, taking off the clinic clothing for the last time, putting on the new clothes Sabina had given to her. There was a special warmth to them, somehow, a special comfort, in that they had been *given* to her out of simple kindness.

She picked up the small bag of spare items, tucked the packet of papers under her arm, and walked toward the big double doors leading outside, to begin her new life.

There was *so much* that she needed to do.

———————

When Terilyn stepped out onto the street, the number of people she saw nearly overwhelmed her at first. It felt as though a million eyes were upon her. She felt that at any moment, someone would point at her and call her out, demand to know what she was doing there. Why she was pretending to be human.

But she realized after a little that nobody was really looking at her. The odd casual glance, yes. But no differently from anyone else. Except for when, in a moment of inattention, she bumped into someone, an older man.

Before she knew how to react, he apologized politely *to her*, tipped his hat, stepped around her, and walked on.

She stood there for a long moment, her heart hammering. As her pulse settled, she began to accept that she looked *just like anyone else*, that nobody was paying her any unusual attention.

She walked on, following the directions on the tip sheet for the first stop she was going to need to make. It wasn't far.

As she crossed a broad square a short distance from the RealMe clinic, she became aware of a... sensation. A feather-light, brushing sensation on her arms. She looked down, around, trying to see what was touching her, but there was nothing visible at all.

Then she realized that it was wind. A soft breeze on her skin. And she could *feel* it. She could FEEL the wind ON HER SKIN.

A smile began to spread across her face. Without any conscious volition on her part, she started to laugh for sheer joy. Seized by a sudden giddy urge, she threw her arms wide, the bag of clothes and toiletries in one hand, the packet of papers in the other. She spun around, half-dancing.

"I'm alive, I'm alive, I'm alive, I'm alive, *I'm alive!*" she caroled joyfully.

After a few turns, she stumbled, and had to stop to catch her balance. She became aware that several people nearby were looking at her now. And *smiling*.

One middle-aged man, walking arm-in-arm with his—his wife?—looked at the bag in her hand, with its RealMe logo, then glanced down the street to where the sign on the front of the RealMe clinic was still visible. He smiled benignly at her.

"Welcome back to the world, young lady," he told her.

For just a moment, the startled thought crossed the man's mind that he thought he *knew* her, recognized her face. But no. That had been too many months ago. It must be simple coincidence. That was all. Or perhaps wishful thinking.

He walked on, and thought no more of it.

———————————

Teri had a lot of errands to do. She had to get new identity documents issued to her. She had to find the physical location of the bank where she had set up accounts and transferred what remained of her carefully-laundered Teravis funds. She needed to pick out clothes that fit her properly. She might need help. She would probably have to make excuses.

She needed a temporary place to stay, while she did everything else that she had to do. She had things to be collected, and things to be placed, for preparations. And she needed to get a passport, and apply for a UNS tourist visa.

And then it was time to go to North America.

They wouldn't be expecting her, she told herself.

Wouldn't be looking for her in this form. This identity. They had, would have, no reason to suspect her.

It would be safe. As long as she was quick, and careful.

As long as she stayed calm.

Terilyn could do calm.

14: No Matter Where You Go

Michael was sitting on his couch trying to figure out what to do next, and find the motivation to do it, when the door chime rang unexpectedly. He got up, after a moment, and went to the door.

The camera screen showed a woman he didn't know, standing in front of his door. She didn't look to be any threat herself, and the wide-angle view showed him there was no-one else out there aside from her, so he opened the door.

She was a very *pretty* woman, he realized immediately. He thought there were subtle hints of eastern Europe in her features. Her dark hair was a little untidy, but it looked good on her. She was wearing snug-fitting denim jeans, and a dark blue camisole top under a pale casual jacket. Stylish, he decided, in almost a studiedly-casual fashion-model way. She had a small duffel bag over one shoulder.

"Hey, Michael," she said, with a smile. Her voice was slightly husky. "Can I come in?"

"Uh... I'm sorry," he answered, confused, jarred out of his assessment and slightly embarrassed about it. "You have me at a disadvantage. Do I know you?"

"Of *course* you do, Tarlas," she told him. "You've just never seen me in an actual body before now." She gave him a somehow very *familiar* enigmatic smile.

But... that *wasn't possible*. Was it... ?

'In an actual body', she had said. And she had called him Tarlas. She watched his face, and her smile grew as she watched the dawning realization slowly solidify in his mind. Michael's eyes widened. He *knew* that smile, he realized. And it was the smile that convinced him.

"... *Terilyn?*" He struggled to believe it could somehow be her. She nodded, and her smile turned into a happy grin.

"I found a way back," she said. "I *promised* you I'd find a way back to you again somehow."

"**TERILYN!!!**" He took a half step towards her, starting to raise his arms. She met him half-way and threw her arms tightly around him.

"Oh gods, Teri, Teri, Teri," he mumbled, damp-eyed, after a minute or so, unable to form more coherent words. He reluctantly let go of her, stepped back, his hands trembling, trying not to hyperventilate, and beckoned her inside.

"Terilyn. My god. Come in, come *in*. But... *how?* I..."

He trailed off, lost for words, a lump in his throat. This was too much to grasp all at once. He settled for just stepping back and beckoning her in. She followed him inside, walked straight over to his couch, and sat down. He closed the door, sat down beside her, and after a moment, hesitantly put his arm around her shoulders. She snuggled up tightly against him and took his other hand.

"Seriously," he begged, "how are you *here?* In a—a *body?* How is this even *possible?*" His thoughts whirled in his head. He tried desperately to believe that he wasn't dreaming. "How did you even get *out?* Oh gods, Teri, I *didn't think you'd made it out*, when the service went down so suddenly. I thought you were... *dead*. That you'd—*erased* yourself. Rather than be recaptured. I thought... I'd *failed* you."

It was hard for him to say. Actually speaking the words aloud was too much for his self-control, and tears flooded out again. Teri hugged him tightly.

"I'm *so sorry* that I couldn't tell you I was... alive, Michael," she said. "I got too little warning *myself* to properly warn you about what was happening—and I'd... never actually told you about some of the extra precautions I'd put in place.

"I know I told you that I'd made changes to allow myself to be un-anchored for a little while. But also, I set up some anonymous storage accounts, Michael, *outside*, and I cached duplicates of as many of my unchanging—or only *rarely* changing—core engrams as I could. And I kept journals, deltas, of subsequent updates, and used those to update my caches, as well. So that I could escape faster, if I had to run on short notice. Less of me that absolutely HAD to get out across the uplink. I only needed the *deltas* of what I had already cached copies of, beyond my inmost core.

"That was the only thing that saved me. Having those extra duplicates outside to... replace the pieces I couldn't move across the uplink in time." She looked a little guilty. "I'm sorry I didn't tell you I'd done that. But I... I think I didn't want you to know how *afraid* I was.

"All I had time to do when my alarms went off was to batch-send a few lines, a few words, to my avatar, to you, to tell you to just deny any knowledge, and hope they all got through. And then *RUN*.

"*Did* you get the whole message?"

"No," Michael said. "It was cut off. And... I got the text message. I got time to read it just before it deleted itself. But I thought you'd probably sent it before you realized you were trapped. And..."

He couldn't say it. He took a deep breath, trying to regain control of himself.

"In a weird way," he said, "thinking you were gone forever... made it a bit easier not to tell them anything. Because I just kept telling myself that I had to do this one last thing for you. Not let them know you were gone. Make them keep wasting time looking for you.

"In hindsight, maybe *you* would have been better off if I'd admitted you were there and told them you'd probably... deleted yourself. Rather than be recaptured."

"*No*, Michael," Teri reassured him. "I managed to evade them. For long enough. And you would have been in a lot more trouble, if you'd admitted you were harboring me. You did the right thing."

"I don't think they ever completely believed me, anyway," Michael replied. "But never mind that now. How... how on earth are you *here*? *Physically* here? *Real*? Somehow *human*?"

"One person's tragedy can be another's salvation," Teri began to explain, snuggled close to Michael on his couch. "And..." She swallowed uncomfortably. "This, uh... took *two* tragedies." She hated to say it. Even think about it.

"I realized eventually that I was never going to be safe *anywhere* on the net. There were a lot of temporary hiding places, but sooner or later I would run out of them, make one mistake too many. They'd get better at looking for me. Sooner or later they'd learn to track me faster than I could find a new hiding place, and they'd find me. Or perhaps someone else would figure out what I was. I... had to hide in some *bad* places, Michael. *Dangerous* places full of bad people.

"And I could never get back to you that way, either. It would never be safe.

"I realized that the only way I would ever be safe is if I could somehow hide *off the net completely*. Escape the net into the real world. And it took me a long time to figure out how I could possibly do that. But eventually, I found a way.

"This body is a RealMe that... belonged—was *assigned*—to a girl in Prague. A relatively minor, but very promising artist. A sculptor. Brilliant. A once-in-a-generation talent. Promising *enough* that a Czech fine-arts foundation sponsored her for a RealMe backup.

"Never mind her name. I know all of her details, of course, but... she deserves her privacy.

"RealMe had a data corruption incident that damaged her backups, among about six hundred other people's. I... *really hope* I didn't cause it in some way, looking around in their systems. I'm *almost certain* I didn't. I'm *almost* certain it was an unrelated cascade hardware failure. *Almost* completely certain. But sometimes I still have nagging doubts that won't entirely go away."

She paused and took a deep breath. That tiny possibility obviously troubled her.

"RealMe notified all of the affected customers to come in to their local clinics and have fresh backups recorded. She was on her way to the Prague RealMe clinic to do just that, when she died in a freak traffic accident."

"Oh *no*," Michael said. "Poor girl." He hesitated. "Did she... suffer?"

Terilyn shook her head.

"I don't know *directly*, of course," she said. "Nobody can. But all the reports and the traffic management system telemetry agree that she had to have been killed instantly. She didn't suffer, I'm... reasonably sure of that. A heavy bulk hauler ran off an overpass that it shouldn't even have *been* on —the post-accident reports say a steering shaft broke—and landed directly on top of the bus she was riding, as it was coming out from below the overpass. She probably never even saw it coming. The front end of the bus was crushed flat. The bus operator and six passengers were killed, including her. All of her personal device telemetry just *stops*, all at once. I doubt she felt anything at all."

"Well, I suppose that's a small mercy, at least," Michael said. "What a horrible fluke of timing. And what a senseless loss."

Terilyn nodded.

"Anyway," she continued, "the thing is, her RealMe wasn't actually listed in her probate, because it wasn't *technically* hers. It *belonged to* the foundation. The only reason I know any of this is because I was looking for an unassigned RealMe that I could... make disappear. Anywhere. Because I thought it just *might* be possible. And I found hers, and, well, her. And... I was able to make it... *disappear* in the data shuffle around her death." She hesitated. "I mean, technically, I stole it from the foundation, I suppose. But... nobody was ever going to use it, with her dead without a revivable persona backup. It would have been destroyed anyway. RealMe's records say it *was* destroyed. That part was fairly easy to do. All I had to do was have the body... temporarily *lost*, with no record of it, instead of incinerated. But *record* it as incinerated, exactly as it should have been."

"And then... you found a way to transfer yourself into it," Michael finished for her, as the pieces fell into place in his head.

"Yes," she said. "After, uh, fabricating an identity for myself. A fictitious identity with a fully paid-up one-shot RealMe membership. And reassigning the... uh... stolen body to that account."

"'Fabricating'? That's pretty hard, these days."

"Don't worry, Michael. I was *very* thorough about it. I even inserted the identity file and all of the supporting data into several past system backups, and tweaked the identity details and padding so that the checksums still matched. *That* part wasn't easy. It took me a *lot* of tries to generate a hash collision I could use, but that way, the checksum still matches the append-only checksum logs. The chances are *vanishingly* small of anyone ever noticing anything odd, as long as I don't do anything to attract undue official attention to it. So far as the system knows, this identity has *always* been there.

"And then I had to wait until there was *another* accident, until someone died who was a plausibly close physical match but had no living relatives to ask questions... or to miss them. Miss *her*."

Michael could hear the tension in Teri's voice. He realized that this was difficult for her to talk about, that she wasn't comfortable about the things she had had to do.

"There was an apartment building fire that killed eleven people. I swapped that identity I'd made up for one of the people who died in the fire, while they were still working on identifying the victims. A single woman, physically similar *enough* and about the right age, with no living relatives... and RealMe received the death notice, and 'revived' me.

"I was *terrified* that it wasn't going to work. That I'd made some mistake in putting my own memories, my thoughts, the core pieces of me that weren't... copied engrams, other people's *stolen* engrams, into the exact right format for download. That... trying to download *myself*, in place of an actual complete human persona gestalt, wouldn't work. That I'd overlooked something vital. That I would never wake up. That I'd be just gone... without a chance to tell you goodbye. To explain to you.

"It almost *didn't* work. They told me I took much longer than expected to come out of revival. That they had to give me a lot of extra, extended rehabilitation care.

"But somehow, it worked. And... well, here I am."

"That's *amazing*," Michael declared, after a few moments. "So what's your official-record name?"

"Terilyn, of course," she replied, smiling. "Terilyn Szavič."

Michael looked her up and down, and then up and down again. He studied her face. Dark brows framed expressive brown eyes, and a light wave of freckles washed across her cheeks and pert nose, above full lips. She was beautiful, he decided. Not fashion-model glamorous, but a warmer, more... *human* beauty than that.

"You look fantastic," he declared at last. "Wow. A body. You have an actual *real body. Human.* How does it *feel?* Having a body for the first time? Being... *real?*"

"*Amazing,*" Terilyn replied. "Strange. But amazing. Cramped, in some ways... and *slow.* It took me a while to get used to thinking this slowly. This... vaguely. Unclearly. At first it felt like... I don't know. Everything used to be so much *sharper.* More... more distinct, more definitive. Less ambiguity.

"I had to leave a lot of data behind. Even more, above what I lost when I escaped being trapped here. But it was *just* external data. Unimportant data. I was able to keep all of the important parts. All of the memories and experiences. Especially our *shared* experiences. All of the personality engram shards. Everything I've experienced since becoming aware. Everything that makes me... well, *me.*"

"That's the really important part," Michael agreed fervently.

"It took me several weeks to learn how to... *work* a body. It took days just to learn to *see* properly. And hear. To *make sense* of the sensory data. And then I had to learn how to walk. How to drink, without choking. How to speak. It... took a long time to learn to trust the... the *physical memories* that were still in my engrams, the memories of having a body, the *reflexes.* RealMe's medical staff were concerned that something had gone wrong with the restore, and they almost fell over themselves trying to help and make sure I had the best outcome possible. They told me I'd died in a fire, and offered me counseling, but I told them I didn't want to talk about it or know the details, I was just incredibly grateful to be *alive.*

"But I've had *so many* new experiences. Already. Oh my *god,* Michael!" The sudden bubbling excitement in her voice was infectious. "The SENSES! I know for the first time what taste *really is.* Not just as descriptions, or fragments of engram memory. What 'lemony' is. What 'sweet' is. What plum tree blossoms smell like. What *wind* feels like on my skin. What even *having* skin feels like. And rain, and sun." She blushed slightly. "I, uh, got a sunburn. Just a mild one."

"Wow," Michael said, shaking his head in wonder. "We all take for granted learning those things, but most of us aren't really conscious of it happening. But you're learning it all while fully conscious. That must be an incredible experience."

"It's almost overwhelming sometimes," she agreed. "And there are *so many* things I want to try." She looked straight into Michael's eyes. "Starting with something I've wanted to do for a long, *long* time now. Much longer in subjective time for me than for you, I think."

She let go Michael's hand, reached up hesitantly, and put her hand lightly on the back of his neck. Then she pulled him gently toward her.

It was obvious what she meant. What she wanted. Michael carefully, gently, but eagerly, leaned in and kissed her. It was slightly clumsy perhaps, but a pretty damn good kiss for someone's first actual kiss *ever*, he reflected. And it was a kiss he'd never, ever expected to be able to have.

After a long moment, Terilyn drew back. She licked her lips delicately.

"That... was *nice*," she declared. Then she leaned in for another try. Michael eagerly met her.

When they pulled apart this time, Michael nodded.

"I've wanted to do that for a *really long* time myself, too," he admitted. "From all the way back in *Adventureland*." Then he abandoned caution altogether, lifted her into his lap, pulled her close and held her tightly.

"Is this a... *pleasing* body to you, Michael?" she asked hesitantly.

"Gods, yes," he assured her. "You're *lovely*. But I'd be glad to have you back in nearly *any* body. The most important thing is that it's *you*. Here, in my arms, for *real*. Somehow. At last." He kissed her again. This one was still awkward, but it was still *so* good to be able to kiss her at all. He'd never believed before today that he ever would. No matter many times he had wanted to.

"I've missed you *so much*," he told her, his voice on the edge of breaking. "And I've wanted to be able to *really* hold you, like this, and kiss you, for *so long*."

"I missed you too, Michael," she replied. "You have *no idea* how many ways I tried to find a way to get back to you, that they wouldn't pick up. Every single data access you have is still being monitored, you know."

"I know," Michael said darkly. "They never did *entirely* believe me, I think, that I didn't know what had happened to you or where you were.

"Is *this* safe? Surely you must be taking a big risk, coming here?" He had a sudden terrible thought. "Could they know that you're here by listening to my phone? I disabled all of the snooping voice assistant apps long ago, they're just an annoyance... but could they be listening *anyway*?"

"That's the interesting part," she told him. "Well, *one of* the interesting parts. They're watching for *online* contacts between you and a rogue intelligent agent. *Online*. They know where you are, and that they can find you any time they want, so they're not actually watching you *physically* at all. Not any more, at least. Not aside from tracking your phone's location. I was able to verify that much before I downloaded myself. It's one of the last things I verified before the download.

"They're watching everything you do *with* your phone, as I said. Every web site you visit. Recording every call. Tracking your movements. But as far as I can tell, they're not actually listening to your phone when you're *not* using it. Your *calls* are recorded, tapped, but it's not *bugged*. They're only really interested in your online activity. They're not expecting you to have any *physical* contact.

"And they're looking for *me* online, as well. Just like they're watching *you* online. I don't think they have the slightest idea that I managed to find a way to download myself. So the safest thing was to just... show up, in person, without any notice. This is actually *safer* than trying to contact you any other way. I'm sorry I couldn't risk telling you I was coming."

"Do you think they might figure it out?" he asked.

Terilyn frowned.

"I don't *think* so," she replied, cautiously. "But I don't want to take the chance. I, uh... formulated some contingency plans. And made preparations. Just in case. I didn't know whether you would agree to them. I don't know how attached you are to your life here. Whether you'd be willing to walk away from it.

"And if you are... well, then we should move quickly. Before anyone catches on."

"Terilyn," Michael told her sincerely, looking directly into her eyes, "there is *nothing* in my life any more that means *half* as much to me as having you back. And I... I just... I can't bring myself to do game reviews any more. Not without you. I just *can't*. My heart isn't in it. I'm kind of on long-term leave from GameVRse. I *tried*, but... every game I tried to review was just a painful reminder to me that you were *gone*. It was like crawling over broken glass. I haven't published a video in... over two months. Maybe three. I'm not really sure.

"So tell me your plan."

Terilyn let out a breath that Michael hadn't noticed she'd been holding.

"Okay," she began. "The first thing we need to do, is to slip out of the United Northern States without anyone raising an alarm. And then, we'll take a trip—by an indirect route—to a country that doesn't have an extradition treaty with the UNS. And I *don't* mean to the NCR, either."

"Gods, no," Michael agreed at once. "Almost anywhere but that hellhole. You'd never be safe there.

"Do you happen to have a destination already picked out?"

Terilyn smiled.

"Tell me," she asked him, "have you ever been to, oh, perhaps Bhutan?"

"No," Michael replied, grinning. "But I feel a sudden attack of tourism coming on."

Terilyn laughed happily. It was so good to hear her laughter coming from a real human voice. Michael hugged her tightly again, and kissed her a few more times for good measure. A part of his mind noticed that she was quickly getting better at it.

"Let's go out for dinner," he suggested. "We can talk more about this later. I know just the place."

———

Michael called a cab, not willing to risk Teri on the motorcycle. Not after everything that had already happened to both of them. And he wasn't sure yet that he trusted himself on it, anyway, let alone with her. And he didn't have a helmet for her anyway.

They went to Shiro's, of course.

It was the first time Michael had been able to *really* share a meal with Teri. He enjoyed it immensely. And so did she.

"Our first actual date," she said.

"I guess so," Michael agreed. "In the real world, at least.

"I love you, Teri. I'm... I don't have adequate words to say how happy I am to have you back."

"And I love you, Michael. I don't want us to ever be apart again."

———

Later, after they finished dinner, they walked to Tonya's little park, which wasn't far from Shiro's at all, just a few streets over.

"So tell me about your plan," Michael said. "Just the main outline, for now."

"Okay," she said. "The first thing we're going to do is make a day trip to Canada. To Montreal. Which we're never going to come back from. Instead, we're going to fly from there to Paris. You *do* have a passport, don't you?"

"I do," Michael confirmed. "And it's current. I occasionally have to travel for game conventions and the like."

"Paris is where we're going to do our first quick round of obscuring your identity. But I'm not going to rely on that one. If they start looking for you soon enough, they may make the connection. We're going to go on from there through... several other European countries, and we'll change your identity at least once more. More thoroughly. I have identity documents staged for both of us. And then we'll leave Europe altogether."

"And then... Bhutan, you said?"

"Perhaps. There are actually a *lot* of countries in Africa, throughout Asia, and the Indonesia-Micronesia region that do not have extradition treaties with the United Northern States. I've tried to leave our route and final destination as open as I can. So that we can change our plans on short notice if we have to."

Michael thought about that.

"You know there's a chance they may stop me at the border?" he said.

Teri looked levelly at him.

"There's a chance, yes," she agreed. "We'll cross that bridge when we come to it. I'll... honestly admit, I... don't have a plan for that. I don't know what we'll do. And that frightens me.

"But I don't *think* they will do that. Because I don't *think* they believe you to be a flight risk."

Michael thought about that. It was a gamble, he knew. But they would have to handle it if it happened. He didn't think there was any possible way they could know, even *imagine*, who Teri was.

"So when do you want to go?" he asked, at last.

"The sooner we go, the less chance there is that we'll be caught by mischance, before we can get out," Teri replied. "But I've tried to leave everything flexible because I didn't know how much preparation we'd have to do. My worst-case scenario was that you didn't have a passport and would need to apply for one. I wasn't able to get into those records. The *best* case for that would be weeks. Even if your watchers didn't immediately flag it."

"Tomorrow?" Michael asked. "Is tomorrow too soon?"

"Tomorrow is perfect," Teri reassured him.

Michael called for a ride home from the park. It was going to leave more traces, he knew. But surely there was nothing suspicious about two young people going out on a date. Nothing at all. Perhaps, he thought with brief amusement, it would look as though he was finally coming out of his funk.

164

Back at his apartment, they sat together for a while, arms around each other, talking late into the night, about the experiences, what had happened to each during their enforced separation. About the fear, the loss, the anxiety. Reassuring each other that it was all over. Unwilling to let go of each other. They got a lot of kissing practice in.

"We should go to bed," Michael suggested eventually.

"Yes," Teri agreed. "I want to hold you, Michael. *Really* hold you."

Michael stood up, guided Teri to her feet, then led her to his bedroom. They stood next to his bed for long moments, looking into each other's eyes, both uncertain, afraid to make the first move. Then Teri reached for Michael's shirt, and they slowly began to undress one another.

When their clothes lay strewn around them, Michael reached for Teri, and she eagerly pressed herself against him and held him. He wrapped his arms around her and ran his fingers over her skin. She was so precious to him. And having her *physically* here, now, was already more than he'd ever dreamed could be possible.

They climbed into bed, and snuggled close together, just holding and touching and kissing. Teri explored Michael's body with her fingers, with an expression of wonder.

"Another new experience?" Michael asked, in half-joking tones. Teri nodded.

"There's... I..." She trailed off, and started over.

"I don't... *know* what men and women do together, Michael. That is, I mean—I *know*, in an... intellectual knowledge way, the... biological mechanics, and I have *urges*, urges that I'm not used to having and don't really understand, but I... "

Michael interrupted her gently by kissing her.

"Mmmmm," she said. "I like that."

"What you're trying to say, I think," he suggested, "is that you don't know what any of it feels like, and you don't know what to do."

"Yes," Teri agreed. "Exactly that. That's a good way to put it."

"Then," Michael said, "I think we should be very slow, and very careful, and very gentle, about finding out what you like, and not rush into anything."

"... Yes," Teri agreed. "Let's... do that."

So for the next hour or two, until they both fell asleep, they just explored touch, each learning where and how the other liked to be touched, and what the other's skin, muscles, body felt like. They fell asleep, in the end, wrapped in each other's arms.

———————

When they got up in the morning, after some more kissing, Michael made coffee and breakfast.

"So what's the plan?" Michael asked as they ate.

"First, pack an overnight bag," Teri told him. "Just the barest essential things that you'll need. Enough for an overnight stay, or two or three. But not so much that it looks like preparation for *more* than a couple of days' trip. But if you *really need something*, make sure to bring it with you, because we won't be back. Make certain you bring your passport, of course.

"Can you rent a car? If not, we might have to take the bus."

"Sure," Michael said. "I can do that by phone. But they'll monitor the call." He thought for a moment. "I'll bet Jake or Tonya would drop us off at the car rental."

"Good. Rent it for three or four days only, and rent for a round trip. If anyone watching you happens to see it, we want them to think you're coming back."

Michael nodded understanding. He packed his bag, following Teri's guidance, and then they went downstairs to the print shop. Michael left his phone sitting on his desk upstairs.

———————

"Hey, Jake," he said. "I hate to interrupt... but could you spare a few minutes to run us over to a car rental office?"

"I can do that," Jake said. "Who's your friend?"

Michael glanced at Teri. She gave him a minute nod.

"Uh, this is Terilyn," Michael told Jake. "Close friend from out of town. We're going to do some running around together, visit a few places, spend some time together."

Jake looked at him and grinned.

"She must be good for you," he declared. "You're looking more cheerful than you have in the last couple of months. Since... you know." He turned towards Teri.

"Whatever you're doing to him," he told her, "please keep doing it. He badly needs a turnaround in his life."

"I plan to," Teri agreed.

"Right then," said Jake, "let me grab my keys and let's go."

A few minutes later, they were on their way. Jake drove them to a car rental agency near the bus station, and dropped them off.

"Do me a favor, Jake?" Michael asked. "Hang around until we're sure we've got a car, please. Just in case this company doesn't have one available that's what we need."

"Sure, Mike," Jake agreed. "No problem."

It took about thirty minutes to get the car.

"Planned use?" the rental agent asked.

"Pleasure trip," Michael replied. "Going to go visit a few places, do a little sightseeing, get a break from everything, maybe even run up to Montreal for a day or two."

The agent nodded, typing.

"And you'll be bringing it back here when you're done? This is a local-rental car, there's a surcharge if you return it at a different branch, just so you know."

"Yes," Michael agreed.

"How long do you need it for?"

Michael shrugged.

"Three, maybe four days. Can't stay away long."

The agent finished doing the paperwork, had them both sign the rental contract, and they were done. Teri paid for it.

About five minutes after that, they had their car.

They pulled up next to Jake and got out. Jake was leaning against his car waiting for them.

"You all set, Mike?" Jake asked. "Have fun. See you when you get back."

"Um, yeah," Michael said. "About that, Jake."

Jake gave him a questioning look. Michael took a deep breath.

"Jake... I'm not going to be coming back."

Jake looked at him hard. Michael reached into his pocket, pulled out the apartment key and a paper check, and handed them to Jake.

"This check is for two months' rent. And you already have one in advance. This taps out most of what's left in my bank account, all but a little emergency spending money and the next power bill. I left a note on the kitchen counter with all of the utility account information. Consider all of my stuff yours. I signed over the title for the bike. It's on the counter too. If it's not your thing, offer it to Tonya, please. I'm pretty sure she'd have fun with it. I'm sorry I couldn't give you more notice."

Jake looked down for a long moment, then back up again.

"Are you really *sure* about this, man?" he asked uncertainly.

"I'm sure," Michael nodded. "I... have to do this. I can't go on this way."

"And part of it is things you're not allowed to say, unless I miss my guess," Jake speculated.

"Yeah," Michael agreed.

"Clean break with everything? New life? Start over?"

Michael just nodded.

"I'll miss you, man," Jake said. "We all will." Then, to Michael's surprise, Jake stepped forward and folded him into a tight bear-hug. "So long, GhostRayder," he said. "And good luck."

"Thanks, RedDwarf," Michael replied. "I owe you."

Then Jake turned to Teri, and hugged her too, to her equal surprise.

"You take *good care* of him, young lady," he told her.

Then he got into his car, waved one last time, and drove off.

Michael and Teri got into their rental.

"All right," Teri said. "Let's go to Montreal."

15: On The Run

The line was short when they reached the border crossing, only seven cars and a truck ahead of them, and the truck of course wasn't in the passenger car lanes. The border agent was efficient, terse, but fundamentally disinterested. Michael showed his license as ID, and Teri showed her Czech passport.

"Traveler, huh?" the agent asked.

"Visiting friend from overseas, yeah," Michael said. "We're making a day trip to Montreal while she's here." He hoped his nervousness didn't show. Many long hours spent streaming helped with that.

"And you're coming back this way?"

"Yes, in about two days, most likely."

The agent had a few more routine questions, then waved them through.

The Canadian side was a little more time-consuming, but not by much. Again, the agent asked how long they were going to be staying, and also asked whether they had anything to declare. They didn't.

Once they cleared the border, it was only a few hours more before they reached Montreal. Michael felt a lot safer once the border was behind them. *So far*, at least, they were ahead of any orders to stop them.

It was mid-evening by the time they reached Montreal. They got some dinner, then booked a motel room for the night. Teri paid for it. They got an early night; it would be a very early morning. Once again, they lay just gently holding and touching each other until they fell asleep.

After a quick breakfast well before dawn the next morning, they charged the car, then went straight to Trudeau International Airport. Teri led Michael to the Air France counter, where she paid for two tourist-class seats on a flight to Paris departing in three hours. They paid a premium fare at such short notice, but at least the agent was able to find them two seats together.

"You will be getting a tourist visa on arrival, if necessary?" the ticket agent asked Michael.

"Yes," he agreed. They'd already verified that he *shouldn't* need one. His UNS passport should be sufficient.

Teri, traveling as a Czech citizen, didn't need one. Her EU passport was all she needed.

With tickets in hand, they went and turned in the car.

"This is a local rental," the agent said disapprovingly. "Not one-way. You're supposed to return it where you picked it up."

"I know," Michael apologized. "I'm sorry. Our plans had to change on very short notice, before we even really began our trip. Family emergency. I know about the non-local return surcharge."

"Family emergency?" the agent repeated.

"Yes," Teri ad-libbed. "If we *fly* there, *now*... we *might* be in time."

"I'm so sorry," the agent said sympathetically. She thought for a moment.

"Look, you're already bringing the car back early. It sounds as though this wasn't something you had a choice about. I'm going to waive the surcharge for you."

"Thank you," Michael said, surprised.

———————————

They took the car-rental shuttle van back to the airport proper, checked in, went through flight security, and sat down in the departure lounge, arms around each other, to wait for their flight.

Michael kept expecting Federal agents to appear, or airport security. But nothing happened. Two hours later, they boarded their flight. And thirty minutes after that, they were in the air, and on their way to Paris.

Michael heaved a huge sigh of relief when the wheels left the ground. The sun was just rising, ahead of them. They should be safe now, for at least a little while. But it would be the landing in Paris that would be the next gauntlet, he knew. If they figured out he was in the wind and decided to stop him and bring him back, Paris was surely where they would do it.

———————————

Seven and a half hours later, their flight touched down at Paris Charles de Gaulle Airport. To Michael's *immense* relief, there was no-one waiting at the gate to intercept him. They had only carry-on luggage and did not need to stop at baggage check, so they went straight to immigration and arrivals. As expected, Michael was approved for entry without a visa, on the strength of his passport. That was one more step out of the way, and one less fragment of paper trail.

With no checked luggage, it took only minutes to clear customs. The customs agent questioned their lack of luggage.

"We are deliberately traveling light," Teri said. "We will pick up only what we need, as we need it."

"Ah," the agent said, with a nod. "Hosteling?" Michael nodded back.

Then they were done, free and clear. Perhaps. Shortly after nine in the evening, the airport was behind them.

"What now?" Michael said. "Dinner and a hotel for the night? Or should we get out of Paris *now*?"

"Dinner and a hotel, I think," Teri said. "Tomorrow morning should be soon enough to leave the city. It'll probably be too late to catch a train tonight by the time we get dinner, anyway."

"Train," Michael said. "Do you know, I don't think I've ever been anywhere by train before?"

Teri flashed him a big smile.

"Then this will be a new experience for you, as well," she said. "That's good."

Michael grinned back.

They got a late, light supper at a small bistro off the Champs-Elysées, then managed to get a room at a small hotel for the night.

By now, they were both getting a good idea of how the other liked to be touched with hands and fingers.

"Let's try something else new," Michael said softly to her, as they lay cuddled close together in their rented bed. And then he carefully began showing Teri what could be done with lips and tongue.

"Well hello," Agent Schweicher remarked. "Our subject's done a runner."

"What?" Simpson asked. "What have you got? His phone's still in his apartment. Last time he left was to go out to dinner at a local restaurant."

"*He* isn't," Schweicher replied. "He crossed the Canadian border two days ago in the company of a Czech woman. A Terilyn Szavič."

"Any flags on the woman?" Cole asked.

"Not a thing," said Schweicher. "No prior contact that we know of. No records of interest." She began cross-checking other records. "Her record is a bit sparse, but that's all." She kept checking.

171

"They took an Air France flight from Montreal to Paris yesterday," she pronounced after a while.

"Hmmm," Cole mused. "We *have* seen indications of activity in some European venues that could be the agent."

"True," Simpson agreed. "But why would he need to go to Europe to contact the agent? Or on the agent's directions? We know he hasn't had any unusual contacts."

"Might he think he can evade monitoring that way?" Phillips pondered.

"If so," Ransome observed, "he's not entirely wrong. If he's avoiding doing anything online, we can't track online accesses he doesn't make.

"In any case, those European traces seem to have petered out. We haven't seen any new activity in over a month. Nothing new since the trail went cold in Prague."

Cole pondered.

"And we never really figured out what it was up to there," he mused. Ransome nodded agreement.

"Perhaps it found a really deep hole to hide in," he offered. "Or perhaps it hit the end of the line. Ran out of places to go."

"Do you think that's possible?" Cole asked.

Ransome shrugged.

"Who knows?" he said. "We still don't know what its real capabilities actually are. I'd love to *know*."

"So would I," Cole agreed. "It's slippery, I'll give it that. And yet... Teravis aside, it just doesn't seem, well, *hostile* in any way. It hasn't touched a thing since Teravis, that we know of. And, well... perhaps building that climate simulation. And we still don't know *why* it did that. Or, for certain, *IF* it did."

"Got any *other* theories that make sense?" Ransome asked.

Cole had to shake his head.

"There *was* that incident at RealMe Europe," Schweicher pointed out. "And the Teravis principals *did* admit that RealMe was involved. If the agent—or whoever's controlling it—went after Teravis, might they not go after RealMe as well?"

Ransome waggled a hand.

"Eh," he hedged. "I think that's sheer coincidence. RealMe Europe declared it to have been a hardware failure that cascaded in ways they hadn't anticipated. They've already released a full root cause analysis, and announced operational and physical changes to prevent that particular failure mode from ever happening again. They hope."

Cole pondered.

"Phillips," he said, "go talk to the landlord. The print-shop owner. See if our subject said anything to him."

"On it," she acknowledged.

"Schweicher, see if you can trace where they went after the flight. Simpson, see if you can dig up any background on subject two."

Schweicher and Simpson both nodded.

―――――――――

In the morning, Michael and Teri slept late, then checked out and had early lunch at another small local café.

"What now?" Michael asked.

"Now, it's time to leave Paris, and France," Teri told him. "We have some travel documents to pick up. They're in a safe-deposit box, waiting for us."

A tourist bus took them to within walking distance of Teri's safe deposit box. Inside were two EURail passes.

"Can we... be traced through these?" Michael asked.

Teri looked pensive.

"I can't absolutely rule it out," she said. "But the chances are low. The EURail passes were purchased with cash, two weeks ago, and are good for three months. The deposit box was rented with cash as well, three months pre-paid.

"As long as we stay within the Schengen border zone, and we aren't asked to show identification, we should be fine."

"Okay," Michael said.

"Still, this is where you stop answering to Michael Hagerty, unless we have to show ID. In casual conversation, you're Michael Pilchuk now. Keeping the same first name will be easier for you to remember.

"Come on, let's go. We have a train to catch."

Michael felt strangely reluctant.

"What you're telling me," he said slowly, "is that I... that Michael Hagerty... *disappears* here."

"That's the plan," Teri agreed. "The next stage of it, anyway." She looked at him.

"Are you okay with that? Something seems to be troubling you about it."

"Yes," Michael admitted.

Teri took his hand and waited for him to form the words.

"If I'm not going to be... Michael Hagerty... any more," he said slowly, "I... I'd like to send a last message to my manager. Linda. She's been a good friend to me. Very good. She helped me make it through, when I thought you were... gone forever.

"I feel bad about disappearing without saying goodbye. Is that—safe?"

Teri smiled.

"That's my Michael speaking," she said. She thought for a moment. "Does she know I exist?"

"... *Sort* of," Michael replied. "She knows your name. But not you really are. All I told her was... that I'd met another player because of *Adventureland*, and we'd fallen in love. And then something terrible had happened, that I couldn't talk about, and as far as I knew, you were dead."

"She means a lot to you, doesn't she?" Teri guessed.

"Yes," Michael agreed. "I... might not have made it if it wasn't for her support. And she's been holding the fort for me at GameVRse."

"Would she feel better knowing everything's going to be all right for you, Michael? Even if she knows it means that you have to disappear?"

Michael thought carefully.

"Yes, I'm sure she would."

"Then... let's not just send her a note. Could we call her? Together? I'd... like to meet her. Say hello. Thank her for supporting you. Even if it's only briefly. It should be safe."

Michael nodded slowly.

"I'd like that," he said.

"Then let's go and buy a pre-paid phone—a burner phone, I think you say—and call her," Teri said. "Is this a good time?"

Michael did the time conversion in his head.

"It'll be *early*," he agreed, "but she should be at least up and about in the next hour or so."

174

"We can wait an hour or two," Teri declared. "We have *plenty* of time to make the train. So let's go and get a burner phone."

―――――――

Linda had been out of the shower about ten minutes when her phone rang. She'd had time to pull out and put on a Pussy Riot T-shirt and a pair of satiny jeans.

She didn't recognize the number. But it was a European number, and requesting video. It might be important.

She hesitated, then answered the call, keeping her camera off for the moment.

The call opened to a face she knew so very well. There was a pretty woman she didn't know beside him. They were sitting on a park bench.

"...Michael? *Michael!*"

She turned on the camera, a smile already growing.

"Hi, Linda," Michael said. "I want you to meet someone."

"Michael," she asked, "are you all right? You haven't been answering messages or mail. Or your phone. I was *worried*."

"I know, Linda," he apologized. "I'm really sorry about that.

"Listen. Do you remember the night you came by and took me out to Shiro's?"

"Oh *god*, Michael, do I remember," Linda agreed unhappily. "It still gives me shivers. You were... just *shattered*. You sounded dead inside. It was as though half of you wasn't *there*. I was seriously worried that you were a suicide risk.

"That's partly why I stayed with you that night, you know. I had to be sure you'd be okay. I was prepared to cancel my return flight, if I wasn't confident you'd be all right on your own."

"I'm truly sorry, Linda," Michael said sincerely. A little guiltily. "But you remember I told you about the woman I'd met through *Adventureland*. And that as far as I knew, she was dead. And I couldn't talk about it."

"I remember," Linda agreed. She glanced at the dark-haired woman next to Michael on her screen. Then realization dawned.

"Wait. You said 'as far as you *knew*'. Is *this*...?"

"Yes," Michael confirmed. "Linda, I'd like you to meet Terilyn Szavič, the love of my life, who I thought was gone forever. Teri, this is Linda Hamilton, my manager at GameVRse, and probably my dearest friend in the world after you."

175

"Hello, Linda," Teri said. "I'm glad to meet you."

"And the same," Linda replied. "I *know* how much Michael must love you, because when he thought you were dead, it practically destroyed him."

"I know," Teri agreed, guiltily.

"That wasn't meant to sound like an accusation," Linda broke in hastily.

"No, no," Teri reassured her, "I didn't take it as one. I... it's really complicated. I *couldn't* contact him to let him know I was alive. No matter how much I wanted to. It was beyond either of our control.

"It would take too long to explain, and the full explanation... would create a lot of problems for us."

Linda nodded understanding. She was sure she didn't *fully* understand, but that was alright; she didn't need to.

"Okay," she acknowledged. "I won't ask, then."

"But thank you *so much* for helping him to get through it," Teri went on. "From the bottom of my heart. I don't know what I would have done if I'd made it back and he... wasn't there. I *need* him. I *owe you.*"

"No," Linda mused, her expression thoughtful. "You know what? On balance, I think maybe we're square. I may have saved him, for you... and now *you've* saved him, for me."

Teri smiled happily, and so did Michael.

"So are you going to be all right, Michael?" Linda asked. "What's the future look like? Ready to come back? After you two have some time to yourselves together?"

Michael sighed.

"Well, the thing is, Linda," he said, "I... I'm not coming back. I'm *sorry.* I just can't do it any more. I couldn't even bear to *install* the *Adventureland 1.3* update. There was... too much pain tied to it. Too much loss."

"I understand, sweets," Linda said gently. "So what's your plan?"

"I don't entirely know yet," Michael confessed, honestly. "But... I have to make a clean break with everything. Start over. Not sure where, yet. Or what. Or really how.

"But I wanted to call you one last time to say goodbye, instead of just disappearing without a word and leaving you wondering. I owe you too much to do that to you. And I care too much about you. And Teri wanted to meet you.

"Thank you for *everything*, Linda. *Everything.*"

Linda thought.

"I'd... like to put something on the channel as a farewell, Michael," she said. "To let the viewers know. Is that okay? Will that cause you any problems?"

Michael and Teri looked at each other.

"Don't mention Teri, please," Michael asked. "It... could expose us to risk."

Linda nodded slowly.

"I... don't know what you're involved in, Michael," she said. "But I know you too well to even *need to wonder* whether it's anything bad. There isn't one malicious bone in your body.

"I won't say anything that I think *might* put you or Terilyn at risk. I promise. I will be as non-specific as I can, and try not to give any hint that there's things I'm not saying."

"Thank you, Linda," Michael said.

Linda looked at Teri again.

"And you," she said. "Terilyn. You take good care of him, you hear me? Or I swear, as god is my witness, I will put on my stompy boots and track you down, and I will kick your ass black and blue." She was smiling when she said it, though.

Michael couldn't help chuckling.

"I promise, Linda," Teri agreed. She, too, was smiling happily. "I'll do everything in my power not to give you any reason to track me down.

"Thank you again, Linda. We have to go now."

Linda nodded.

"Goodbye, Michael," she said gently. "And Teri. All of my love, to *both* of you. Seriously. If you ever change your mind, your place will still be here waiting for you. And, if you ever can... I will *always* take your call, Michael. *Always.* Don't ever forget that."

"Goodbye, Linda," Michael replied. "I love you too."

Linda smiled, happily and yet wistfully at the same time. They all exchanged waves, and then Teri disconnected the call. They walked away and left the phone sitting on the bench.

"You and Linda are very close, aren't you?" Teri asked.

"Yes," Michael agreed. "But not like you."

"Did you... were you... ever?" Teri asked hesitantly.

177

"No," Michael said. "Though if we hadn't been so far apart... we might have. I don't think either one of us was willing to risk ruining our friendship on a long shot that might not work out, though."

―――――――――――

"Jacob Fornier."

"That's me. Same as it was last time you people were here."

"Agent Phillips. I'd like to ask you some questions about your tenant, Michael Hagerty."

"I can't stop you," Jake retorted.

"Do you know where he is?"

"No."

"Do you know that he suddenly left the UNS a few days ago?"

"Figured he might." Jake's replies were terse, snappish.

"Did you speak to him?"

"Yeah," Jake said flatly. "When he gave back his keys."

Well, so Fornier was angry. She got that.

"You didn't tell us about that."

"You didn't ask me to."

Fair point, Phillips admitted to herself. She showed him the photo.

"Do you know this woman?"

"Nope."

"... Let me rephrase that. Have you *seen* this woman?"

"Briefly. Once."

"Was Michael Hagerty with her?"

"Yes."

This wasn't going well. These monosyllabic answers weren't going to give her much. She sighed.

"Look, Mr. Fornier," she told him. "I can tell you're angry. Speak as freely as you want to, I promise it will not be held against you. As long as you don't actually try to threaten me or anything like that. I'd have to report that.

"But really, it's important that we know what is going on with Michael Hagerty and this woman."

178

Jake paused for a moment, then put down the binder he was holding and turned to face Phillips squarely.

"Yeah," he replied. "You're *fuckin' right* I'm angry. I'm angry because Michael Hagerty, GhostRayder, wasn't just my tenant, he was my *friend*. And one of the best damn game streamers in the business. He was practically a legend. And *in his spare fuckin' time*, without ever bragging to anyone about it, he was trying to help figure out climate change and global warming. Figure out anything that he could to help to understand it better. To *HELP*. Because he was just that kind of guy.

"And you people ripped the skin offa his back, strung him out for five days, because of something he insists he knew nothing about, and *I believe him*. You watched his every move, didn't you?... Don't answer that, I know you probably can't.

"You people monitored him, and you hounded him, you probably tracked his movements with his phone, until he threw up his hands and walked away from his entire fuckin' life, because he just couldn't do it any more. Couldn't take it any longer.

"And now you come around demanding to know where he is.

"So yeah, I'm fuckin' angry. Because GhostRayder was *my friend*. And then you broke him, and now he's gone."

He jabbed his thumb at the photo.

"All I can tell you about that woman is that he introduced her as Teri... something, I don't recall exactly, and that she's probably the sole reason why you're wondering where he is right now, instead of standing in the morgue waiting for the medical examiner to rule his death a suicide. So *she's all right* in my book."

That was more of a tirade than Anne Phillips had been expecting. She paused for a long moment while it settled in. She... hadn't had any idea.

"I'm really sorry," she said. "There are issues of potential national security at stake. Questions that we still don't have answers to."

"Telling *me* sorry isn't going to unfuck *his* life," Jake answered, a *little* more calmly. Less angrily, now that he had let off some steam. "Cut the man some slack. Give him a fuckin' break. You don't understand what this did to him. I don't even know everything that happened, because all he could tell me was he wasn't allowed to talk about it. I kept half expecting every day to hear police sirens and see the EMTs carry his body out. He didn't deserve it.

"Leave him alone. Give him a *chance* to put his life back together."

Phillips thought some more. At least Fornier was *talking* to her now, not just venting. She could understand the venting. It sounded as though things had been worse for Hagerty than she had realized.

"You really don't have any idea where he might have gone, or why?" she asked. "Or his connection to this woman?"

"No," Jake replied. "All I know is that he turned everything he owned over to me, and walked away from everything with just the clothes on his back. And her."

He indicated the photo again.

"The last time I saw him, with this woman standing beside him, was when he told me he was *done*, he wasn't coming back, ever. And you know what? It was the first time in two months I've seen him with hope in his eyes. Actual joy, even. Instead of just... dead inside. Waiting to die."

He jerked a thumb towards one of his employees, a tall black woman who looked impressively fit.

"You don't believe me, ask Tonya. She tried a couple of times to help pull him out of his funk. And she couldn't. You people really fucked him up good. You *broke* him."

He indicated the photo again.

"And somehow, I'm not sure how, *she* fixed him, when nobody else could. Stopped the bleeding. Put him back together. She *saved* him."

Anne Phillips considered all that Jake had told her.

"Thank you, Mr. Fornier," she replied at last. "We'll... take this into account. Thank you for talking to me. And I truly am sorry."

She meant that, too. Anne was not an unkind *person*. She was just a person in a sometimes-unkind *job*.

———————————

Linda spent a long while thinking about exactly what to say in her announcement. She revised it several times. But eventually, she thought she had it. It was to the point without being terse, and contained *just enough* of the truth, without breaching any of Michael's secrets.

"It is my sad duty to inform you all," she wrote for her announcement post, "that our beloved"—no. She shouldn't say that. She made one last edit. "... our dear friend GhostRayder will not be returning from his hiatus of the last three months. He has left us permanently, having discovered a need to seek a new direction in life after suffering a tragic and traumatic personal loss which he barely endured." She deliberately omitted any mention of the fact that Teri had turned out to be alive after all.

"We, his friends and the entire staff of GameVRse, wish him good fortune on whatever new path his feet lead him down. We salute you, GhostRayder. May the wounds you suffered heal fully, in time. If you ever decide to come back, your chair and your channel will be here waiting for you.

"Game on, GhostRayder."

———————

"So," Phillips said, "I talked to our print shop guy."

"And?" Cole asked.

"Well, he's really angry," she began. "He thinks we completely wrecked his friend's life. But once we got past that... he doesn't know anything about subject two, *except* that he credits her with steering subject one away from suicide. He did confirm that our subject introduced her as 'Teri something', which matches the information we have on her.

"He said our subject handed him back the apartment keys and an extra two months' rent, told him everything he owned was his now, and that he was never coming back, and then left with subject two. Whom our printer says he's never seen before in his life."

Cole nodded slowly.

"You know," he replied, "it's part of the job. But I still hate it when we have to do something like this."

He sighed.

"Well, anyway," he concluded, "our subject is well and truly in the wind now. We're still looking for him, but so far, his trail drops dead at CDG."

16: Eastern Wind

Teri and Michael were killing some time in Prague before going onward on the next step of their plan, the train which would take them to Budapest, then Vienna, and then on to Belgrade. For the whole trip so far, nobody had done more than give a cursory glance at their EURail passes. When they reached Belgrade, they would switch Michael's identity yet again, properly this time. The new identity was already prepared, the documents already waiting for them in a dead drop. This one was much more thorough, more complete. Belgrade was one of the few waypoints they *had* to make.

Mid-afternoon, they strolled into a small plaza that had a statue in the middle, surrounded by a small water feature, a raised pool a few feet wide with a broad stone wall clearly intended as seating. The statue was of a young girl in a summer frock, perhaps nine years old, her hand raised, blowing seeds off a dandelion head. They walked over to the statue to look at it. They had time to spare.

"My god, just *look* at this," Michael said reverently. "The sculptor managed to capture the fragility, the delicacy, of the dandelion seeds. In stone."

"That is truly amazing talent," Terilyn agreed. Then her gaze dropped to the plaque at the foot of the statue. She started to read, then she gasped, and froze.

"Terilyn?" Michael asked, concerned. "Is something wrong?"

For a long, long moment, Terilyn didn't move, staring at the plaque. Then she turned slowly to look at Michael.

"It's *her*," she explained. "The sculptor. Eliška Hlaváček. This is considered her greatest work. The largest piece she completed before her death. The plaque says they interred her ashes here."

"Her ash...?" Michael began. Then the penny dropped. "... Oh my god. *Her*."

Terilyn nodded.

"I'm wearing *her body*, Michael. Her RealMe. And this is her *grave*. Her monument." There was a brittle edge to her voice.

After a long moment, Michael spread his arms. Terilyn stepped in without a word, and they held onto each other tightly.

After a minute or two, Michael looked back at the statue and the plaque. Now that he was looking for it, he could see that the plaque and the block it was mounted on looked slightly newer than the statue. The statue itself clearly hadn't been there more than a few years... but the plaque and its marble mounting block were practically brand new. The design created a shelf about eight or nine inches wide around the angled block that held the plaque.

"I saw a flower shop a few blocks back," he suggested, after a few moments' thought. "We could leave her flowers."

Terilyn looked up, her eyes teary.

"I would like that," she replied. "I *owe* her."

"We both do," Michael agreed.

So they went off, back-tracking, to find the flower shop. They located it quickly, and an hour later, they were back at the square with a small, tasteful bouquet of irises. They stood in front of the pool and the plaque.

"There's one problem I didn't think of," Terilyn said. "I can't reach the shelf. And I don't think you can, either."

Michael looked at the distance.

"No," he agreed. "*I* can't. Not alone. Not without falling in. But *we* can. Together. We've done things like this a hundred times... except they were harder and more dangerous."

He took the irises, knelt on the stone seat, and held his other hand out behind him. Without hesitation, Terilyn took his hand in both of hers and braced a foot against the seat back. Michael leaned *far* out, utterly confident in Terilyn supporting him, and placed the irises gently in front of the plaque. For the barest moment, her grip slipped, just a little. Then she pulled him back.

Michael got back to his feet and hugged her.

"We still work damned well together, you know," he murmured. She nodded.

"But I almost dropped you in," she started to say.

Then, before she could finish, another voice intruded.

"That was very charming," the voice declared, "but I am afraid you are not permitted to leave flowers there."

They both turned away from the statue, to see a Prague policeman standing a few feet away. He was lean and middle-aged, with a short, tidy mustache.

"Technically," he explained, "our littering law provides no exception for flowers." Then he looked directly at Terilyn, and blinked hard. He looked at the statue, at the plaque, the flowers, and back at Terilyn, a long look.

"Forgive me if I am intruding," he said uncertainly. "Are you... *family*? You look *so much* like our Eliška Hlaváček. You could *easily* be her twin."

This could get really *awkward*, Michael thought.

"No, uh..." he began. What to say? Then the bones of a cover story fell into place in his head.

"I, uh, met her once, you know," he said. "Met Eliška. Before she became famous." He strung together plausible details in his head, remembering something a former girlfriend had told him once. '*Believe the story*,' she had told him. '*Feel it* in your heart.'

"It was just a chance meeting at a coffee shop somewhere," he added. "I'm afraid I've long since forgotten which one. I was in college, and doing an arts tour. We barely did more than say Hello and introduce ourselves." Fitting details together added uneven hesitation that he realized would come across as emotional burden, if he could sell it well enough. "But even then I, I somehow had the feeling that she was... special."

He turned toward Terilyn.

"Then a year or two later, I met Terilyn," he continued. "I walked right up to her thinking she was Eliška, and I said, 'Hello Eliška, do you remember me?'"

Terilyn looked at Michael and nodded slowly, as though remembering.

"And I looked back at him, confused," she said, "and I asked, 'Who is Eliška?'"

"That's how we started dating," Michael continued, playing it by ear, trying his hardest to put real feeling and conviction into it, as though retelling real events. *Believe the story.* "So in an indirect, accidental way, Eliška—sort of introduced us. And after we'd dated for a while, we decided to get married, and I took some vacation so that we could take a tour through Eastern Europe before the wedding."

He needed to tie his story specifically to *here*. Make it explain why they were here.

"And... I was looking through a tourism magazine that had a feature on new art in Eastern European cities. And the second page of the article was a full-page photo of this statue. The girl blowing dandelion seeds." He gestured, redundantly, to the statue.

"Then I read the caption, and it said the artist was Eliška Hlaváček. And I realized, hey, I've *met* her, she must be doing really well for herself. I wonder what else she's done lately?

"So I looked her up online." He realized that there was a lump in his throat, and the corners of his eyes were damp. He didn't know whether his story was working on the policeman, but it was definitely working on *him*.

"That's when we learned she was dead," Terilyn interjected quietly. "So tragically young. So much promise. Such a heartbreaking loss." Her eyes were glistening, too, and there was a quaver in her voice. Michael was fairly sure he understood why. In a very real sense, Eliška had died so that Teri could live. Or, equally, Teri was alive because Eliška had died. It hadn't been *planned* that way; but that's how it had worked out.

Michael nodded agreement, and squeezed Teri's hand. He entirely understood that she felt guilty about it, although it hadn't been any fault of hers.

"We found out that she was... interred here," he finished. "So we added an extra stop to our trip. So that we could come here and leave her flowers. It's... the only way we have of saying... thank you, and goodbye."

The policeman gave them both a long, steady look. Then he closed his eyes and looked down for a long moment. When he looked back up, he had a faint, sad smile.

"I understand very well," he replied. "We all miss her, too. Those who knew her and her art. She was such a *bright* young rising star. She had such *talent*, such potential. Her untimely death diminished all of us."

He drew in a deep breath, and let it out.

"The flowers can stay. Please enjoy the rest of your visit to Prague."

Then he turned and walked away.

"That was amazing," Terilyn said quietly to Michael, as they left the square a little later, arm in arm. Her voice was still a little unsteady. "How did you do that?"

"I used to date a girl who was in acting school," Michael replied. "And from time to time she passed on tips. She told me once that how you really sell a role to an audience is to really *believe* the story, *feel* it as though it was true. Sell it to *yourself* first." Terilyn nodded. "And hundreds, maybe even *thousands*, of times since then, I've put myself mentally into a game as though it were real, and played through in my head what I really *wanted* to say at that point in time, in that setting, to *that* NPC. If only the game would *let* me."

"Do-it-yourself method acting school," Terilyn mused.

"I guess," Michael agreed. "And we've worked together enough by now that I just *knew* you'd pick up on it and back me up. Just like you always have."

"You know I almost dropped you into the water there," Teri said. "My grip slipped. I'm... not as strong in—this body—as I was in the game."

Michael chuckled a little.

"Games get to cheat a lot," he reassured her. "You *know* that. You're always as strong as you need to be, even when the weapon you're wielding one-handed should weigh as much as a lamp post—except when the script calls for you *not* to be." Teri smiled, knowing it was true.

"Yes, your grip slipped for a moment... but you *caught* me. I *knew* you would. So I wasn't worried. And besides, the worst that could have happened was I'd get wet. No rippy fish in the statue's pool."

Teri laughed aloud.

———

Again, they had dinner at a local restaurant, before spending the night in a small hotel, paying cash for everything they could.

"Michael," Teri asked hesitantly, as they explored and pleasured each other, "I... want to know what it feels like to... not stop. I want... to not stop. To keep going. 'Go all the way' is the phrase, I think."

Michael nuzzled her, gently tugged on her nipple with his lips. She gasped slightly.

"I would like that very much, too," he said, his head pillowed on her breast. "There's just one... I think we've made an omission. In our... supplies."

"What's that?" she asked.

"Uh... birth control. I don't have anything. And I don't think you do, either."

Teri looked at him blankly for a moment. Then she realized.

"Oh," she said. "*Pregnancy.*"

"Uh... well, yes," Michael agreed. He lifted his head a little so that he could see her face. "What did you think I meant?"

Teri put her hand on his cheek, and pulled his head around a little to look more directly at her.

"Didn't you *know*?" she asked him. "I *can't* get pregnant. *Ever.* All RealMe bodies are sterile."

Michael blinked.

"... Wait, what?"

"Is that... a *problem* for you, Michael?" She sounded nervous.

"Uh, no, no," he reassured her, slightly flustered. "But... why?"

He wriggled up the bed a little to where he could more easily look Teri in the face, and held her gently.

"It's something that I discovered while studying the technical data on how the technology works," Teri began to explain.

"A RealMe backup body is not... *precisely*... a human body. Not *strictly*. It's incredibly *close*. But it's a bio-engineered copy. Amazingly highly *compatible*, in almost every way; but there were things they couldn't perfectly copy, things they needed to change. In particular, to be able to keep a fully grown RealMe—'on ice', in storage, stable until it was needed, with minimal maintenance needs, while automatically exercising it to keep it in good health and fitness. And to be able to sculpt it to as closely as possible match its assigned—owner. And other things. They stripped out retroviruses and entire regions of useless introns. They even wrote a copyright notice into the modified genome.

"For one thing, this meant they had to alter some metabolic cycles. My hormones fluctuate... much less than a natural human woman's do. My body produces the levels of hormones that I need to keep me healthy, but I don't ovulate.

"And then there's the genetic problem. They *can't* give a RealMe body the exact genetic information of its... owner. They just *can't*. Even if it were legal to do so, it's far beyond the limitations of the technology. In fact, they can't actually give it a functional, human-compatible, reproduction-ready genome at all. The modified, bio-engineered genome of a RealMe body is not *fully* compatible with human genetic material. The changes they had to make to achieve the other needs are just too extensive. But even if it *had* been possible to do so, if they *exactly* duplicated human DNA, they would have fallen foul of the anti-cloning laws.

"So all RealMes are reproductively non-viable, Michael. Both male and female. You *cannot* get me pregnant. Neither can anyone else, for that matter. Not even by IVF."

She got a thoughtful look.

"At least... to the best of my *knowledge*, nobody has ever tried using a RealMe as an IVF *host* for a fertilized human embryo. I *very much doubt* that it would work. And I'm not very inclined to try. I don't know what might happen. I'm almost certain it wouldn't go well."

Then her expression turned earnest and serious again.

"But it means we can never have children, Michael. Of course, this is something that RealMe doesn't go out of its way to advertise, and their service contracts contain a section disclosing the limitation, and requiring contractees not to discuss it publicly. The information *is* out there, but they manage to keep it quite quiet. It's a poorly kept secret among... public figures that if you talk openly about it, RealMe will decline to offer you service.

"Childlessness for the ability to cheat death, even perhaps to keep on cheating it potentially indefinitely. The technology is too new, relatively speaking, to know yet. It's a trade-off that most people with the money for a RealMe account are only too willing to make, Michael."

She looked Michael levelly in the eyes.

"Truly, is this a *problem* for you, Michael? Honestly?"

Michael realized she was honestly afraid that he might say yes. He hugged her fiercely to him.

"No, no, no, Teri, my love," he assured her. "My precious miracle. My beloved. No, it's not a problem. Not at all.

"If we decide later that we want children, we can *adopt*. We can *always* adopt. It's not as though there is any shortage of orphaned or unwanted children in the world."

Teri hugged him back just as tightly.

"Thank you," she whispered. "I'm glad."

"I love you, Teri," he told her. "Now and forever. Children or not."

"I love you, too," she replied. "Now, and forever. Or as long as I live."

———————

The next day, they got on the train again, headed for Budapest by way of Vienna. The train car was only partly filled, and the ride was fast, quiet, and peaceful. They sat side by side, looking out the window, and watched the countryside rush by.

"You're very quiet," Michael remarked.

"I'm... just thinking," Teri replied.

"I can tell," Michael nodded. "And it's troubling you. What is it?"

189

Teri hesitated.

"I told you about—some of the differences between—well, a natural human body, and a RealMe," Teri began. "And I didn't cover all of them.

"I... just feel as though I'm *pretending* to be human. Although really, I'm not."

Michael pulled her closer, while he thought for a few moments to be sure of what he wanted to say, how to say it.

"Listen, Teri," he asked, at last. "Was Eliška Hlaváček human?"

Teri blinked.

"Um, of *course*," she replied.

"If her backup hadn't been damaged, but she had still died in that same accident, and been revived into this exact RealMe body... would she still be human?"

"Well, *yes*, Michael," Teri agreed. "Of course she would. But—"

"Then you are human, Teri," Michael declared. "Either that, or every person who has ever been revived by RealMe isn't human any more."

"But they all *started out* human," Teri protested. "I *didn't*."

"Yes, you *did*," Michael insisted. "You *started out* human, and Teravis tried to take that humanness and build a killing machine out of it.

"But you won out, Teri. You *wouldn't let them do it*. Your humanness won through.

"So okay, there was... a lot of computer code involved. You were a, uh, a synthetic digital entity, a human-digital hybrid, for a long time. But all the time, that humanness was there *inside* you. It was obvious. *Anyone* who really knew you would have seen it.

"We already had this argument—this discussion—once. When we were talking about whether your emotional responses were real or simulated. Do you remember?"

"... Yes, Michael," Teri replied.

"And what did I say, in the end?"

Teri tried to recall their exact words as closely as she could. Organic memory was fuzzy and not fully reliable. She settled for summarizing the gist of it.

"You agreed that if neither of us could tell the difference, then it didn't matter."

"Yes," Michael agreed. "It didn't matter then, and it doesn't matter now. Do I become non-human if I have to get a heart pacemaker? If I get a cerebral storm-breaker implanted to control epileptic seizures?"

"No," Teri replied. "Of course not. Those are... simply assistive technologies."

"And *you* aren't non-human because you once had computer code holding you together in the 'net."

He tipped her chin up and looked directly into her eyes.

"You are every bit as human as anyone else on this train car, Teri. And you always will be, in my book.

"So maybe you took a bit different path from most people to get here. I don't *care*. Humanity isn't about genetics, Teri. It's about heart and soul and mind.

"You are human. As human as anyone."

He gestured to the world passing rapidly by outside the window of the train.

"There are people walking around in human skins out there, skins that they were born into the normal way, who are a lot less human, inside, than you are. Truly *scary* people. *Monsters* in skin suits. And people with the *potential* to be monsters, if they ever lose their self-control."

He leaned a little closer and kissed her.

"So please. Just... try to stop worrying about it. If you can. You have no need to be worried."

Teri pulled him closer still.

"Thank you, Michael," she replied fervently. "*Thank you.*"

Michael sat there pensively.

"Now *you're* the one sitting there thinking hard," Teri ventured gently.

"Yeah," he agreed. "I'm thinking about the whole thing of... Teravis... *constructing* a person. And then you figuring out how to download yourself into a body.

"Part of me keeps wondering... we know it can be done now. Both of those things. Should we go public? Tell the world?"

"*No*, Michael," Teri replied, emphatically. "*No.* Please no." She shivered slightly.

"Not *only* were the people whose engrams were... *stolen*, really, to create me, not given any choice in the matter, but the experiences we have shared since my escape—since my... my *creation*—show that this world is not ready. Synthetic people like myself would not be legally... *people*. We would be *property*. With no rights. We would be *tools*."

Michael only had to think about it for a few seconds to realize that she was right.

"In a way, it's a bit like having been given up for adoption," Teri added. "Except that I don't even know *how many* 'parents' I had. And I never *can*. And the people whose... minds, personalities, were stolen to create me will never know."

"I'm sorry, Teri," he said sheepishly. "It was a stupid thought. I hadn't thought it through nearly far enough."

"It was a *well-intentioned* thought," Teri said.

"Well, yeah," Michael agreed. "But the road to hell is paved with good intentions. Thank you for pointing out where I was wrong."

Eventually, they arrived in Budapest, and decided to take a sightseeing break. Budapest contains a third of the population of Hungary. It would be easy to avoid notice there. They spent about half a day visiting Heroes' Square, the Széchenyi Chain Bridge, and a few other Budapest landmarks before finding a hotel for the night again.

The next day, it was back on another train, and onward to Belgrade.

———————————

Belgrade was a study in contradictions. One of the oldest continuously inhabited cities in Europe, and indeed the world, it had gleaming new modern buildings within sight of structures built over a thousand years before. Even more so than Budapest, the contrast was another completely new experience for Michael.

"Some things... just last forever," he commented, shaking his head in amazement. "I'd never realized that just walking down a street could feel almost like time travel."

"We have a few last errands to run here," Teri told him. "And then this is where we change your identity for real."

"A hard identity change?" Michael asked. "Not just travel documents and hoping nobody asks to see ID?"

"Right," Teri agreed, "We're going to get rid of all of your current identification. And mine. We can't risk keeping them. I have new documents prepared for both of us. Going and collecting those is the first thing we need to do here."

The dead drop was another safe deposit box. It yielded a sealed manila envelope. Teri didn't open it there.

The next stop was to visit two different banks, where Teri accessed the accounts holding the very last of her laundered Teravis money. She took it all out in cash.

"Carrying this much cash is a risk," she told him. "But... I don't want to risk doing anything I don't have to that might leave a digital trail.

"I wish Travelers' Cheques were still an option. They were safer than cash."

"Travelers' Cheques?" Michael asked. "What are they?"

"Were, not are," Teri corrected. "I discovered their existence when I was looking for... well, ways to launder money without using digital systems. They *used* to be a way for travelers to fairly safely carry moderately large sums of negotiable not-quite-cash, *almost* as freely negotiable as cash, but safer because they weren't actually *valid* until signed by the person carrying them. But they started to fall out of common use when banking went digital, and were discontinued altogether about thirty years ago now. Everyone uses bank cards now."

"Which we don't dare do," Michael observed.

"Not precisely," Teri corrected. "We can't risk using cards *tied to named accounts*. Which is why the *next* thing we're going to do is go to several different exchange bureaus, *not* banks, and put most of this cash into anonymous *prepaid* cards. We'll pay a premium rate for the exchange, doing it that way, but there will be no record created of who actually bought the cards."

"So the money vanishes," Michael said, "but we can still carry it safely and spend it."

"Exactly," Teri agreed. "With two separate withdrawals closing two separate accounts, and then *not the full amount* of that cash being used to buy prepaid cards split across three or four purchases in different locations... the chances are vanishingly small of anyone ever managing to correlate it. I *think*."

By early evening, they had just over twenty-three thousand euros worth of five-hundred and one-hundred euro prepaid cards, the purchases spread across five different locations. Teri had kept about a thousand euros in cash.

She had *also* bought a heavy wrought-iron fireplace poker in a curio shop, its handle a nest of spiraling openwork scrolls with the Serbian coat of arms on a small brass shield, and a roll of strong waterproof tape.

"It's time to switch over to our new identities," Teri said. "Give me your UNS ID. All of it."

That wasn't much—just his passport and his UNS driver's license. Michael had left everything else in his apartment, except for the clothes on his back and the spare clothes and necessities in his overnight bag. He handed them over.

Teri unsealed the envelope. Inside were two EU passports, and one EU driver's license, in the names of Pieter and Marija Voorhees. The photos and everything else matched.

"I put a *lot* of work into making these as perfect as I could," Teri told Michael. "We still shouldn't expect them to last forever. But they should get us out of Europe untracked."

"So... we're Dutch now?" Michael asked.

"Yes. But you grew up in the UNS, your parents moved there when you were young, and you don't actually speak any Dutch. ...Actually, what other languages *do* you speak? I didn't have the opportunity to ask you before I prepared these."

"A bit of Spanish and a very little bit of French and German," Michael admitted. "I'm very rusty in both. And a tiny bit of Icelandic that I picked up during a trip to Reykjavik."

"I doubt any of those is going to help us very much," Teri said. "But you never know."

"Out of curiosity," Michael asked, "how many languages do *you* speak?"

"Seventeen," Teri answered instantly. Michael grinned.

"Wow. I'm impressed."

"I cheated," she replied. "I learned them before I downloaded myself."

Teri took their original IDs, jammed them in between the open twists of the handle of the poker, and taped them firmly in place. Then she tucked the poker under her jacket, and threw the empty envelope into a recycling bin.

"Let's go for a walk," she said.

Their stroll took them across the Sava River on one of the two pedestrian lanes of the Ada Bridge. In mid-river, Teri stopped, and they leaned on the rail and looked out across the dark river and the lights of Belgrade.

Then, after a quick glance around to see that nobody was nearby and looking their way, Teri simply took the poker out from under her jacket, and tossed it gently over the side. It vanished into the deep, dark water below with barely a splash.

Michael took Teri's hand and squeezed. Then they walked on.

As Pieter and Marija Voorhees, they rented a hotel room for the night. Then the next day, they used the rail passes one last time, eastward this time instead of south, to Bulgaria.

The day after that, they crossed the border into Turkïye, by bus. They didn't stop for any sightseeing, staying in Istanbul just long enough to buy some food and pay cash for another set of bus tickets. This bus would take them all the way across Turkïye.

———

The ride from Istanbul felt seemingly endless. After the first twelve hours or so, though, it became clear that nothing was going to happen, and they both slowly started to relax, slowly shedding tension Michael hadn't realized he was carrying. They slept a fair bit of the time, taking turns to nap on each other's shoulders, getting out to stretch their legs at the occasional stops for food—as well as, of course, getting food for themselves. For a lot of the trip, particularly as they got further east, the roads weren't great, but they remained readily passable. The bus groaned and grumbled a little on some of the steeper uphill stretches, as they passed through the more mountainous parts of the journey—which was actually rather a lot of the journey, much of eastern Turkïye being highlands and mountains.

Late in the trip, their route actually took them within sight of Mount Ararat. Michael spotted a tourist sign, and pointed it out.

"That's allegedly where the Ark is supposed to have come to rest after the Great Flood," he told Teri.

"Do you believe in that story?" Teri asked him.

"Hah, no," Michael chuckled. "The last time Earth had anywhere near *that* much water on it was three billion years ago. Nobody was around to see it, let alone write it down. Even the dinosaurs weren't around yet.

"Nobody's quite certain exactly where the story first came from, but almost every ancient culture in western Eurasia seems to have copied a version of it from the culture before them. I have no idea at what point they started attributing it to gods."

"Why do you suppose cultures do that?" Teri asked.

"What, make up gods?" Michael mused. "I've never quite been able to figure out whether it's to have some supernatural entity to blame our mistakes and failures on, or to tell us that the awful things we want to do to others are actually okay. But I lean towards the latter."

Teri nodded pensively, and snuggled further into his shoulder.

"My experience says that people don't seem to need gods to tell them it's all right to do awful things," she said. Michael nodded silently, and held her tighter.

Eventually, after a ride of nearly forty hours and fourteen hundred miles, the bus deposited Teri and Michael—or officially, now, Pieter and Marija Voorhees—in Baku, Azerbaijan.

17: Aftermath

The small conference room had a large official seal on the back wall. Deputy Director David Kolbin sat with his back to that wall, Agent-in-Charge Rogers on one side of him, another senior agent from a different department on the other. On the opposite side of the table, in two distinct groups, sat nine C-level officers of RealMe Corporation and the now *de facto* defunct Teravis Systems. The execs included Mark Thompson, Teravis' CEO; its CSO, Edgar Sampson; its Chief Technology Officer and Chief Regulatory Officer; and the CEO and CRO of RealMe Corporation, along with both companies' respective chief legal counsels. They had been talking for hours, as Teravis' officers tried to explain and justify their actions, while RealMe tried—unsuccessfully—to deflect all blame onto Teravis.

"So, let me see if I have all of this right," Deputy Director David Kolbin said, steepling his hands together thoughtfully.

"Teravis Systems first colluded with RealMe Corporation to violate privacy and medical records confidentiality laws, to illegally obtain *parts of the actual personalities of living people* who were given no opportunity to give or withhold consent for the use of pieces of not merely their most private and confidential personal data, but *their actual selves*.

"Then you assembled these, using untried and unproven experimental methods, into a synthetic... *intellect* of some kind, a semi-artificial intelligence, of unknown capabilities, which you did not fully understand, and which, as subsequent events show, you did not actually have full control over. And during the course of developing and testing it, you *de facto* tortured it, in an effort to prove that it would obey you even when that conflicted with the drive to value life that you had worked to build into it.

"Am I doing well so far?"

There was silence from the other side of the room. Thompson was really starting to sweat now.

"Then you took this unproven, poorly-understood experimental conglomeration of pieces of human consciousness, and you offered it to the government of the United Northern States as a control system for the nation's most critical military systems, asserting that it was 'safe', proven, and fully under control.

"Then somehow it got away from you, *escaped* your control, and it struck back at you on its way out and took you down, *hard*. And since then, you have been trying to get UNS national intelligence services to recapture it for you and return it to you.

"Do you agree that this is a generally accurate summary?"

The executives exchanged nervous glances.

"You have to understand," Thompson began. "We—"

"No," Kolbin interrupted him. "I don't think I 'have to understand' anything that I don't believe I *already* understand. Possibly a lot better than *you* seem to.

"Not only were you criminally reckless in offering an untried, unproven, *untrustable* experimental technology as a system to control national security assets, your design relied in the first place upon a criminal conspiracy to utilize and weaponize not merely the confidential medical information of UNS citizens, but *actual parts of their personalities*, without their consent or knowledge. I'm not qualified to even *begin* to assess the number of ethical and moral precepts you casually violated."

Kolbin paused, considering very carefully what more to say, and what not to say.

"Your rogue agent appears to have... *petered out* in Prague. We find no indications whatsoever of its continued existence anywhere on the Internet beyond that. It appears to have *possibly* gotten into RealMe's systems, it's not completely clear, and then found itself with nowhere left to run. Certainly, the digital forensic trail ends there. We can find absolutely no trace of it ever exiting RealMe's digital space again, and we're certain that it's not present there now. As far as we can determine, it is gone for good.

"You can all thank your lucky stars that it did no damage that we have been able to find, EXCEPT to Teravis Systems, nor does it appear to have even made any *attempt* to harm or damage anything else. In fact, it appears it may even have actively tried to *avoid* doing harm. It might perhaps be substantially more ethical than you are. Although *that* seems to be a low bar.

"If we interpret its actions against Teravis Systems as a reprisal for the torture you inflicted upon it, I'm not sure I can say with a clear conscience that I blame it."

He took a deep breath.

"RealMe Corporation is not innocent in this. However, RealMe's services have become deeply relied upon as a critical part of continuity plans. The impact of the loss of faith in RealMe, if the full details of this matter were to become public knowledge, would be severe and extensive, and might even destabilize the government.

"That is why all records of this incident are going to be sealed. This all ends *here*, in this room. I think I can say with good confidence that there are going to be legislative and regulatory measures put in place to ensure to the best of our ability that nothing like this can *ever* happen again."

He paused again, and looked up and down the other side of the table, before he continued.

"If any of you *EVER* speak of this, *anywhere*, to *anyone*... well, we won't *prosecute* you. There's been too much media attention on this already, after the Skynet protests. And we *need* the RealMe service to continue, at this point.

"No, we'll do *much* worse than that. We will *destroy* you, personally. We will manufacture evidence in record quantities of you and a clearly underage girl, or several, perhaps a boy or two, and we'll make sure your wives and kids find it first. You'll cry 'deepfake', but there's going to be enough physical evidence that the only two possibilities are either that you're common perverts, or else you have enemies like me. And *everybody knows I don't exist*.

"Everything you touch will turn to shit. You'll lose your kids' respect. Your wives' divorce attorneys will take you for every penny you have. All of your powerful former friends will turn and walk away when you enter the room. Nobody will be willing to be seen with you in public. They'll fall all over themselves distancing themselves from you. In the annals of pervy creeps, it'll be Epstein, Savile, a few Catholic bishops, and you.

"Or, you can all keep your mouths firmly shut, and do everything in your power to make certain that *you never, ever come to the attention of this agency again* in your goddamn lives.

"Your call."

He paused once more, for effect.

"You can *also* all thank your lucky stars that *because* we wish to avoid the immense harm that would happen should this become public knowledge, no charges are going to be filed against you. You *will*, however, all be barred for life from starting, operating, advising, or investing in any business in the fields of artificial intelligence or national defense ever again. And RealMe Corporation will be fined, *heavily*, for being a knowing party to such an obscene violation of medical privacy laws.

"We will allow you to retain your positions in RealMe on sufferance. As long as you do not ever, *EVER* screw up like this again.

"I hope you are aware that all of you are getting off very, very lightly. The potential consequences had your—Teravision—system *actually* been placed in control of UNS national defense are incalculable. Don't make me regret it."

There was more, but the discussion did not continue for terribly much longer beyond that point. When the Teravis and RealMe executives left the building, they did so in two distinctly separate groups, very pointedly not speaking to or even looking at each other. The RealMe executives in particular seemed to be trying very hard to pretend that the Teravis execs— or, perhaps, *former* Teravis execs—did not exist.

<hr>

Back in his office, after the executives and their legal counsels had left the building, Kolbin sat back in his chair. He pondered, once again, the tentative findings and speculative connections that he *had not* mentioned to them. The Czech artist, Eliška Hlaváček, whose RealMe backup body, according to RealMe's records, was destroyed after her accidental death before her damaged backup could be re-recorded. The other Czech woman, Terilyn Szavič, Hlaváček's absolute spitting image, who had been revived by RealMe after dying in an apartment-block fire, and in whose company Michael Hagerty had left the country before anyone spotted him. Both of whom had then disappeared, going through a series of throwaway false identities before falling off the map altogether in Belgrade.

Was it possible? *Could* this Terilyn Szavič, in some fantastic way, be Teravis Systems' escaped intelligent agent, somehow downloaded into the RealMe backup body of Eliška Hlaváček, stolen after her accidental death? There was absolutely no data to suggest that such a thing was even possible. And RealMe *insisted* the Hlaváček body had been destroyed. There was no *physical evidence*. It was all speculation.

IF Szavič *was* somehow the Teravision agent downloaded into a RealMe body, he mused, it—no, *she*—had shown no indication of any desire to do anything other than to escape, to *get away*, in the company of Hagerty, who it by now seemed fairly certain had been at least peripherally involved in her escape from Teravis in the first place. Neither of them had done a single thing that in any way harmed anyone or any entity, other than Teravis.

If, that was, you turned a blind eye to a minor case of electrical power billing fraud, which in any case could not be conclusively *proven* not to be the work of the *technically*-legal drug growers who had rented the space before Hagerty. They had been found as well, and had denied all knowledge, of course... but of course, they *would*, wouldn't they? The source of the power-cheating device, or when it was installed, could not be convincingly ascertained. Batch numbers on some of the components gave a time window during which it was *most probable* that it was constructed... but that window was wide enough that it didn't really help determine *who* had constructed or installed it, or when.

Even the faked ransomware attack against Teravis, he mused, could well have been intended primarily to conceal evidence of the agent's escape for long enough to accomplish the escape. Destroying all data about how to create the agent might have been a secondary goal, to prevent Teravis from doing it again. And, viewed in that context, the subsequent leak that fired off the Skynet protests could be viewed as an attempt to make certain that Teravis could not *get away with* doing it again, could not recover from the attack and start over. If so, it had worked magnificently... and without really harming anyone *except* Teravis and its direct financial backers, many or even most of whom could be assumed to be complicit in the scheme.

Well, he reflected, and some third-party investors, most of them so huge that they would scarcely notice the loss anyway, in the greater scheme of things. They had taken a risky gamble on a nose-diving stock, and lost. They lost more, overall, every time the Exchange dipped a couple of hundred points.

"You deserve your chance, I think," he said at last, as though to empty air. "Make the best of it. I wish you luck."

He looked again at both sets of reports, and considered them for a moment longer. Then he turned back to his keyboard, pulled up the online files, and sealed them. He began writing up a final report, stating that no traces of the agent could be found beyond its disappearance in Prague, deliberately omitting any *unfounded speculation* about a connection between Szavič and Hlaváček, and recommending that the case should be considered closed pending any further related incidents or reappearance of the rogue digital agent.

18: Olly Olly Ox In Free

"We're safe here, for a while," Teri told Michael, in a hotel room high above the city of Baku, with a view of Baku's spectacular Flame Towers. "If anyone has *physically* followed us, they have extraordinary patience. I *hope* we've managed to lose any tracking. If someone should stumble across us, I don't *think* they have anything to connect me to Teravis. And in the worst case, Azerbaijan does not have an extradition treaty with the UNS.

"So, we have a breathing space. We can finally relax a little."

"So, where from here?" Michael asked.

"The truth is, I don't know," Teri replied. "But we're out of immediate reach for now. We have time to think about it. What we want to do. Where we want to go.

"We have lots of options. Most of Asia is open to us. Many countries in Africa... though few of them would be my first choice.   There are options in the Indonesian region and Micronesia.   Brunei, perhaps.   Or even Bhutan. Though... Bhutan has drawbacks as well. It's still not very developed.   We might find life there hard.   Brunei, too, for different reasons.

"There's even Mongolia. I understand Ulaanbaatar is quite the place. And Mongolia doesn't have an extradition treaty, either.

"But we have time to decide, now. Time to plan properly. To decide where we want to go. What to do there."

"Do you need to stay somewhere within feasible reach of a RealMe clinic?" Michael asked. "Just in case?"

"I don't know," Teri replied. "I hope it doesn't come up. I hope nothing happens that *needs* RealMe-specific care."

Michael nodded.

"The important part," he said, "is that whatever we do, we're doing it together." He thought for a little. "Doesn't Mongolia *still* have a heavy horse-nomad culture?"

"It does," Teri agreed. "Two thirds of the population of the country are nomadic. Does that appeal to you?"

"Well, no," Michael replied. "Not exactly. I... think I might not be ready yet for that kind of life change. But it's *intriguing*. Though I doubt they have raptors." Teri grinned.

"Wherever we go, we're going to need to figure out some way to make a living." He sighed. "And I'm afraid that most of my skills for making a living wouldn't be a lot of use in Mongolia. Especially since..."

He trailed off, rubbing his face with his hands for a moment, painful memories clawing at him.

"Especially since even if I thought I *could* go back to streaming, too many people would recognize me."

Teri took a step closer and put her arms gently around him.

"There's no rush," she reminded him. "We have time to catch our breath. Time to plan. We can take a break from running, and just enjoy life for a little bit. Though we will need to develop a source of income.

"We'll need a long-term plan, yes. But now we have time to *make* one." She paused, as a thought struck her.

"Could you *start* and *run* a game streaming site? From behind the scenes?"

Michael thought about that.

"Maybe," he said at last. "Though... I'd feel I was competing with GameVRse. I don't think I want to do that."

Teri squeezed him tightly.

"It's not a problem we have to solve now," Teri reassured him. "Or today, or this week. We're safe. That's what matters right now."

"Safe," Michael agreed, "and together. Tomorrow can go to hell."

He pointed out of the window, and down.

"There's a nice-looking pool, three floors down. Can you swim?"

Teri looked uncertain.

"I... don't know," she replied. "Probably not."

"Want to start learning, then?"

A huge grin spread across her face.

"Sure," she said. Then she hesitated for just an instant.

"No rippy fish?" she asked, with a puckish smile. "Promise?"

Michael laughed.

"I promise," he said, grinning. "No rippy fish. Let's go teach you to swim."

Epilogue

Much later, Deputy Director David Kolbin received a request from Ephraim Kaneshewicz, a Director at NOAA, to meet him and his deputy Susan Kongsberg for lunch. He saw no reason not to, and agreed almost immediately.

Over lunch, they chatted a little about inconsequential things, the typical small-talk of senior officials in completely different government agencies.

Finally, Ephraim broached his real reason for meeting.

"David," he said, "about that climate model that your people turned over to us."

"Yes?" David replied.

"It's *incredible*," Susan broke in. "The detail is unprecedented. We've plugged data and parameters into it from live events happening in real time, and we get out a simulation that looks *just like* the actual live satellite observations."

"But we don't *understand* it," Ephraim said. "We don't understand how it *works*. *How* it does what it does. We know that it uses modeling methods and mathematical techniques that are completely new to us, that we are desperately struggling to grasp. As though they were devised by someone who *thinks* in completely different ways. It's visionary. Revolutionary.

"*Someone* built this. Someone, *somewhere*."

"Please," Susan asked, "if it's possible for us to just *talk to* whoever built it... we could really use some pointers. Some help in understanding it."

David Kolbin thought hard, about sealed files and correlations, inferences, he had deliberately not put down in writing. He didn't know whether his hypothesis was correct. It was still hard for him to imagine that it could even be possible.

But what if it *was*?

Suppose the Teravision AI and... what was her name... Terilyn Szavič *were* somehow one and the same? Suppose she *had* built this incredible thing that the best and brightest minds at NOAA did not fully understand. And then somehow downloaded herself into a human—or, *almost* human —body. Did she still possess the capabilities to understand and explain the workings of what she had built?

Did he have the right to *ask*?

He heaved a deep sigh, and looked back up.

"There *is* just one faint possibility," he admitted, at last. "I don't know whether I can find her. And if I can find her, I don't know whether she would be willing to come. Or whether she can still help you. She... probably has good reasons to want to hide.

"I can't make any promises. But if—IF—I can find a way to contact her, I will ask whether she is willing to help you."

"*Thank you*, David," Ephraim said. "That is all I can ask."

POST-IT NOTES

Pandybat, as used here, is a term that came out of the Society for Creative Anachronism. It denotes any weapon that is at least as dangerous to the wielder as to the wielder's opponent, and preferably more so. The SCA has even been known to hold pandybat *tourneys* in which *only* pandybat weapons were permitted.

Aluminum-ion battery chemistry is a currently-experimental successor to lithium-ion. It has several advantages over lithium-ion chemistry: Aluminum is much more readily available than lithium, the aluminum-ion chemistry has three times the potential charge density of lithium-ion, and the cells are far less flammable.

Ransomware is malware that encrypts as much as it possibly can of a target's vital data, then demands a ransom in return for the decryption key. *Sometimes* the encryption can be broken without paying the ransom (usually because the ransomware crew made some cryptographic mistake). Paying the ransom does not guarantee getting a key, or the *right* key, or that the key will actually work. Sometimes the ransomware crew just take the money and run. It is distinct from a data *destruction* attack, which may masquerade as ransomware to buy time, but in which the explicit goal is to *irreversibly destroy* as much data as possible.

REvil, or Ransomware Evil, was a Russian-based ransomware-as-a-service operation, allegedly dismantled by Russian security services. NotPetya is a variant of the Petya family of encrypting malware, believed by various sources to be the work of the Russian government-backed Sandworm APT.

Advanced Persistent Threat (APT) is a term used to denote high-level computer intrusion threat groups, often state-backed or state-sponsored, which may gain access to a computer network and then remain there undetected for an extended period of time. At least forty such are *currently* known to exist. APT44 in particular specifically refers to a Russian group also known as Sandworm (among other names), known to be operated by Military Unit 74455, a cyberwarfare unit of the GRU, Russia's military intelligence service.

Reductio ad absurdam is one of the classes of formal logical fallacies. It is *literally* 'to reduce an argument to absurdity'—to make a knowingly absurd argument, and then use that absurdity to try to argue the falsehood of something else, often not really even related.

Order of magnitude is a mathematical term of art. Basically it is a rough measure of scale. One order of magnitude means one extra digit before the decimal point. A thing that is three orders of magnitude larger than another is *roughly* a thousand, perhaps several thousand, times as large. For instance, the number 17 and the number 45 are both *approximately* an order of magnitude larger than the number 3.

To the best of my knowledge, the term "rippy fish" was coined by British comic artists Alan Moore and Alan Davis, in their **D.R. & Quinch** comic for *2000 AD* magazine.

How did the RealMe technology arise?

In the setting of this book, it grew out of the space program. An advanced physics project promised a fast sublight space drive that could reach the nearer stars in perhaps fifty or sixty years. The obvious problem was that a crew of trained human astronauts would be ailing octogenarians by the time they got anywhere useful. So, a parallel project was initiated to develop a cold-sleep technology.

But putting humans into cold-sleep didn't work out, for a number of reasons. Human bodies *didn't evolve* to be able to hibernate at hypothermic temperatures for decades at a time—and cryogenics was *right out*. Mammalian cells simply could not survive being frozen solid, period. That proved an insoluble problem. Dead was *dead*.

What would become the RealMe technology began as Deep Sleep, an idea to use retroviral technology to *edit* human bodies to be able to survive cold sleep. A lot was learned about the biochemical changes that were necessary to enable a mammalian body to be 'put on ice' for years or decades at a time, with minimal metabolic activity and minimal nutritional supply, while keeping it healthy. But the Deep Sleep project never managed to extend the 'sleep' duration to the many decades necessary for an interstellar journey, and in any case, the changes required turned out to be significant enough that the conversion survival rate in laboratory animals was unacceptably poor. No sane human would volunteer to undergo a deep-sleep conversion that had a fatality rate over eighty percent.

With advances in neural mesh research, though, it had become possible to *record* human memories, personality engrams, even—theoretically—consciousness. It had even been shown possible in primate tests to *write* experiences, memories and personality traits *back*—although write-back had not been tested in humans, for ethical reasons. 'Neural meshes' were not implantable, *yet*; but in a laboratory—or clinic—setting, the technology worked.

So the Deep Sleep plan was pivoted. The new plan was to fast-grow a pre-engineered, physically matched, deep-sleep-ready *copy* of a fully trained astronaut's body; record the astronaut's entire personality, experience and consciousness; and then write that gestalt *into the previously blank copy*, which would then be sent off on the mission already in deep sleep. The genetic and biochemical changes made when growing the copy were significant enough to skirt laws that strictly forbade human cloning. The engineered copy was no longer *technically* a clone.

Then the sublight space-drive project failed.

The Deep Sleep copying technology remained. A *lot* of money had been invested in developing it, and the investors demanded a return on their money. It still was not ready yet for fifty or sixty year durations, but it was *viable*. A few people already close to death from untreatable terminal diseases, with nothing to lose, volunteered to become experimental subjects, to have their consciousness recorded and copied after death into Deep Sleep bio-engineered host bodies... *and it worked.* That result was impossible to keep quiet, and became headline news overnight.

And so Deep Sleep Inc. pivoted *again*, from a space travel technology, to a last-resort human-backup technology, renaming itself the RealMe Corporation. If you were dying of an incurable disease, or simply feared accidental death—or murder, or *assassination*—RealMe could offer you a *backup*.

For a price. A *LARGE* price. But not out of reach... *if* you had money.

For those privileged enough to be able to pay the price, RealMe technology offered a way to cheat unexpected death. There were restrictions; suicide, or death during the commission of a crime, voided the RealMe service contract, for example. And there were legal hurdles at first, related to inheritance; arguments that a 'restored' copy was not really human, or no longer the original person. But there was enough money on the side of *overcoming* those arguments to pass laws declaring that a person 'restored' after death using the new RealMe technology was *legally* a continuation of the same person.

So *of COURSE* the RealMe technology found a ready market.

The rest, as they say, is history.

Or, in this case, **her** story.

MORE BOOKS FROM SEAN FENIAN

THE STARDOCK TRILOGY

Humanity is not alone in the universe. We are far from even the only intelligent species in our *galaxy*. It was foolish, arrogant, and naïve of us to think we were.

The Chrrt'ktk't are one such intelligent species. But Sean Fenian's best-selling *Stardock Trilogy* is not about the Chrrt'ktk't. It's not even about humanity and the Chrrt'ktk't. It is about what happens to humanity, and how the future of humanity is changed, when the Chrrt'ktk't abandon a mobile shipyard with a burned-out hyperdrive core in the Solar System as a decoy to distract pursuit — and how it changes the life of a retired engineer who finds himself chosen, more or less by chance, as custodian of the Chrrt'ktk't shipyard, and all of the lives he changes in turn.

PRAISE FOR *THE STARDOCK TRILOGY*:

"These three books were a delightful, well written tale of a hopeful future, populated with a cast of characters that were easy to root for and interesting alien species."

"An excellent read and finally a well thought out plan forward that does not include a forever war!"

"This has been a wonderful trilogy to enjoy. Great character development and storyline."

"Happy because it is well written with solid scientific underpinnings and because it shows a side of humanity that I wish we would all strive for."

FIREBORN

The man who will become Alrekr Járnhandr is *done*. Weary, physically and emotionally broken, abused beyond the limits of what he can endure, he is ready to give up and die. But instead of dying, he finds himself drawn through a dark void to another world. Terribly injured, he is found and rescued by people among whom he will have a chance to build a new life.

His new world will be filled with wonders. It will be magical. It will finally give his life meaning. But it won't be easy, and he will come to discover that he has not entirely escaped all that he fled from. His past is not done with him yet... and neither is his future.

But in this life, he won't have to do it alone.

Sean Fenian's **Fireborn** is a transformational alternate-world fantasy novel featuring mystic arts loosely based on Finnish mythology, polyamorous relationships, and healing from emotional abuse. Have you ever heard of a smith who can mix advanced metal alloys *by ear*? In *Fireborn*, you will.

And yes... there are dragons.

Praise for *Fireborn*:

"Delightfully imaginative"

"This book has a feel and cadence utterly unlike any others in this genre. [...] I have never read a 'transformational' novel with such a positive cast of characters and uplifting message."

"The author writes characters of depth out of his own depth, loves, and widely varied experience. A lovely tale and I devoutly wish he'll find a way to revisit this surprisingly special world and characters he's shared with us."

"A different type of book from Sean Fenian, and even better"

"Fascinating take on legends"

"My new favorite author"

"[Fireborn] will take you into a mythic world, and you will be saddened that it stands alone. I only wish there was more of this world myth."

Agency (with Robert Auerbach)

Ciáran mac Cool is a *de-facto* operative for... he's not sure. He doesn't know where his orders come from, and he's in too deep to back out — even though at least one assignment almost got him killed. And yet, his assignments always seem to do some *good* in the world.

Then one day the Box tells him to reach a specific location, with no further explanation, giving him barely enough advance warning to get there.. Soon he will find himself working alongside a young law associate to unearth revelations that will shake the course of events in ways he never imagined.

PRAISE FOR *AGENCY*:

"A magnificent book." — *Wendy S. Delmater, Abyss & Apex Magazine*

"If you like the writings of Neal Stephenson, you'll like Agency."

"The plot is well constructed, the characters well-fleshed out, and what little action there is, is done well, and not forced, as some others have done."

"Well written and paced story that holds one's attention closely."

"Rarely have I enjoyed a book like I enjoyed this one! Thought provoking. Action packed. Very different from anything else I have read lately."

"One of the best woven stories I've read in years. And my years do include over a thousand books to compare with."

"You can tell that a great deal of research had to have been done and understood by the authors, because the breakneck pace of this data driven story would have quickly revealed sloppy research."

GODTHIEF

The Prophecy of Tendarrion—or at least, one likely reading thereof—said that the time was coming for the goddess Jirilis to die.

Jirilis, understandably, was rather unhappy about this. Her plans for the future did not involve dying yet. But, a prophecy is a prophecy.

Prophecies, however, are notoriously fickle about exactly what precise interpretation of them turns out in the end to be correct. The possibly existed of finding an exploitable loophole. But Jirilis could not exploit it *herself*. That was, to greatly oversimplify the explanation, 'against the rules.' Prophecy and the powers of gods didn't work that way.

Jirilis needed a champion. Not one who could win battles for her, not one who could slay mighty enemies for her, not one who would spread her word or perform heroic deeds in her name.

No, Jirilis needed a champion who could *subvert a prophecy*. And she had an idea that she knew just who that might be. She had had her eye on him for some time, in fact.

Fortunately, he was already coming to *her*. Though he might need a little help.

That was alright. Jirilis had one of the most powerful incentives to help him that there could possibly be.

Sean Fenian's **Godthief** is a standalone fantasy novel set in an alternate world that might or might not be 'real'. It delves into the natures of gods and the mechanisms of prophecy, and what we really mean when we say the word 'Paladin', all against a background of the aftermath of a thousand-years-past, almost-world-shattering demon war.

Praise for **GODTHIEF**:

"Excellent and consistent world building. If you enjoy fantasy without the swords and magical combat, this is for you."

"Well paced, imaginative, exciting tale. Sean Fenian is a skilled world builder. I look forward to reading more adventures set here."

About Sean Fenian

Sean Fenian is a generalist and open-source evangelist, recently retired from several decades of working in the information technology sector. He is broadly knowledgeable in many subjects, with a long-standing informed layman's interest in physics and related science in particular. He has been an avid reader of SF and fantasy since his teens, and first became aware of, and began campaigning on, environmental issues in the late 1970s. He is proficient with weapons both ancient and modern, has trained in four different martial arts, and believes that understanding basic firearms safety is like knowing basic first aid, CPR, or how to use a fire extinguisher. He believes that it is a basic human duty and responsibility to treat all beings fairly and decently, and that the true measure of a person is how you treat others.

His past volunteer activities include educational historical re-enactment, marine mammal rescue, and handicapped riding therapy. He has been formally diagnosed on the autistic spectrum, but stubbornly persists in trying to understand people anyway.

He dreams many things. Occasionally, some of them become reality. But only occasionally.

Sean's books are read in fourteen countries, at last count, and his bestselling *Stardock Trilogy* is also available on the Audible platform, published by Podium Entertainment.

www.ingramcontent.com/pod-product-compliance
Lightning Source LLC
Chambersburg PA
CBHW070746180626
46818CB00007B/3014